TRITON'S DAUGHTER

THE TRITON SERIES BOOK ONE

EMORY GAYLE

1st Edition

Copyright © Emory Gayle 2018

All rights reserved.

No part of this book may be reproduced in any form or by any electronic or mechanical means, including information storage and retrieval systems, without written permission from the author, except for the use of brief quotations in a book review. All characters in this publication other than those clearly in the public domain are fictitious, and any resemblance to real persons, living or dead, is purely coincidental

Cover design © Lori Follett of www.HellYes.design

In loving memory of Lewis and Ike.

Two of the kindest men to walk this earth.

Note from the Author

Triton's Daughter is set in the same world as the *Water Series*. It takes place just before the events in *Water: Book One of the Water Series*.

PROLOGUE

A GENTLE SMILE spread across his face. My heart fluttered when his eyes met mine. I was captured in them, the same way I was every time. Every time I dreamed of him.

The startling violet of his eyes. The angle to his face. I knew it all; I had known it all since I was a child. We grew up together, and yet, we had never met. Not really. Only in my dreams.

His dark blonde hair was lazily styled. Deep set eyes peered at me from under a thick, dark brow. A low chuckle came from him, bringing out a smile that stretched across his full lips. The sound seemed to come from the very core of him; no matter the day that I had it always made me smile.

We used to play together. We used to tease and talk. Now…things were different. There was more between us than ever before. Somehow, somewhere, he stole my heart.

"You stole mine too," he whispered, his lips so close to my ear that I could almost feel them on my skin. A shiver ran down my neck and across my body.

It happened every time, just the same. Every time we came close to touching.

But we never did.

It was just a dream.

A dream that would never come true because that's what dreams were. Fantasy. Lies. Make-believe. Simply…a *dream*.

…and I was impossibly in love with the man from my dreams.

Though my heart wanted him, my head knew better. Dreams don't come true. That's a child's game. I was no child. Not anymore.

At least that's what I thought the morning before I saw him.

I
JETT

THE WATCH CIRCLED IN THE WATER. The ten of us kept a keen eye on the open sea as we soared above the city. Keeping a tight pattern, our weapons were drawn and at the ready.

"She was spotted coming from the north," Rayna called to us. Her raven black hair cascaded around her in the water, adding darkness to the light of her flawless porcelain skin. I grasped my spear in my hand harder and swam to her side. Her daggers flashed in the dim light as we swung around, watching and waiting. There was always a chance that our info was wrong and that the Siren wasn't alone. When Sirens were involved, we had to be vigilant.

Over the last week, there had been a Siren spotted looming over the city of Triton; one of the vast underwater kingdoms in Mer. Taking up residence at the bottom of the ocean, the Mer lived in safety and seclusion from the world around them; and, that included the violent and malicious Sirens. It was never good when the evil creatures started coming closer to the city limits; it usually meant that an attack was imminent. The Watch wanted to prevent that, so we were taking her in for questioning. The Watch's job was to dispatch with the Sirens quickly and quietly, without the Mer finding out.

That was how The Watch did things. Protect the city. Don't get caught doing it. By anyone.

The Sirens and the Mer didn't know we existed. Even though the Sirens and Mer were at war, we treated them both the same. It was The Watch's job to make sure that neither side knew we were there. Unfortunately, we weren't always successful. Being seen was an automatic death sentence to anyone that laid eyes on us. The Watch was deadly and quick when protecting our secret. None survived to tell about us. *None*. That may seem cruel, but it kept our people safe, and that made it worth it.

Rayna circled around and stopped in the water; her violet eyes narrowed as she watched for any signs of movement. We had been part of The Watch for a few years together and Rayna was a fierce fighter, one of the best. Our people had set up The Watch to hunt down rogue Sirens and protect the citizens of Triton from Siren attacks. We were determined to put a stop to the Sirens taking Mer.

It had nothing to do with a love for Mer. We didn't love Mer. How could we? We weren't welcome in it. But, we didn't like the Sirens either. What we did care for were the innocent lives that were destroyed by the Sirens when they took a young Mer. Her life would be turned into a living nightmare. It was that life that we fought to protect.

I moved quickly, twisting around next to Rayna. We had worked together for a few years and were good friends. She took her role in The Watch as seriously as I did…maybe more, if that was possible.

We got along really well, but lately I had gotten the feeling that there was something more coming from her end. A longer look. A lingering touch. Rayna had been a friend for a long time and I respected her more than most, but romance was not something that I saw with her.

"Jett."

I turned at the sound of her voice. She pointed off into the distance, never breaking her eyes from the shadow in the water. I could just see what she was talking about. A dark spot was making its way to the city and it was moving *fast*. Rayna stiffened at my side.

"What do you think? Whale?" I asked her.

"Too fast for a whale. Shark?" she countered.

"Too big," I answered.

"You don't think…" she uttered, not wanting to say what she was thinking and give it merit.

"Yeah, I think so. It's a swarm," I stated, confirming her fear. She didn't need to be told anything, but knew what to do without me saying a word.

"To the west!" she yelled and the others turned, lining up in formation, waiting for my word.

"We wait for my mark," I called to the group.

I was the commander of The Watch. Rayna and I both sat on our people's Council - a group of twelve members of our society that governed our people. Even though we held equal positions on the Council, she took my appointment as commander very well. When you were dealing with the danger that we did, there could only be one leader. That was me. I didn't have to worry that Rayna would oppose me, though. She always followed orders and never argued a decision I made. She was unfailingly loyal and tough as nails. All reasons I respected her so much.

I cast my gaze out into the open water, and the swarm of deadly Sirens approaching. My powers were tingling, ready to be unleashed. I could feel the pull of them in my core as the shadow closed in. Strength wasn't a recipe alone for leadership; I also knew when to use my powers, and when to hold back. I didn't take pleasure in killing Sirens even though my distaste for them ran deep, but I knew that it was a necessity of our job. Either we kill them, or they kill us. I knew which I preferred.

"You ready?" Rayna asked, flipping her daggers in her hands, a smile tipping the corner of her mouth. She was always up for a good fight.

"Always," I answered, smiling back. I might not have *liked* killing Sirens, but knowing that they were coming to do worse took the sting out of it.

"You think the Mer can see us?" she asked.

"Not from this distance. We're safe," I assured her.

We had gained information that a possible attack was coming. I had pulled together a larger group for the night, ten strong. Sirens tended to travel in swarms up to thirty. We may have been smaller in numbers, but we were trained in Siren killing. They had no idea what was waiting for them.

When the shadow got close enough I gave the order. "Take them," I commanded to the group. Rayna shot off into the water, the others trailing behind. I stayed back to take on those that would go around the flight and make their way to the city. We had sustained more injuries in the last year than ever before. The Sirens were showing up in greater numbers, and they were gaining in skill. I wouldn't go so far as to say we were struggling with it, but it was definitely more of a challenge than it had been in the past.

As our group engaged the first few Sirens, the rest of the Sirens went over the fight and straight for the city. Just as I guessed.
My turn…

2
JETT

I SHOT FORWARD, following the Sirens. They were streaking through the water, aiming for the entrance to the city. The people of Triton were protected from the sea by a huge dome that reached over it. Impenetrable as it was, the dome kept the harsh sea waters and its creatures away from the Mer. Without it, they would have been open to attacks from all sides. They looked like a city in a snow-globe at the bottom of the ocean. With only two entrances, they were well protected. However, that didn't deter the Sirens from trying to do damage when they could.

As the Sirens got closer to the entrance, I feared that the Mer guards would see them. I didn't need the Mer guards, who would just be doing their jobs, coming out and seeing The Watch. The rule was clear: *Leave none alive that have seen us.* I wasn't up for killing the guards; they were innocents. I would have to move fast.

A new group of highly skilled fighters had been put into action in the last year, taking up the role of guarding the city. I personally liked it, but it did pose a possible sighting issue. That was something that we needed to avoid. The group would be out soon, and killing their whole guard was not in my books. They were just trying to do the same as we were, protect their people.

Streaking through the water, I came up behind my group of Sirens, counting sixteen. The nine of The Watch were behind me engaging the other half of the Siren swarm. I wouldn't have a problem with these but it, also, wouldn't be easy. Pulling my power from my core, I could feel the energy vibrate up my spine and down my arms.

I had discovered at a young age that I was different than the others in my community. No one was like me, and that made me both special and a target. My people had been driven out of their home because they were different. Exiled and humiliated, they were thrown from everything they knew and loved, but that didn't mean that they embraced diversity within our own community. It took a long time, and a lot of work, for me to be accepted as who I was and not as a threat to others. My fosters had a lot to do with that; and so did my brother.

The day that I discovered my powers, I was mad at Jasper, my older brother. In a tree with a low hanging branch, I had draped a huge table cloth that my foster had on the line to dry. Using clothes pins and some ingenuity, I had pinned together the edges to make a cozy tent. Inside it was warm and free of wind and bugs…mostly. I had my toys in there with me, and was playing peacefully when I heard the sound of a plane - at least that's what I thought it was. It turned out to be my brother.

Pretending to be a plane whose engine had failed, he crash landed into my fort, tackling me from outside. In the process, he ripped the table cloth and kneed me in the face as he went. When I finally got out of the mess of my mangled tent, I looked for Jasper, who was hiding behind a tree…laughing.

I let my anger get the best of me, feeling a rage build to a boil; and, that was when I felt it. A snap in my core with a tingle that spread through me fast and free was ignited. I yelled, releasing my anger at him and feeling the surge of something new within me. Without intending to, pink electric light exploded from me and slammed into the tree bringing it down to the ground and setting it on fire. Jasper tucked and rolled out of the way just in time to miss the fiery tree collapsing on him.

Jasper got up with a bounce and ran to my side. We both stood there as the tree burned away. He looked at me in astonishment, and then anger. Turning, he punched me in the gut. I doubled over.

"Okay, I might have deserved that," I groaned.

Jasper clapped his hand on my back. "Yeah, just a little."

"I'm sorry," I apologized, pulling myself up.

"I know. But, I *might* have deserved that," he said pointing to the smoking tree.

"Huh?" I uttered and looked at him.

"Well, let's face it, it *was* my fault. But, you're going to have to work on keeping that power in check. We can't have you starting pink fires every time you're mad," he pointed out so nonchalantly, I thought I was hearing things for sure.

"You're – you're not scared of me?"

"What? Why would I?" he answered, his brow furrowed as if I was speaking Latin.

"Because, I just tried to *kill you*!" I yelled, trying to knock some sense into him.

"Meh. I deserved it," he shrugged and looked over at the demolished pile that once was my fort. "I saw how long you worked on that. I was just mad when you said I couldn't play too," he admitted.

"I – I don't know what to say," I uttered, truly astonished at Jasper.

"Don't look so surprised. Come on, let's get a pail of water to put out this fire," he laughed as we both ran for the hose on the side of the house.

That was the last day I stopped inviting Jasper to play, and we haven't been apart since. Not even after our fosters died a couple years ago.

Something shot past my shoulder, and I was jerked back into the moment. The Sirens had seen me and three had changed directions. I could feel my power at my fingertips and a grin spread across my face. I aimed, waiting for the right moment when I could take out more than one with a single shot. No point wasting my energy. Plus, there were a lot of them.

Taking careful aim, I released a bolt that shot with such speed it sliced through three of them. Sirens liked to line up one behind the other to try to hide their numbers and protect each other. But, that made them really easy to shoot straight through. A typical weapon wouldn't be able to do that, but they had never faced a weapon like me. I nodded, satisfied with my aim and swam right through them as they fell to the seafloor, away from Triton.

"Hey!" I yelled, trying to gain the attention of the group swimming toward the entrance; but, it wasn't working. Killing a creature in the back wasn't in my code of ethics, even when it came to a Siren; I needed them to turn. I summoned my power again and flashed. It was another gift I had - the ability to become light and flash like lightning to where I needed to go. It only worked for short distances; but, for hunting Sirens, it was perfect. They didn't see me coming before I was right in front of them.

Hovering in the water between the party of Sirens and the entrance, I threw my hands out. Pink jagged lines of light cut through the water from my fingertips. Forking out, the lightning slammed into the chest of the first Siren and then into the chests of the three that turned at the sound of their sister's wail.

I now had the attention of the rest of the group, and they weren't going to hold back just because they outnumbered me. Turning, I shot out the spear in my hand with a strength that was all mine and followed it with zap of energy. The spear pierced the chest of a Siren, eliciting a scream from her as the bolt collided with the other two Sirens. All three were stopped as their cries died on their lips. They sank from sight, and I turned from them, focusing my attention on the remaining Sirens.

I didn't have time to grasp where they were as I was tackled from behind and twisted up in the water. In a mix of limbs and weapons, I tried to get my bearings. I hadn't seen the one sneak up behind me.

Damn it, Jett. Pay attention.

I grasped the hand that had wrapped around my neck and poured my power into the flesh. A scream like rusty train breaks sounded in my ear, and her arm loosened. I flipped around, grabbing the dagger on my side and thrusted it into her ribcage. A sickly crunch sounded as the knife broke bone on impact. *Twelve down, four to go.* Those four drew their blades and wailed as the bodies of their sisters fell from view.

I watched more carefully as they started to circle me, their daggers flashing in the water. I knew damned well I was lucky that I hadn't been cut by the last Siren. A Siren blade was tipped in poison. One scratch would kill you, or at least render you useless enough that you were easy pickings for the Sirens to finish off.

I put the dagger away, drew the two short swords from my back, and faced the four Sirens. Hand to hand was not how Sirens fought. They weren't ones for following the rules of battle. They would gang up on you or stab you in the back without hesitation. Sirens had no honor; it was something I struggled with. I liked to think that I fought with honor; but, sometimes, it nearly got me killed.

"Ladies," I said and flashed a smile. "What are you doing out on this lovely evening?"

One of the Sirens literally hissed at me, like a cat. *Lovely.*

"I take it you're not talkers," I added as they glared at me, saying nothing. "Okay, well as fascinating as this conversation has been…" I paused and threw a sword full force at one of the Sirens. It lodged deep in her chest before she could move. The rest of their eyes shot to me from their sister and they launched into action. I smiled.

This is going to be fun.

Pink flashed and I was in the midst of them before they knew it. Dodging the first, who swiped out with her poisoned blade, I spun and drew my sword across her abdomen, cutting deep into it. With a twist to dodge another blade, I sliced through the water and deep into the neck of another Siren. With a gurgle she was gone. The last one tried to swim away, but I grabbed the dagger from my side and flipped it in my hand.

Damnit, turn around.

My stomach flopped as I realized that if I was going to stop her from getting back to Midira, the Siren queen, I would have to violate my rule of combat. I held the dagger tighter in my hand and cursed at the damned Siren under my breath. Swinging out with my arm, I sent the knife soaring through the water. I could hear the *thunk* as it buried deep in her back, but took no pleasure in it. I didn't like shooting anything in the back. Sometimes my personal standards had to be put aside for the greater good.

I flashed back to Rayna and The Watch, helping to dispatch with the rest…all but one, the one we would take back home to have a chat with.

Rayna clapped me on the back, as we regrouped, "Nice work Commander!"

"You too! You guys got a nice catch," I complimented, looking at the snarling Siren that was spitting and swearing at the ones holding her.

"Yeah, she's one of the leaders. Will be tough to break, but she'll have the most information. I called her early so that the rest stayed back," she shared.

"Hopefully she knows what's going on with all this new Siren movement," I replied. Rayna nodded.

"Let's head home," I announced to the rest of The Watch. All ten of us took off for the outcropping of rock near Triton. Our entrance, which was a portal home, was hidden among the hills and valleys of the rough surface. Within a tiny cave that we had to squeeze into was our way home. On the other side was safety from all that lurked in Mer - which included the Mer.

Letting everyone through, I took one final look to make sure that we weren't followed or watched before I entered the cave.

3
KYLAYA

"YOU'RE LATE!" he shouted at me as I bustled into the room furiously fixing back the last two hairs in my bun.

"I'm aware of that," I bit back. Commander Hasp was always on time, ahead of time. He was perfection in every bleeding thing that he did. That was why the citizens of Triton loved him so much. He was dependable.

I took a seat across from him at the large desk in the small meeting room. He narrowed his intelligent eyes at me, and I knew he was judging me already. A long-time friend of our family, Hasp had been around me since I was a child. He was more of a second father to me than a work colleague. His greying hair was cut military short, his dark suit was neatly pressed, and his white collar was sharp enough to cut yourself on. Always impeccably dressed, he never looked like anything took him by surprise or worried him. It was really intimidating. Especially considering, at that moment, everything flustered me. For weeks, I felt like I was doing most of my job wrong in some way.

"It's rude-"

"To keep a guest waiting. I know, Hasp," I finished for him, as I had heard his speech a million times before. "You know, it's not like I don't have just a few things going on myself."

"Your responsibilities aren't going anywhere, KyLaya. You'd better get used to that, my dear. Your father would expect nothing less of you, and neither do I," he retorted, watching me closely as I took out the material for our meeting.

"Don't talk to me about Father. He'll be fine and back in his place as Prime soon. He's already doing better under Doctor Freewater's care," I said, even though it was a complete lie. Father had taken ill weeks ago and had slipped into a coma. His care had been given to the best doctor in all of Mer. That should have comforted me, but Doctor Freewater was an idiot. He had *no idea* why my father was ill and no idea how to help him. So, it was left to *me* to take over for my father, as Prime and leader of Triton, until he regained consciousness. If he ever did.

"Well, I am certainly glad to hear of that. He had us all very worried," Hasp said with a grateful nod. I just nodded back and clicked my papers on the table, as if they needed straightening. Since I had taken over for my father, the weight of running a kingdom had fallen on me and I wasn't the least bit prepared for it. At least I didn't feel I was.

Hasp brought a large file out and slammed it on the table. I inwardly groaned. His steal grey eyes looked over the papers from underneath a thick greying brow. Though he might have been getting up in years, Hasp still looked as strong and capable as he did twenty years ago. There was no denying the power and leadership capabilities that he had. Anyone that crossed him soon found themselves with a black eye and sore jaw, and washing out the jail cells for a couple of months for disrespecting him. I should know. When I was younger I tested that line to see how far I could push him…turned out not far. And my father didn't do a thing to stop Hasp from sending me to clean the toilets all around High Hill, where we lived.

I learned my lesson. *Don't push Hasp.* And, don't depend on Dad to bail you out when you do something disrespectful like that. From then on I respected Hasp and my father all that much more…after I stopped being childishly mad at them.

"I'm here now, let the meeting officially begin," I decreed and opened my book to write notes.

Two hours later I emerged from the meeting depressed and stressed beyond measure. Hasp was the commander of our army and defender of our city, Triton, which is the sister city to Mer's capitol Titus Prime. Titus was ruled by King Zale, a good man whom my family had always got along very well with. We followed under the laws that he and his family set forth, but we functioned on our own for the most part. Our cities were far from each other, and my family, the Constantilly's, had been in charge of Triton for generations. We were the caretakers of the city and the ones responsible for keeping it running smoothly and safely.

It was a job that I was supposed to take over when I was much older and my father had taken ill of old age. Not something I was thrown into before I even turned twenty! I was not prepared to take on Father's job, not yet. Maybe it wasn't so much the job; I just wasn't ready to let go of Father. He was the only family I had left, and I just couldn't imagine my life without him in it. I wasn't prepared for *that*, and I didn't want to be.

There was still so much that I hadn't learned when Father took ill. But, I was trying and working my bleeding ass off to do the job justice. Hasp was doing his best to keep me up to speed with everything that was under his job description. He took on more than he was supposed to in an effort to help me, but he wouldn't be able to keep that up for long. I was grateful for his help even though it didn't seem like it most days.

I walked with purpose to my chamber, my heels clicking off of the white tiled floor and echoing through the hall. Pristine walls in white and grey welcomed me, reminding me of all the advances that my home had. Triton was a beacon of modernization in the world of Mer. We prided ourselves on it and we showcased it. My room was on High Hill, named for the giant building that was created to house the prominent members of my family long ago and the hill it was built upon. To me, it was just home.

All I wanted was a moment's peace…some time to just be myself for a moment and forget all the things that I had to do and all the things that I was failing at. That's what I was hoping for as I threw the door open to my room.

The soft pale shades of rose and gold welcomed me in like a hug. My room was the one thing that hadn't changed when father became ill. I refused to move to another room. I was just down the hall from him; and if there was anything that happened, I wanted to be close. I knew it wasn't the best room in the house and really not one for the leader of Triton, but it was mine. It had always been mine, and I wasn't ready to give that up.

I flopped down on my bed, pulling my hair from the tight bun it was in and massaging my scalp. The headaches from tight hair were just one of the pains that went along with the new position; that and the blisters from my shoes.

I used to be fun. I used to have fun. I lamented as I scrubbed my face with my hands effectively ruining the make-up I had meticulously put on that morning.

A knock rapped at the door, and I was drawn out of that depressing rabbit's hole. I knew it was best not to pull on that thread, but sometimes…

The knock came again.

"Damn it," I whispered under my breath. I stalked to the door and opened it. "What?" I barked. A set of big eyes met mine. Eyes that I had known since I was a kid, and knew almost as well as my own, looked back at me.

"Whoa, good to see you too, Ky," a deep voice answered.

"Oh geez, Mazz, I'm sorry," I apologized and waved him into the room. Tall and lanky, Mazz walked through my door and into my room. His dark brown, short hair was perfectly shaped and styled, just as the clothes he wore and the way he smelled. Mazz had been my best friend since we were kids. He was a Hasp, and our families had worked closely together for a very long time. We grew up running the halls of High Hill making mischief and mayhem and having a blast. But we were now adults, and with that came a responsibility that neither one of us would have guessed as kids.

We were engaged to be married.

But, we weren't in love.

I loved Mazz a lot actually, but not as anything other than a brother. I simply couldn't imagine what that would be like. It just seemed…wrong. I wished that I could love him more, the way that I was supposed to. I had even heard of families in the past using a betrothal spell that would make you fall in love with the person that you were to marry. I had asked Father to do one on me so that I would be in love with Mazz, but he refused. He said that kind of love wasn't true and had consequences beyond what we could see. I didn't understand. We all knew that Mazz and I were supposed to marry. What was wrong with a spell to make us fall in real love with each other? It wasn't like I was going to marry anyone else.

Mazz and I had been determined as mates by our families when we were both kids. Taking over for my father was my job, would be my job, no matter what happened. Mazz would take over for his father, no matter what. Our life paths had been determined since we were born. A marriage was just part of the deal. It just made sense that we should end up together.

A betrothal spell wasn't going to change that.

"Hello?" a hand waved in front of my eyes. "You there?"

"I'm here," I said with a huff and flopped down on my bed.

"You met with Dad, huh?" he asked sitting next to me and brushing my hair off my face.

"Yep, and according to him the whole of Triton is going to fall into despair if I am two minutes late for another meeting with him," I lamented.

"Why are you surprised, Ky? You know how my father is," Mazz pointed out.

"I know," I answered.

"Then why were you late *again*?"

"Because I was dealing with something else that took longer than I was anticipating, that's why," I answered.

"*What* were you dealing with?" he asked looking at me with a pinched brow and squinted eyes. His steely grey eyes that he got from his father pierced right through my story.

"I – uh – you know, city stuff," I shrugged.

"What city stuff, KyLaya?" he asked using my full name for effect.

"Alright, I was getting a dress fitting," I revealed with a sigh, placing my head in my hands. "I didn't think that it would take that long. I swear."

"Don't *ever* tell my dad that," Mazz emphasized.

"You *think*? He would outlive me just to finish his lecture over my grave," I replied. Mazz nodded.

"While that is *true*, it's not just that. He's been under a lot of pressure lately," Mazz added.

"I know, there was another sighting today," I shared.

A Siren sighting. Sirens were a breed of mutated Mer that had turned violent generations ago. They lived in a city called Stronghold, where Queen Midira plotted her revenge on all of Mer. She harbored some serous hate for Mer. Titus Prime had it the worst with the Sirens, though. Mer-born Sirens were still being born and banished to the open water in their city while we hadn't had a Mer-born Siren in the city for over a decade.

In Titus Prime, when I was a kids, the Sirens broke through the dome that protected their city and killed a bunch of Mer. It devastated the city. In Triton, we have been lucky. Our dome had never been breached. We were far enough removed from the Siren path that they hadn't shown much interest in our city. At least that was one theory.

In truth, we really didn't know what was keeping the Sirens from our city. Still, we weren't stupid enough to think that they would never be back.

Sirens had disappeared from our waters for over a decade. No one had been taken, no one had been turned. It was as if we were forgotten about, as far as the Sirens were concerned. Since then, we have been training for the day when they would return, because we all knew that day would come, eventually.

Of course that day would be when my father was in a coma and his untrained, unprepared daughter was in charge of the city's wellbeing. I knew it was falling heavily on Hasp's shoulders to keep the city safe. Even though that *was* his job, it had always been a joint effort between him and my father.

"Another one, huh?" Mazz mumbled. "That makes, what, the third this week?"

"The fourth," I sighed.

"What are you doing about it?" he asked.

"What *can* I do?" I asked back. "They come out of nowhere. They stay far away. They haven't even come close enough to the city so that we can really see them. It's as if they are waiting for something. And to make things worse, they disappear into nothing!" I fumed in frustration. I had sent out scouts to watch and wait. They found nothing and saw nothing. Five minutes after they were called back, the Siren showed up again. It was infuriating.

"Are you even sure that it is a Siren?" Mazz asked.

"Who else would be lurking around the city like that?" I asked him as if he had a better idea.

"I don't know," he shrugged. "Is that who my father thinks it is?"

"Your father thinks a whale fart is a Siren attack," I answered. Mazz full out laughed.

"That's so true," he chuckled. "Okay, so the Sirens are checking us out. What for?"

"I don't know. How about you go ask one?" I said, lashing out at him. Mazz turned and leveled a class 'A' glare at me. There were few people that could shame me into an apology, but Mazz was one of them. My sister was the other, but it had been a long time since she had been around to do it.

"Sorry," I apologized.

"Ah," he said with a shrug and wave of his hand, "I know you didn't mean anything by it. I just like testing you every once in a while to see if you can still utter the word 'sorry'. You passed!" he said clapping and smiling like a child

"You're-"

"Charming?" he interjected. "I know."

"I was going to say an idiot," I pointed out.

"I like mine better; we'll stick with that one," he said and wrapped a long arm around my shoulders. "I'm always here for you; you know that right?"

"I know," I answered and pulled an arm around him too. He rested his head on mine, and my heart warmed. But that was as hot as it got. Never more, never…what it should be when you are going to marry someone.

"Okay," I said, pulling myself away from Mazz. His arm released, and I stood pulling my hair back into a bun.

"Oh, boy, I know you mean business when your hair goes back like that, all severe and scary," he said with a dramatic shiver.

"You scared of me?" I asked looking at him.

"You wish," he chuckled deeply.

"Well, I don't actually," I said, meaning it. He was the last person that I wanted to scare away.

"Want to get a bite together before you get all serious and stately again?"

"That sounds perfect," I sighed. Mazz offered the one thing I didn't know I needed, some Mazz time, even if it *was* while the other girls in Triton all stared and smiled at him. He was a catch - a big one - and everyone else seemed to see it. Everyone but me. Mazz linked his arm in mine, his smile deepening as he opened the door.

"My lady," he said with a sweeping motion. Something that he did when we were kids.

"Why, thank you, kind sir," I said with bravado and walked through, only to be shoved back as he went through before me. I laughed, shaking my head and kicked him in the butt. He chuckled heartily, putting an arm around my shoulders and shaking me.

No one could cheer me up like him, and I needed it.

4
KYLAYA

I WAS BACK IN THE SAME PLACE, the place I dreamed of at night and thought of in the day.

Light was all around me. Under me, over me, everything was light.

And then, there was him.

I didn't know his name, but I knew his face. I had known his face since I was a child.

My heart pulled and pulsed rapidly when he closed the space between us. He sat so close to me, but he didn't reach out. We didn't touch, we couldn't. If we did, the dream ended. I don't know why; but every time we would make contact as kids, I would wake up. Dream over. So now we stayed away from each other, which was becoming increasingly more difficult.

His violet eyes wandered my length.

"You look beautiful as always," he said and smiled a crooked smile that had my heart pounding in my chest.

"You're a charmer," I said, a smile sneaking out.

"Only to you, trust me. No one else thinks I'm charming," he laughed and it felt like a million butterflies took flight in my chest.

For years we had been in this place together. We were kids when I first saw him. Since then, he has graced my dreams through all the stages of my life so far. Everything that life had dropped on me I shared with him. In this world, it was safe to say everything that scared me, everything that I felt, and be honest to a fault. I could really open up to him with no fear. After all it was just a dream; and, a part of me always knew that while I was in the midst of it.

"How is your father?" he asked, as he had every day since father had fallen ill.

"No change," I said sadly, dropping my head down.

"He'll come back to you, Laya. Don't you worry about that. He's a strong man. I can't imagine him not fighting to get back to you," he said.

"Thanks. But, it's not just that. It's everything that I've had to-" I stopped myself remembering another dream stopper. Life details. It seemed that if I ever tried to tell him where I was from, the dream ended - just as it did if we touched. I frowned, wishing that I could just tell him everything about my life and not have to leave out where I was. I didn't see the difference; it was just a dream.

"Dream stopper?" he asked.

"Yup," I said with a frown and a nod.

"Well, if it makes any difference, I have a few that I would like to tell you too; but, I would prefer to stay here with you instead. I can complain about my job later," he smiled.

We might not have known where the other lived, but we did know what our jobs were to a certain extent. He was responsible for safety in his home and often had to do guard duty. He knew that I was having to take over for my father but really had no idea how big that was. That was a dream stopper. As far back as I could remember, it was like that. Anything that might give a clue to where the other was from was a dream stopper. That included his real name. I told him mine was Laya, and that didn't dream stop; but, every name that he said to me was a dream stopper, so we stopped trying. I've just been calling him Handsome. Mostly to make him blush.

"I wish…" he began and then trailed off.

"Me too," I finished for him. He smiled. It wasn't the first time we had wished the same thing. That it wasn't a dream.

Do people age in dreams? Cause we did. We used to play together. We'd run and pretend, having fun in a world of light and sun as kids. It was glorious. But as we started to grow up, we went from playing to talking. From a childhood friendship based in play came something better, something deeper. Sometimes when I was having a particularly bad day, I would dream of him. We would lay together in the clouds and talk. I would spend the night venting and chatting; and, in the morning, I would feel better. Handsome had a way of lifting my spirits no matter how hard the day. I loved him for that. We fit together in a way I didn't have with anyone else, not even Mazz. It was always easy with him...and fun.

About a year ago something shifted. Our conversations were more...intimate. I looked at him differently. I noticed his long eyelashes and the different shades of violet in his eyes. The single dimple on his left cheek. The way that he looked at me was new and suddenly my blood pumped faster and stronger when we were next to each other. I couldn't stop the smile on my face.

It was new and exciting. A fantasy that I knew, when I woke, wasn't real.

"What are you afraid of?" I asked him a couple of years ago.

"Of losing those that I love," he answered. His eyes darkened, and I wanted to reach for him, to comfort him.

"You think something is coming for your family?" I asked.

"I lost two people I love very much," he said and a tear trickled down his face. "I feel...lost."

"I'm here," I said, looking at him as he turned to me. "I won't leave you." He smiled.

"I wish I could hug you," he uttered and then blushed realizing what he had said.

"I wish you could too," I replied, matching his blush.

Since then, I ached to sleep so that I could see him. A part of me blamed him for why I couldn't fall for Mazz. I would vow to stop feeling something for him, determined to end the ridiculousness of having feelings for someone that didn't really exist. But then I would fall asleep, and he would be there and all my feelings would rush forward and break down every wall I tried to build. I just couldn't get away from him; and, the worst part was, at the heart of it, I didn't want to.

I sat down enjoying the sun on my face and the relaxation settling in. Then, I started thinking about Mazz, and the life that I was supposed to build with him. I knew, to some extent, that Handsome was the reason I couldn't get to the place I wanted to be with Mazz.

"You are ruining my life," I said to him without thinking.

"What? How did I ruin your life?" he questioned.

That's when I realized that I was about to admit to him that I had feelings for him. I froze. It was the strangest feeling. Logically, I knew he wasn't real, but I couldn't get my heart to wrap its way around that;

and, I didn't want to embarrass myself if he didn't feel the same way…even though he wasn't real. *What the heck is wrong with me?*

"I – you…never mind," I bumbled.

"No. No way am I letting you off the hook that easily," he said with a wave of his hand and shake of his head.

"It's nothing. I didn't mean it. It's stupid," I answered.

"What is it? What did I do?" he asked, his brow furrowed as he looked at me. I could see the concern across his face and suddenly felt guilty for saying it.

"You didn't do anything, specifically," I admitted.

"So, just being *me* ruins your life," he retorted crossing his arms.

"Yes. And no," I said and gave him a weak smile.

"Fine. If it is any consolation, you have ruined my life too," he shouted sitting up and throwing his hands in the air. I looked at him in complete shock as he leaned over to me, looking deep in my eyes and placing his hands on either side of my body - not touching, never touching. My heart was in my throat. He leaned over and whispered in my ear, so close, for a moment I thought I could feel his breath on me.

"I can only hope that I have ruined your life the way that you have ruined mine."

My breath was short and came with the hammering of my heart. I looked in his eyes as he gazed down into mine. I wanted to touch him more than anything in that moment. *Why can't we touch? Why?*

"You know…you know this is insane," I whispered, barely able to find my voice.

"All I know is that I want you…more than I should."

I watched with amazement as his eyes intensified on mine and then flicked to my lips. My gods, my heart was going to explode.

Like a man starved, he dipped his head, pulled me hard against him – and kissed me.

My body exploded in sensation as his lips wrapped around mine. In that moment I knew I was lost and there was no coming back from where I was going.

The scariest thing was…I didn't care.

5
JETT

WHOA...

The feel of her lips was still on mine as I sat up in bed. We had never touched, at least not since we were kids and just playing. My heart was still hammering in my chest at the thought of her in my arms.

My feelings for the girl in my dreams had grown over the last few months. Suddenly, I was thinking of her in the day. I looked forward to seeing her at night. It was like I was in a relationship with someone that didn't exist! It was insane and I wanted to bash my head in every time my heart flipped thinking of her.

What's wrong with me?

6
KYLAYA

THREE KNOCKS SOUNDED from the door. *What?* I turned over, my pulse racing and my cheeks flushed.

Whoa…

Three knocks again. I touched my lips lightly, as the dream let go. I sighed, heavy and long, letting the feel of Handsome against me float away. Easing from me, like a slow bleed was the sadness of realizing that, again, he was only a dream.

Damn it! When did I fall asleep?

I didn't remember climbing into bed or closing my eyes, but I obviously had. Five meetings and two meals later, I had gone back to my room and got ready for the night. At some point I must have drifted off.

Three knocks again.

I hadn't seen Mazz for two days; not since we had lunch together. It had to be him.

I groaned and rolled off the bed. I had changed into something comfortable, some soft pants and a shirt. Both of them were in a light pink, a color that no one would have ever thought I wore, as black was generally what I had on outside of my room. My foot hit the water glass on my bedside table, as I shuffled to get out, spilling water onto the floor and rug.

"Of course," I groaned. Grabbing the tipped glass off the floor, I summoned my water power and drew the water from the carpet. Hovering the water in the air, I flowed it to the sink in the bathroom. As a Mer, we could control the water around us giving us the ability to swim at great speeds; but, some of us could control it outside of the ocean, too. I was one of them. Though my powers weren't as advanced as some, I was getting better with them. Satisfied that that carpet was dry, I walked to the door and pulled it open to the sound of another set of knocks.

"What?" I sighed, my eyes closed and a frown on my lips.

"My lady, Doctor Freewater would like to speak to you." A guard stood at the door his eyes shifting away from me as his weight went from foot to foot. A blush appeared on his cheeks, and that was when I realized that I wasn't wearing a bra.

"Very well, I'm coming," I said and walked to get a sweater. Part of me just wanted to point to my boobs and say "yes, I have breasts. Get over it," to him. The guy was around the same age as me; and, like the others in High Hill, now looked at me as this sexless being with no discernable female parts. Whenever I wasn't in my meeting clothes, I got looks from the High Hill members like a teacher gets from a student who sees them outside of school for the first time.

My gods! She wears pajamas! It's like she's a real person or something!

I bit my tongue, though, and wrapped the sweater around me.

What does that moron of a doctor want now?

Walking down the hall toward my father's room; I braced myself for more bad news about him. My slippers shuffled across the cold floor as the boots of the guard echoed around us. My room was close in case of an emergency; the only other room in the hall. I had been in that room since my sister disappeared. On my father's orders, it was remodeled for me out of the servants' quarters it had been before. He didn't want to take any chances after what happened to KyLena. I stopped at the doorway to his room and took a deep breath.

I placed a hesitant hand on the brushed silver latch and took another breath. I needed to be calm going in, or I would say something that, while true, wouldn't be helpful to my father. As I pushed the door open, the stale air hit me hard and my breath was cut off. I didn't hide my glare at the damned doctor who thought breathing that foul stench was good for someone who was ailing. The room needed to be aired out…and fast.

Doctor Freewater was standing over my father administering some kind of medication, useless medication I was sure. His thinning white hair was combed over the top of this head in a desperate attempt to hide the gleam of his smooth scalp. His beady eyes squinted over his pointed nose at the instruments before him. I walked to the window and opened it, sending a much needed gush of fresh air and light into the room. The doctor looked up, and I threw him my best death glare, which shut him up momentarily. I then walked slowly to my father's side and took his hand. It was warm, and the feel of his skin was like having a little part of him back again. If I closed my eyes, it would be like he was awake and joking around with me and Mazz, teasing him about all the girls that loved him.

"Miss?" Doctor Freewater's voice broke through my memory.

"Any change?" I asked, opening my eyes and looking at him.

"I'm afraid not," he said with a shake of his head, swirling some blue liquid around in a glass and squinting at it.

"There has been no change in him for a *month*! What are you doing to help him?" I asked, frustrated with the doctor's lack of care.

"I am doing all I can, my dear," he answered the same way he did every time.

"Don't call me that," I ordered, not liking the familiarity that he was trying to have with me. Not to mention that I was his leader and, not some little girl to be placated.

"If I might, miss," he started. "I think that your father is in need of a move."

"What? Why?" I asked, my voice getting louder and higher.

"Well, this room isn't adequate for the tests that need to be done on him," he replied, indicating the space with a broad sweep of his pale, thin arms.

"What tests?" I asked.

"In my lab, there are some instruments that I think will help me determine what is going on in your father's mind. I just have to make an incision and have a look around," he said in a light tone that was all together not appropriate for what he was telling me.

"Incision *where*?" I asked through gritted teeth.

"On - or rather - in his…head," he answered hesitantly.

"You want to cut open my father's head and have a look around? Is that what you are saying?" I shouted, utterly shocked at his gall.

"There are many things that could be going on in his mind right now, and if I could just get a look at-"

"No," I said slowly.

"Miss, if you would just-"

"No," I said louder and stood from the bed, placing my father's hand at his side.

"If you come within a foot of my father with a scalpel, I will make sure that you leave with it lodged in your jugular. Do you understand me?" I threatened.

"But, if I might just-"

"Get. Out," I said through clenched teeth. He opened his mouth to speak again and I reached over, grasping the book my father kept by his bed for evening reading and whipped it at him.

"You can't treat me that way, *young lady*!" he yelled in disgust.

"You will address me as Mistress Prime Constantilly, or you will find yourself in the cells for disrespect!" I said slowly and clearly. "Guard!" I shouted.

The door opened and the guard that had come to get me stepped in. "Doctor Freewater isn't to come back in this room, do you understand? He is to stay the hell away from my father!"

Doctor Freewater turned toward me and charged. The Guard stood there, unmoving in shock.

Useless ass.

I saw the glint of a scalpel and knew at once that the doctor meant business. He swiped out at me, the instrument cutting through the air. I dodged to the side and turned, punching the doctor in the face and breaking his nose. Blood leaked from behind his fingers as he groaned into his hand.

"Take him to the cells," I said to the guard who finally snapped out of his trance. The doctor uttered a few less than kind things at me, while the guard was yanking him out of the room. I smiled.

I had been itching to punch the ass-wipe in the face for weeks, I'm not going to pretend it didn't feel really good.

I looked back to my father. He would have been proud. I walked to the door and slammed it shut. Resting my body against it, I banged the back of my head on it a couple of times.

Cut open my father's head? Is he insane?

Walking slowly and quietly back to my father's bed, I sat at the edge and took his hand again.

"What am I going to do, Father?" I asked him. "I'm scared for you. What's wrong?" I knew there wasn't going to be an answer; there never was, no matter how many times I talked to him.

"Doctor Freewater is gone. He wanted to cut you open and look around your brain. Can you believe that? It might not have been the most stately action, but punching him in the nose sure felt good. Wish you could have seen the look on his face. I think Alastair Sands is going to get a strongly worded letter from me on his recommendation of Freewater," I huffed.

"I wish I knew what to do for you, Father. I'm scared. I don't know what I'm doing and I just - I don't want to be left alone. Please, fight, and come back to me," I said as tears started to run down my cheeks. I buried my head in his blankets and just let go.

Pouring everything I had been feeling right out of me, for the first time since he got ill, I just let myself be a lost, scared daughter.

It felt good.

It was refreshing, relieving, and exhausting to the point where I just passed out, right there, at my father's side.

7
JETT

IT HAD BEEN A LONG TIME since we had brought back a Siren for interrogation. We didn't do it as a normal practice, but there had been some occasions that had called for it. This was one of them. A large swarm attacking the city was cause for concern and we needed to know what was going on. If we could figure out what Queen Midira's end game was, maybe we would be able to stop her.

Queen Midira had been the leader of the Sirens for an unnaturally long time. Her mother was the original Siren, Queen Sireana, The Evil One. She had the power to turn Mer to Sirens through their dreams, something that she passed down to Midira. But, Midira wasn't blessed with that precise gift, instead, she needed the Mer to *agree* to come to her - something that she was exceptionally skilled at manipulating out of young mermaids. There were a lot of my people that would have loved to wrap their fingers around Midira's throat. There would be a long line for the thrill of doing that, though. Midira wasn't winning any popularity contests among the Mer, either. But, her Sirens were terribly loyal, and she had friends from other races that had formed allegiances with the Sirens over the years making her a powerful force and not one to be taken lightly.

The Siren that we took was a Siren-born, meaning that she was born to a Siren at Stronghold. A Mer-born was from Titus Prime and was born to a Mer family - she later turned into a Siren once Midira got to her. They could be told apart by the color of their skin. Siren-born Sirens had pale colored skin in shades of blue, green, and purple, where the Mer-born Sirens only had the violet eyes that all Sirens had. They looked like Mer in every other regard.

And we would know better than anyone.

My community existed because of the Sirens. Most of our females were turned at young age by Midira but were saved from being taken to Stronghold. Rescued from a life of torture and humiliation, they were brought to a place where they could live in peace - away from the dangers of the Sirens and the Mer. Being away from the sea, they weren't susceptible to a Siren call anymore, thus living their lives free of Midira.

And then there was me and my kind…

I am a Siren's child. A male Siren. Stronghold, the Siren City, is a female only society, shunning all males unless they are used for procreation purposes; and that included all male children that they gave birth to…like myself. For a very long time, those male children were just killed or left for dead in the ocean. Something unimaginably cold and heartless. Now, they are rescued and brought to my town; saved from certain death and allowed to live.

I am a Sirenite.

A Siren's son.

8
KYLAYA

I SAT UP WITH A GASP, thrown from the dream as if I had been slapped. He wasn't there this time; instead, there was a set of red eyes and a voice I didn't know. I could sense the energy in the air just being close to the power that was in my dream.

"I'm coming for you," he said.

My hand found my forehead as I tried to catch my breath. I rubbed my hands hard against my face, trying to rid myself of the dream and the anxious feeling that I had in my gut. I shuffled to the edge of the bed and to the bathroom on shaky legs. Leaning over the sink, I splashed cold water on my face and took deep cleansing breaths. Through the bathroom window I could see that it was mid-morning. I had slept in.

Damn it to Hades. I cursed to myself and ran to the shower. Hasp was going to have my head

THE DAY WAS SHOT the moment I ran from my room and smacked into Hasp. My eyes burst open, knowing that if he had come looking for me, I was in epic trouble.

"I'm sorry! I slept in! I don't know how it happened. I don't want a lecture; I just want to get on with the day," I said before he could get out a word. But he didn't say a thing, he just grabbed my hand and hauled me back into my room. He closed the door quietly but not before looking through it to make sure that there wasn't anyone else out there.

"What's going on, Hasp?" I asked. "You're scaring me." He turned and something about the look on his face had me stepping back from him. I couldn't explain it, but something was…off.

"Stay back from the door," he said in a voice that wasn't his own.

"Who are you?" I demanded, knowing immediately that I wasn't looking at the man that I respected and loved like another father.

"Oh, pardon me," he said and waved a hand in front of his face. Hasp melted away to reveal the stunning face of a young man. His bright blonde hair shone like the sun and was only dimmed by the icy blue of his eyes. Somehow he grew, standing well over seven feet tall. His bronzed skin was chiseled and strong. The air in the room buzzed with a power that I knew came from him.

A switch was flipped in me. *Where is Hasp? Who is this guy and how dare he come in my room under the guise of a friend!* I did a quick twist, and with a high kick, planted a foot against his face. He was thrown to the floor.

"Ow!" he yelled at me. I wasn't through. I rushed at him, slamming a knee into his stomach and straddling him, pinning him down as he gasped for air. Drawing a knife from the table by the door, I placed it against his neck.

"Who are you? What have you done with Hasp?" I asked, glaring at him and pushing the sharp edge harder against his skin. His hands flew up in surrender as he looked innocently back at me.

"I am a *friend*, KyLaya. I promise you," he said with a tentative smile.

"Yeah right," I argued. "Where. Is. Hasp?" I asked slowly.

"I knocked him out. He's fine!"

"What do you want with me? Why are you here?" I yelled.

"Can I get up? You are kind of hurting me," he asked. I turned the dagger so the tip pressed sharply against him. He yelped and his brow furrowed.

"Okay, you know, I really didn't want to do this, but you leave me no choice," he said.

"Don't threaten me," I growled at him. He scowled at me and I glared back. Pale pink mist rose from his skin toward me like a thick cloud.

"Nice try, but I'm not afraid of a little smoke," I said to him.

"Oh, you should be," he answered. Suddenly I was smacked with a dizzy spell that toppled me off of him. I laid on the floor as the man stood.

"I'm not here to hurt you, KyLaya," he said again.

"How am I supposed to trust you?" I slurred at him. I stood on wobbly legs and tried to charge at him. He maneuvered out of my way with ease and sighed.

"Alright, you asked for it," he uttered. More mist poured from him. I didn't have enough control over my body to move out of the way of his powers this time. When it drew to me, I could feel it sink below my skin, making its way to my chest…to my heart.

When it did, I was struck with an all-consuming desire for the man that stood before me. He was stunning. His skin perfection. His eyes ethereal. I wanted to touch him. To be closer to him. I stepped forward, but he held up a hand and I found myself stop.

"Listen. There is someone here that has come for you. He wants you dead. I'm here to protect you. I won't hurt you," he said. I smiled lazily.

Sure, sure. Someone else is killing stuff…blah, blah.

"Okay. What's *your* name?" I asked, reaching for his silky skin and hard pecks. He ducked out of my hands quickly, avoiding my grasp.

"My name is Eros," he said in a quiet voice as he shoved his hand into mine. I wanted to hug him…maybe more…

"Stay here and…try to be quiet," he said, pushing me towards the bed. I smiled as he ran to the door and listened. Not being able to fight the attraction I felt I went over to him and laid against his back.

"What is going on?" I said rather loudly, running my hands along his skin.

"Shh! He'll hear you!" Eros stated in a hushed tone, looking back at me over his shoulder. I laughed and blushed like a preteen girl as his eyes met mine.

"Okay," he sighed. "This isn't working. Just remember that I did it so that you would listen to me, okay?"

"Anything you say," I answered and giggled. I watched as pink haze seeped out of my skin and retreated back to Eros. There was an enormous drop in my happiness, like something in me was taken and then I realized exactly when he had done. He made me desire him so much, that I would have done anything for him. *Anything.*

"What the hell was that?" I seethed.

"You weren't listening to me, I had to do something!" he answered, glancing at the door.

"That was a dick move," I said to him.

"You really left me no choice. You were going to stab me," he said, pointing to the red gash on his neck from my knife. I shrugged.

"Fine. Eros, is it?" I asked. He nodded. "What is going on?"

"Deimos - or Phobos - I can never tell them apart, have come for you," he answered scrunching up his face.

"Me?"

"Yes, you."

"And who are *they*?" I asked, standing close to him, but not nearly as close as I had been.

"My brothers," he answered.

"Why do your brothers want to kill *me*?" I asked in a hushed voice

"I- I don't know?" he said, looking sheepish.

"What? You say that they want to kill me but you don't know *why*?"

"Sorry. All I know is that they already killed your guardian. They've found them all, I don't know how," he said with a heavy voice.

"They killed someone? Who? Who did they kill?" I asked, stepping forward and placing my hands on his shoulders, shaking them.

"Sorry about this, but you really need to be quieter," he said and placed a finger in the center of my forehead. There was a flash and the world spun. Darkness took me and I was out.

When I came to, I was in my bed. The light from the bathroom window showed that it was mid-morning. It was as if no time had passed at all.

Did I just dream all that?

The room was empty with no evidence of Eros having been there. I sat up in bed.

What a way to start the day…

9
JETT

"WHAT WERE YOU DOING OUTSIDE TRITON?" I asked the Siren.

We had all rested up for the interrogation. Standard procedure to make sure that we weren't acting out of exhaustion, but with a clear, level head. However, with the dream still playing in my mind, I was more distracted than I would have liked. The touch of Laya's lips on mine left me with more to think about than I liked and though I knew, deep down, that it was only a dream, this time it was different. It was like, for the first time, she was really there.

I shook my head to rid myself of the sight of Laya and focused on the job in front of me. The Siren was strapped to a chair in the basement of the old house on my farm. We never used it, and to keep it from falling into disrepair, I volunteered it as a kind of headquarters for The Watch. With a holding room and interrogation room in the cellar, it served our purpose nicely. Not the most ideal use of it, but the building received general maintenance which kept it standing; and, that was more important than anything else.

The room was small, only enough space for a chair at the center and for someone to walk around it. Stone, cement, and mud made up the walls which were crumbling from years of wet weather and age. A musty smell penetrated my nose as I stood in front of the Siren; the air thick with moisture and decay. The floor was a mixture of dirt, sand, and, from the time before we were able to get Sam on board, blood.

I won't say that I enjoyed what we did in that basement. I didn't. But, the fact was, Sirens were evil creatures and though killing them wasn't the greatest for my soul, there was a degree of satisfaction to getting rid of some of the truly nastiest creatures I had ever spoken to.

The things that came out of their mouths was nothing short of shocking and disturbing…at first. After months and years of hearing it, those words didn't affect me as they used to. In the end, the safety of my people was at risk; and, that was what mattered the most. It was something that I would do anything to protect. That included killing Sirens.

"You know I'm not going to talk to you, *Mer*," the Siren uttered, glaring at me. "You can beat me all you want; you'll get nothing from me." The room was dark for two reasons. It was harder on her vision when the light shone on her, and it kept the true color of our eyes hidden.

"I suppose we'll see, won't we?" I said. "You aren't the first Siren I have questioned," I answered with a shrug. "I don't *want* to hurt you, I really don't; but, I will if you don't tell me why you were in Triton tonight."

"Dirty Mer child! I'm not telling you anything! Rot in Hades!" she yelled, and I cracked her across the face with the back of my hand. Her head flew to the side and stayed there as she tried to make sense of what just happened. Every time I did it my stomach turned and my conscience screamed at me. I hated this part of my job. *Hated* it. But there were some of my kind that would enjoy it too much; and, so to keep *them* out of the room, I took it upon myself to do it. Every time.

"Why were you at Triton?" I asked, placing my hands on hers and leaning into her.

She turned her head slowly to me, her eyes narrow slits, and she spat in my face.

My hands lit in pink energy, as my temper got the best of me. She screamed in pain as my power zapped into her hands. Her head shot back, her eyes wide, as her body went rigid with pain.

When I withdrew my hands, she sagged in the chair. Rayna walked in the room in that moment and looked at me with a question on her face.

"She spat in my face," I said, bringing the bottom of my shirt up and wiping the Siren spit from around my eyes and across my nose. *Ugh, gross.* Siren spit was disgusting and almost always ended up making you sick. I had no idea why; but, it did, at least for everyone else. It didn't seem to affect me.

Rayna always sat in on interrogations with me. The Council ruled that there were to always be two of us in the room in order to keep each other accountable. No one liked Sirens; in fact, most hated them with a passion, but what kept us separate from the Sirens was that we refused to act like them. We wouldn't stoop to their level, to their violence. Sometimes I wished that we could stoop just a little, though; it would make getting answers easier from Sirens like this one. But it was that principle that kept me from overstepping and regretting what I had done…like pulling her fingernails from her hands to get her to talk. Besides, we had other means. Gentler ways, but just as effective.

"He's here," Rayna said from the door. I nodded.

"Good," I answered. Sirens were ready to die for their queen. They were pawns in her grand schemes, and they threw their lives away willingly…never really knowing why. We knew that we were only touching the tip of the iceberg with whatever information we got, but the tip was better than nothing.

The Siren sat up in her chair, regaining her strength a little, yet not offering any information. I expected that she wouldn't talk, they typically never did, not through pain anyway. But, I always had to try. It took less energy for me to attempt to get a Siren to talk through interrogation than it did for Sam through his power. He offered them something that they had never had…total and complete relaxation. Euphoria.

The door darkened as a tall figure came through.

"Hey, Sam," I said to the man. Sam had a gift for healing; his touch could pull fear and pain from you and heal whatever injured you. It took a lot out of him though, and we knew when we asked him to come to an interrogation we were taking the healer away from our people for a day or two. The only thing was…Rayna and I were the only ones who knew he could do this. His involvement in this manner was a complete secret from everyone else. They thought that he was there to make sure we didn't get injured. They couldn't have been more wrong. Even his husband – my brother – didn't know what he really did.

Jasper and Sam had been together for over a decade, but Jasper was completely against interrogating Sirens for information. It was one of the few things that we stood on completely different grounds with. Sam was on my side. He understood the need for information, but he didn't want Jasper to know that. When he offered to help we were only too happy to have his assistance. The only thing that he requested was that we keep it a complete secret. Rayna and I had never betrayed him, nor would we.

Sam was not a small man. He had to duck to get into the room, and he towered over the Siren in the chair. Next to Sam, she looked like a child. Sam knelt in front of her, his eyes meeting hers. His light brown hair glowed in the overhead light that hung from the ceiling as he leaned toward her.

"My name is Sam," he said quietly.

"I don't give a shit," she snarled.

"I will not hurt you," he said as he reached out and placed his hands on hers. She flinched, anticipating pain; but, when none came she looked at Sam with a furrowed brow. A light grew under his hands and sank into her skin. Her eyes widened and then softened as a lazy smile appeared on her lips.

"She's ready," Sam declared, keeping his eyes fixed on the connection he had with her.

"Perfect," I answered, stepping forward. The Siren slowly lifted her eyes to me and smiled. She was pretty, they all were, once the Siren in them was tamed. I leaned in and smiled back.

"Hi there," I said slowly. "What's your name?"

"It's Hellia, Sexy. What's yours?" she asked, leaning toward me. Sam chuckled, I smacked him on the back. We went through this every time. Sam's power lowered inhibitions to almost nothing. Getting hit on was almost guaranteed when he was working on a Siren.

"My name is Jett. Could you tell me what you were doing at Triton tonight?" I asked gently.

"Just trying to get our hands on someone," she smiled and shrugged, her eyes glazed over and her head swayed.

"Who?" I asked.

"Some girl," she answered, not looking at me this time.

"Do you know her name?" I asked again, trying to get more from her.

"Constantilly," she answered with a slur.

"She's starting to slip away," Sam said. "Be quick."

"What do you want with her?"

"Midira…wants her…" she answered slowly.

"For what?" I demanded, leaning toward her, and looking her in the eye.

"Prophesy…" she said quietly, slumping over in the chair. The light in Sam's hands dimmed and disappeared. He stood shaking his head.

"This one was tough. Never seen a Siren go so fast before, everything in her fought against the relaxing power I put into her. Her heart gave out," he said with a wave of his hand.

"Well, we got something, at least. A name," I reiterated. "Constantilly. Ever heard of her?"

Sam and Rayna shook their heads.

"Well, we'll have to find out who she is. If Midira wants her, it can't be good," I reasoned. "Thank you, Sam," I said shaking his hand as he got up, swaying slightly.

"You okay?" Rayna asked him.

"Yeah, will need to go lie down for a while. Same deal as always?" Sam asked.

"Of course," Rayna and I answered. Sam would be weak and Jasper would figure that out. Our job was to corroborate that Sam had healed someone. This time it would be a car accident that we happened upon.

"Go home, lay down," Rayna urged as she wrapped an arm around Sam's wide shoulders. "We'll call Jasper and let him know."

"Thank you," he uttered as he showed himself out. Rayna came to my side.

"What are you thinking?" she asked.

"I'm thinking that we need to find this girl before the Sirens do," I replied.

"And then what?" she asked. I knew what she was getting at. If we found her, what were we going to do with her?

"I don't know," I said, being honest. I didn't know what I would do with the girl. But I knew that she wasn't safe in the hands of the Sirens. Whatever they were planning on using her for we couldn't let them.

"You know we'll have to kill her," Rayna determined.

"What?"

"Well, we can't bring her here and we can't let her go to the Sirens. What options are left?" she asked. I shook my head. Taking a Siren's life was one thing, but to kill a Mer just so that the Sirens couldn't get her was another. One that did not sit well with me at all. But I nodded in agreement anyway. The chances of finding the Constantilly girl were slim to none.

No way I'm going to have to worry about it anyway.

10
KYLAYA

"I DIDN'T SAY WE *WOULDN'T* DO IT! I said I would *think* about it," I exclaimed.

"With all due respect, Miss Constantilly, there has to be more done about this Siren problem," Councilman Trewly insisted.

I was stuck in another meeting, a council this time, with the elected members from Triton. We met to ensure that the people of Triton were being heard and that they knew that there was honest and open communication between people and state. But the thing was, my mind was still a blur of what had happened in my dream, or not dream. Was someone really trying to kill me, or did I dream up the whole thing? Either way, it left me with a little less concern for their petty fears about one Siren lurking about in the water and more that there may be some psycho wandering the halls of High Hill looking to slice my throat open in my sleep.

"We don't have a Siren *problem*! We have one *possible* Siren that doesn't know when to buzz off!" I yelled.

"You can't sit here and ignore the fact that this may *mean* something! We haven't seen a Siren in years! Why is she here?" he asked, throwing his hands in the air and looking to the other members to back up his line of questioning.

"We don't know! No one has been able to ask her! She disappears before we can confront her every time," I answered, throwing my hands up too. "If any of you have any suggestions on how to talk to someone that vanishes into thin water then now's the time, gentlemen! Speak up!" I challenged them. They all looked around the table at each other.

I knew this wasn't how things were done in there. I was yelling, and slightly less than professional doing so, but they had been asking and demanding the same thing for weeks. I was done.

"Didn't think so," I answered for them. "Look, I will go up with the guards today when she is spotted and see for myself what she wants if that's what it will take for you to back off and just let me do what I need to do. Commander Hasp and I are working together on this! Surely, you have faith in his abilities to see this through," I looked around the room at all the mermen gathered there and hoped they weren't daft enough to challenge Hasp.

Grumbling agreements resounded around the room, and we were done. I stood from the table and left, without a glance back, knowing that their grumbles would turn to me as soon as I was out the door.

I stalked down the hall to the echoing sounds of my high heels, something that tortured my feet but I was never without. At only five feet six inches, I needed as much of a lift as I could get. I worked with mostly men. Even though a female leader was something that they were accustomed to, as my mother was leader alongside my father until her death, they had known me since I was a child and some of them still thought of me as one. I learned from the start that I needed to look the part of a leader just as much as I needed to act the part. Just one more adjustment that I had to make. Gone were my comfy clothes and flat shoes…never to return most likely.

Going out on duty with the guards was already a plan of mine. I wanted to get a look at whatever it was that was lurking around the city. If it was friendly, what was it doing? If it wasn't, we needed to do something about it.

I turned a sharp corner, my mind on the meeting I just had, and ran right into Hasp. My papers went flying and so did a curse or two on my part.

"What are you *doing*?" he shouted, and then backed off when he saw my face.

"I was walking, same as you," I answered, glaring at him.

"Sorry," he uttered, not looking at me. "That wasn't about you."

"What's going on?" I asked him, seeing the worry deepening his brow. "Something I should be aware of?"

"There's been an…incident," he answered hesitantly.

"What incident? I've heard nothing," I answered slowly standing and handing him the papers I had gathered that were his.

"I haven't given word, yet. I wanted to tell you first," he said in a low voice.

"What is it?" I asked, my heart starting to thrum in my chest. He had never looked so worried before, so unsettled.

"Come with me. Quickly," he said and turned back the direction he came from. I grabbed my papers and hugged them to my chest, in terrible disarray, and followed after him as best I could in my pencil skirt and heels.

"What about Mazz?" I asked.

"I sent for him; he's meeting us," he answered and quickened his gait. I was about to ask where we were going when I figured it out at his next turn.

"The Archives!" I whispered in fright. "Please tell me…" But I didn't finish, the answer was before me, as was Mazz.

"It was like this when I got here, I swear," Mazz said holding up his hands. I didn't have the energy to smile at his joke; I was too disturbed. The door to the locked tomb, where we kept Triton's most sacred archives, was thrown off the wall as if someone had grabbed the handle and pulled the door from the wall itself. Bits of stone and cement were strewn over the floor, and the door still had chunks of it attached to the hinges. I looked at Hasp; now I understood his need to keep this a secret.

"When?" I asked, stepping up to the door and running my hands over the cracked and split wood.

"I'm not sure," Hasp said shaking his head heavily. "There was a mess up with the guard. No one was here. When I went to check the schedule, someone had tampered with it leaving it unguarded. No one was here all day today. It's hard to pin down a time."

"How did you know?" Mazz asked his father.

"I didn't, I had come down to retrieve a document from the vault and saw this. I went straight to get the two of you."

"What's missing?" I asked as we stepped into the room inside the vault. Hasp lit a lantern and the room came into view. Gasps rang out from all of us when we saw the devastation. The place looked like a hurricane had gone through it. Furniture and shelves were toppled over. Papers, scrolls, books, ancient texts were tossed around the room with no care. My heart was breaking. I had spent a lot of time in there studying the ancient texts when I was a child. This was like a second home to me, a place of peace and history.

"My gods," Mazz breathed as he took in the destruction. "Why would someone do this? *Who* would do this?"

"Sirens," I answered, and he looked at me and then his dad. "It's got to be," I continued. "There's no way it's a coincidence that there's a Siren around the city and then there's a break in. There's no way they're not related." I stooped and picked up a chair that leaned on its side. Old and plush it normally sat in the corner of the room with a light behind it. The perfect little reading nook for someone wanting to dive into an old text, someone like me. I swallowed the rising pressure in my throat as I looked around the place I had always run to as a child – even as an adult.

The three of us circled the room, picking up what we could but not really making a dent in the mess.

"Mistress Hol is going to flip when she sees this," Mazz said with a shake of his head.

"That old crone flips when a dust bunny dares to take up residence in a corner of the room," Hasp grumbled.

"Hush," I hissed at him. "She's a kind woman who takes her job as the caretaker of the vault seriously. She's going to be devastated."

"Actually, I think she's got other problems," Mazz uttered from around the corner of the stacks.

"Why?" I asked, and he stood back and pointed to the corner in the far rear of the vault. When I turned the corner, my heart hit the floor and my hand flew to my mouth. There, under a fallen shelf, was Mistress Hol. A pool of blood spread across the floor, saturating the books that touched it.

No it can't be…

Hasp walked quickly around the corner. When he saw her, he took off his hat.

"She was a good Mer," he said solemnly.

"Why would someone want her dead?" I asked, still not able to tear my eyes away from the sight of the woman that had nurtured my love of reading and research as a child. Her grey hair was a mess of thick blood from a wound across her neck. Her eyes stared into space as her mouth sagged open in a silent scream.

It was enough to make my stomach lurch.

She was the kindest, most inspiring teacher that I ever had. Why would someone kill her?

Mazz stepped forward and removed the shelf from her. Stooping down he grabbed some of the books that had tumbled onto her, in the ransacked mess of her beloved vault. That's when I saw something else.

"What is *that*?" Mazz gasped, pointing to the same thing I was staring at.

Mistress Hol's shirt had been torn open at the collar and on her chest, just below her collarbone, was a mark. I had never seen it on her before. Mistress Hol and I had become friends as I had grown into a woman. She had told me about where she grew up and her family, we talked books and history, shared stories about life and beyond; but, never had she mentioned a mark like that before.

"It looks like the mark of the gods," I answered, not sure I was really seeing it. "Mistress Hol showed it to me once in a book. The gods mark those that they have in their protection…or service…"

My dream. Eros said that they killed a guardian. Was that Mistress Hol? It couldn't be a coincidence. It couldn't. Which also meant that it wasn't a dream and someone was really there to kill me. My blood chilled.

Knees buckling, I settled ungracefully to the ground.

"Ky? You okay?" Mazz asked, placing a tender hand on my shoulder and leaning down to me. I couldn't look at him, he would know there was something wrong, instead I looked at Mistress Hol.

"I just…can't believe it…" I uttered slowly.

Hasp went over, gently moving books and debris from around Mistress Hol so that he could get a better look at what caused her death.

Mazz sat down next to me and grasped my hand. I looked at him.

"I know you were close to her, Ky. I'm so sorry. We *will* find out who did this," he said, his grey eyes storming as he looked at me. My heart warmed, I rested my head on his shoulder for a moment, letting the sadness of Mistress Hol's death take me. She was one of those teachers that inspired me beyond when I was just a student. She had fostered my love to learn to that day. Her teachings had helped me become who I was. She deserved better than such a violent death. But who was she really? If she was a guardian for the gods, who was she guarding? Was it me? Was that why Eros came to me?

"What do you think?" I asked Hasp as he made his way carefully over to us.

He stood, placing his hands on his hips. Clearing his throat, he stepped gingerly back from the debris that we had sat on. He brought his hand around my arm and guided us away from her, and around the corner.

"Dad?" Mazz asked, as he looked at his father with a furrowed brow and concerned eyes.

"I've never seen anything like it," Hasp uttered. "She was cut across the throat, but the cut was cauterized. It takes intense heat to cause burns like that. I don't know of any weapon that can do that." His eyes closed and he shook his head. "I – I just don't know what to think."

"Well, it was the Sirens, right?" Mazz asked.

"Sirens depend on their poisonous daggers. They have no need for a weapon like that. I don't think it was them, son," Hasp answered. Mazz moved his weight from foot to foot and looked around the room, as if the answer was in there somewhere.

"We should go and get the healers to come and take Mistress Hol to the care center to prepare her for her ceremony," I said quietly, knowing that there was nothing else we could do for her now.

I couldn't shake the feeling that I was somehow tied up in her death, and that didn't sit well with me. Mistress Hol was a friend; why would someone want to kill her? Why would someone want to kill me? It all made no sense.

II
JETT

EVERYTHING WAS LIGHT, like always. The world around me as familiar as my own.

I had been in this dream many times before, and I would be in it again. But I wasn't going to argue or fight against it. She was there.

Her long blonde hair hung in great curls around her shoulders and down her back. When she turned and looked at me, my heart nearly jumped right out of my chest. It was like that every time. All it took was a look from her and I was gone. I was done.

"Hey you," she said in a voice so sweet.

"How was your day?" I asked, a smile spreading wide across my face that I couldn't help no matter what I did.

"Honestly?" she asked. I nodded. "It was terrible."

"What? Why?"

"I lost someone close to me. She was killed," she shared.

"Killed?" I blurted. "How? Why?"

"I don't know," she answered, lowering her head.

"I'm so sorry, Laya," I said, aching to reach out and hold her. She sighed again and that ache pulled even more.

"What is it?"

"It's just…I'm so confused. First, Mistress Hol was killed, and then I had this dream the other night. I think they are connected. I think it's my fault she's dead. But, that's insane right?" she shook her head and drooped over. "I feel like I'm going crazy," she uttered placing her head in her hands.

"You're not going crazy, Laya," I said, trying to comfort her without touching her. Something that I was aching to do.

"I honestly think I am," she answered.

"You're the most sane person I know," I pointed out.

"Really? I doubt that," she argued.

"Really."

"It's not just the loss of my friend. It's everything. It's me. It's you. I mean…what would you say to someone that was falling for a person that only existed in their dreams?" she asked me, her eyes on me, waiting for the answer.

I didn't know what to say to her. I felt like I was going crazy in that department too. She was only a dream, and yet I felt more for her than anyone in my real life. That *was* insane. Truly insane.

I sighed and smiled at her. "I think that dreams are a way to experience things that we really hope and wish for, but that we can't experience in real life."

"Wow. That's good actually," she said with a light chuckle and smile. "How long have you been practicing that?"

I laughed, "Only a few weeks." She laughed and leaned back, laying down and placing her hands under her cheek as she turned toward me. I laid down beside her. Not touching her, not dream stopping, and yet aching so badly to kiss her the way we did last time. It was worth it. I turned to her, and looked into her blue eyes that were already on mine.

"Do you really feel something for me?" she asked. My heart hit the back of my throat, and I swallowed hard. If she would have been real, I would have been terrible awkward and shy. I was sure of it, but it was Laya. We'd been around each other since childhood, and she knew me so well, it seemed wrong to lie to her.

"You know I do," I said back. She bit her lip and nodded once. "Why are you asking?"

"You are the closest thing to a relationship that I have ever had, and we can't even touch," she began. "I want to touch you. I want to feel my hand in yours. To know what your arms feel like around me. It seems cruel that the person I want more than anything I can't have…because he isn't real," she finished in a quiet voice. A tear appeared on her cheek. An ache opened in my core that I didn't know what to do with. Acting more out of instinct than anything else, I reached for her. Expecting a dream stop immediately I was shocked to feel her skin. I drew her into my arms, hugging her tightly to me.

"Don't cry, Laya. Please," I said quietly. She looked up at me, tears still wet on her cheeks. I lifted a hand and wiped them away with my thumbs as I placed my hands on her beautiful face. Her long lashes, her delicate skin, her blue eyes, all of it was stunning; and, I felt myself fall even further for her as I looked into her face.

How could there ever be another when I had her?

"Laya," I whispered as she tipped her chin up towards mine. Her gaze held mine, beautiful blue and sad. My heart thundered in my chest, beating hard and steady. Beating for her. My lips tingled as my eyes flicked to her lips. Smooth as silk, they called to me, and I found myself lowering to her.

She didn't wait for me, instead she wrapped a hand around my neck, threading her fingers in my hair and brought her lips to mine.

I SAT STRAIGHT UP. Wrestling with the covers, and swearing at them in the process, I untangled myself enough to realize that I had fallen out of bed. Like a two year old.

What the…

Moonlight poured in through my open window. My white curtains blew in a warm summer evening breeze. The sweet scent of night in the country always made me feel at ease, restful, and settled. But, even with all the wonderful smells of the farm, my dream clung to me.

Laya. Her stunning eyes, her soft skin…

It was different this time, I held her in my arms. Just the thought of it did things to me that I was not prepared for, but that I wanted to do again.

Like now.

Why were these dreams so realist? I knew that it wasn't normal. I told Jasper about Laya when I was a kid and asked him who his dream person was. He had no idea what I was talking about. I found out quickly that I was the only one, but I just didn't know why. Now I was tortured with falling for a person who was literally the girl of my dreams; but, didn't exist in real life.

I grumbled and got back into bed. Throwing myself into it, I placed a pillow on my face and groaned into it. *Why me?*

I closed my eyes and begged my dreams to keep away from Laya. I needed sleep, not a turn on. It had already been a tiring day with the Siren attack on the city and then the interrogation. I needed rest.

There would be a council meeting to attend soon. That was the way of things if we had to bring a Siren back. But the Siren was dead and didn't give us much information. We buried her in the forest behind the house, it might have seemed unceremonious, but it was better than what she would have had with the Sirens.

Sam always gave them a quiet, easy death. He didn't like it, even though his hatred of Sirens was deeper than the rest of us. He actually *remembered* being abandoned. It was a by-product of his power, deeper memory. He was in a dark place when he met my brother. Sam had said, for a long time, that Jasper was the only reason he was still there. I never doubted that. Sam was not one for exaggeration. He was a good man and one I was very happy and grateful to have in my family.

I stumbled to a stand and put on a pair of sweat pants. The house was dark when I walked into the kitchen. The farm evening offered the dead silence that I craved.

Jasper wasn't home; and, for once I was grateful. He was already in town at Sam's helping him recover. Did I like lying to my brother about Sam? *No*. I *hated* it. I knew one day he would find out, and the look on his face when he did would break my heart and Sam's. But, in the meantime, the information that Sam was able to get from the Sirens had saved lives…many lives.

Constantilly…who are you?

I was nagged by an unsettling feeling. I didn't know if it was my dream or what the Siren had said, but it wouldn't leave me. Propelled to do something, I put my gear back on and, without checking in with the rest of The Watch, decided to go back to Triton.

12
KYLAYA

THE NEXT EVENING I prepared to go out on patrol with the guards. I still had a promise to keep about seeing into the Siren who was circling the city. With Mistress Hol's death leaking out, I was happy to get out of the castle for a while anyway. The letters were flocking in and the summons were being made, and I was not answering them. *Let the poor woman rest in peace and her family mourn.*

I knew that Hasp would deal with the majority of the issues and details surrounding the death in the castle. I was really just running interference to give him time to do his job, but it was all so meaningless.

An innocent, good woman had been killed. Stop asking me what she was wearing, what she was doing that day, if she had any enemies.

I shook my head to clear it. I had to focus on what I was doing. A clear mind was needed when you went out into the open water. Distraction was a sure way of getting killed, or at the very least injured.

I pulled on my tight black leather jacket. It fit like a glove and was my favorite piece of clothing. I earned it while training with the Elite, the guards that protect Triton. Father thought that it was important for me to learn how to fight. I was going to be in a position of power and authority, and there may come a time when I would need to protect myself. I argued that my personal guard would take care of me, but I lost that argument and was sent for training anyway.

Turned out that Father was right to send me but not because I really needed it; I actually *liked* it. I liked learning to fight. Even after my standard self defense training was done, I didn't stop. Weapons, hand to hand, advanced offense…I learned it all. And to top it all off, I was good. Really good. So much so that the Elite took notice, and I was asked to start to train with them. The Elite were the guards that patrolled the city in open water. They were the best, and it was an honor to be asked to train with them. It wasn't until Father got sick that I was forced to quit my training.

It had been a while since I had sparred with anyone from the Elite, and I was missing it. They had become my friends, and then suddenly I had become their boss. Being the Prime meant that I could command them. They didn't mind, but it put a distance between us that I didn't see coming. I guess, I never thought that I would be taking over for my father at such a young age. I was nineteen and the only child left, the only family left, of the Constantilly's.

I took a look in the mirror as I strapped on my blade belt over the tight leather pants that went with the uniform. I always felt more powerful in my gear than anything else I wore. Like a second skin, I felt more myself in it than my heels and skirts. I flipped a knife in my hand and placed it in the holster at my hip. Two more went in the holsters on my tall boots. Blades were my choice of weapon. I was deadly accurate with them, more than any of the Elite; though, most of them chose larger weapons than mine.

Just for fun, I flipped a dagger in my hand and shot it at a notch in the wall. It sailed through the air and right to the center of the spot I was aiming for, sinking into the wall and sticking there.

"Still got it," I said with a smile.

There was a knock at the door. I took one last look at the black leather gear that I wore, feeling stronger and more in control and crossed the room to the door. Mazz stood in the doorway when I opened it. When he turned, his eyes took in the length of me.

"Yes?" I asked him, as his eyes made their way up to mine.

"Yeah – umm – why are you wearing that?" he asked and cleared his throat. He bit his lip, which was a sign that he was nervous and trying not to say something stupid.

"I'm going out with the Elite, Mazz," I answered, turning and walking to the wall where I had thrown the knife. Pulling it out, I shoved it back into its place on my leg.

"You can't go out looking like that!" he blurted.

"What? Why not?" I asked, utterly stunned at the ridiculousness of that remark. My suit was what all the Elite wore. It protected our skin from the water, from getting cut, and held our weapons. What was he expecting me to wear? Heels?

"I – it's just not appropriate for you to wear that…that…," he bumbled pointing to me.

"What are you *talking* about?" I questioned, staring at him.

"It's revealing! Okay?" he blurted.

"You're an idiot," I declared and moved him out of the way so I could leave my room. "What did you come here to tell me?"

He huffed. "I wanted to see if you were okay. I know it must have been hard on you to see Mistress Hol like that," he explained.

"I – I'm fine," I answered him with a shrug. Truth was I was far from okay, but I couldn't explain to him why. That I might have been the reason she was killed was still eating at me.

"Well, I seriously doubt that you're *fine*; so, I thought that you could use a pick-me-up. I brought you a little treat from town," he said and held out a wrapped package that I hadn't even noticed he was carrying.

"Mazz," I uttered and took the package from his hands, unwrapping it. Under the paper was a box from my absolute favorite sweet shop. I smiled. Candy always made me feel better. Or maybe it just made me feel like a kid for a moment. "Thank you, that was really *sweet* of you." I leaned over and gave him a kiss on the cheek, plucking a gummy candy from the box and tossing it in my mouth. I sighed and smiled as the sweet fruity taste invaded my taste buds. *Heaven!*

"So good," I said. My silly grin faded as I came back to reality. "I will have to wait to finish this after guard duty. And, you know I *will* be finishing it. Thank you, again," I said grinning at my friend.

"Anytime, Ky," he said and pulled me in for a hug. I rested my head on his chest for a moment and just enjoyed the support of the man I loved like a brother. He pulled my door open, and I placed the package on the table beside it as we exited my room.

"You okay?" I asked.

"Yeah! Yeah, why wouldn't I be?" he asked, placing his hands in his pockets.

"Just with all the stuff that happened today, plus you seem…off," I implied.

"Off? Nope," he said with a shake of his head and a dip to his lip.

"Okay," I said unconvinced. But, I was late and had to run to catch the Elite; so, I would have to drill him for a real answer later.

"I guess I'll see you tomorrow then?" he asked as we left my room and travelled down the hall.

"Of course!" I said.

When we came to the intersecting hall where I had to part ways, I turned to go and was surprised to feel a hand on my shoulder. I looked back and Mazz reached around me, pulling me against him.

"Be safe, Ky," he whispered into my hair as he hugged me.

"I've been out with the guards a million times. I'll be fine," I said, trying to comfort him. He had never liked that I went out with the Elite before. He was more against it than my father was, but this felt different. His eyes lingered on mine a second too long, and I found myself feeling awkward for the first time with him. I stepped back and cleared my throat. He placed his hands in his pockets and gave me a stiff nod before he walked off towards his father's chamber.

Okay. Why did that feel so weird?

13
JETT

THE PORTAL WAS BEHIND OUR HOUSE. It was one of the reasons that we had the farm so far away from town. Resting at the bottom of a slough, under the guise of disgusting looking water, was the entrance to Mer. It was all a magical rouse to keep onlookers away from it. The water was clean and clear the moment you passed through the barrier. I walked through the field toward the portal, each step shushing the blades of grass around my dark green gear as I went. The crickets were singing and the moon was bright. It was promising to be a beautiful night; too bad I was going to miss it.

I placed a foot in the water and immediately it jumped up, swallowing me whole as I was taken.

No matter how many times I travelled by portal I would never get used to the feel of it - being stretched and pulled in all directions and then snapped back into place, and cold…so cold.

When I came out the other side, I was in the salty water I was born to. Even though it was in my blood to breath, it still took a moment to adjust to filtering oxygen through my lungs. Sirens and Mer could breathe both water and air, thanks to a blessing Poseidon bestowed on us a very long time ago. The more you practiced transitioning between the two, the better you got at it and the easier it was. I was at the point where there was almost no time to adjust. However, there were some that felt like they were drowning every time they switched between air and water. I remembered what that was like. Not fun.

The water was calm and dark as I travelled toward Triton. Evening had set in, though not as late as it was back home. Our portal was hidden amongst the sharp edges of a rock cliff, just outside of the city's dome. It had been placed there when our town was created so that we would have access to come home one day. The Watch was really the only people that used it, though. The rest of our people stayed away from the sea for fear of being caught and persecuted for being of Siren blood.

I didn't blame them.

Even though we weren't Sirens, the Mer wouldn't hesitate treating us as Sirens, thanks to the violet eyes that we shared with them. We had to be careful.

Normally, when we came through as a team, we would start for the top of the dome to get the best view, but I was alone and needed to be careful. I didn't know what Midira's plans were now that her attack had been foiled. Would she try again or just give up?

When I saw the entrance open, I sank down into the rocks and watched. The Triton guards emerged into the water in a tight formation, which they only did when there was a cause for alarm. Something had spooked them.

They were just as good at transitioning as we were, maybe better as they had more opportunity to get into the water than we did. But, their fighting skills weren't as good as ours. That didn't mean that I wanted to face off against them, though. They were on high alert; I could tell by their numbers and the way that their eyes searched the water. Something was up and they were on the lookout.

Did they see the fight from before? Is that what this was?

I sank down low and stayed there, just out of their sight. They were on their own in a fight against the Sirens if they returned. I wouldn't be able to help them; it wasn't worth the risk of being seen. I hunkered down and waited.

14
KYLAYA

"WELL, LOOK WHO DECIDED TO JOIN US!" a voice rang out as I entered the water just outside the dome. I was late, as usual, having talked to Mazz for a moment too long. The Elite didn't wait for anyone, even me.

The dome spread over the city like a huge bubble within which we lived. Without it, we *could* survive, all Mer can breathe water; but, we would be exposed to the elements and dangers of the sea. Strong currents, sharks, whales - not to mention Sirens - were just a few of the things that the dome protected us from. To leave, there were two exits, both guarded. I left through the main entrance at the front of Triton. The back entrance remained sealed unless we were expecting a high influx of Mer or a shipment from Titus Prime or Aquious, the other Mer cities.

"Don't start with me," I scoffed back at the Elite's leader, Reqet.

I looked ahead at the Elite, sailing in perfect formation in the water as they made their way to the top of the dome to get the best view of the city and all surrounding area.

Reqet lead as usual. His wide frame was strong and agile in the water in a way that was unexpected from a man that was shaped like him. He had been the leader of the Elite for a long time and had trained everyone on it, including me. He only took the best. Which made my presence there an honor, as I was a welcomed member, even to him. He wouldn't have let me join if I wasn't good enough, no matter who my father was.

Reqet had always given me a hard time; but I earned his respect. I had worked harder and longer than the others in the group during training and afer. He was an abrasive kind of guy, but that was okay with me. I was surrounded by people wanting to get on my good side because now I had a job with power. Reqet could have cared less what my job was; all he wanted was good guards to protect his city. I respected that and knew that whatever he told me was honest and truthful; he didn't have an agenda unlike a lot of the Mer I had to deal with.

"You're late!" He called back at me.

"I know, but I'm here. Let's go talk to this Siren," I yelled back as we soared through the water.

"She's not out just yet. We've been watching but have seen no movement," he explained.

"You think she got discouraged and left?" I asked, coming to the front of the line next to him.

"No self-respecting Siren would leave a post she was sent to man. No, she'll be back," he answered with a determined nod.

We moved over the dome to the top. It was always a strange sight, looking down on the city from so high. Everything looked small from outside, and fragile. If anything happened to that dome, we would all be caught up in the devastation that would rain down on us. Titus Prime had been the victim of that many years ago and we learned from their mistakes. Now there was a guard that kept the dome protected and more safeties put into place against an attack.

"There!" someone shouted and all heads turned. Off in the distance a shadow could be seen.

"What *is* that?" I asked. It looked too big to be a single Siren, yet it was moving with a speed that was too fast for a whale or shark.

Reqet moved beside me. "Stay back," he said, taking out his sword.

"What? To Hades with that," I answered, pulling out a knife.

"Listen," he responded turning to me, "You are a strong fighter; you wouldn't be allowed out here if you weren't, but you are our Prime now. I wouldn't be doing my job if I allowed you to come to harm. You stay back, you hear?"

"I'm perfectly capable of defending myself, and you know it!" I argued.

"Not going to tell you again! You are our *leader* now and with that comes responsibility bigger than charging into a fight. Stay *back*!" he yelled at me, putting an end to the argument. There was no talking to him when he was like that. I knew I wasn't going to get anywhere with him; the question remained if I was going to listen to him.

"I can help," I responded lamely as he took off away from me. I wanted to argue and follow him, but a part of me knew he was right. Frozen with indecision, caught between wanting to help and knowing I should go, I got a better look at what was coming for us. I watched in horror as the shadow closed in and focused.

It wasn't *a* Siren, it was a *swarm* of them.

Gods.

"Get inside!" Reqet shouted at me. "Close the gate and don't open if for anything, you hear me?"

"I can't leave you out here! They out number you-"

"Go!" he ordered and shot a wall of water at me, moving me toward the door without my permission.

Reqet was the strongest in the Elite, able to move a great amount of water at his will. My father was another, born with the ability to move mass amounts of the sea. I was still working on my abilities.

The Siren swarm descended on the Elite with deadly purpose. I watched in horror as they crashed into the guards, breaking their line and scattering them. The Elite fought hard to avoid the poisonous blades of the Sirens, moving quickly around the sharp tips of their daggers. That's why the Elite wore such thick gear – the Siren blades couldn't slice through them. It prevented scratches from getting to their skin and poisoning them. However, there was nothing that could stop a direct hit.

They're going to be slaughtered! I can't leave them!

I just floated there, stunned and immobile watching the battle rage in front of me. Guards that I had worked with and sparred with were fighting off real, live, Sirens. Most of us had never seen a real Siren before, nor fought one. Though Reqet and his fighters had been training for a day like this, there was no training them for the challenge of battling a real Siren and all that went with it.

Sirens were stunning creatures, long hair and battle gear that clung to their bodies like the Elite suits. They moved with agility and strength that echoed that of the guards, but they fought with no honor, slicing and stabbing even at those that they weren't facing off against. Attacking a foe in the back was no cause for pause with them.

I shook my head and summoned my courage. I wouldn't leave my friends to die in such a way. I shot out toward the battle pushing myself through the water with my power and entering a fight I should have run from.

Pulling the daggers from my boots, I flipped them in my hands and charged the first Siren I saw. Flying over the Siren, who was attacking a guard from behind, I tumbled in the water coming around with all my force. Holding the daggers up high, I jammed them into the neck of the Siren, all the way to the hilt. A scream sounded from her as the knives dug deep. With a twist of the blades, she was silenced. I pulled the weapons from her as she fell from the water, landing on the seafloor below.

Oh my gods...I just killed a Siren. A real, live Siren!

With no time to celebrate, a punch landed on my cheek and I was stunned for a second. My training kicked in and I whipped around, slicing the air with my blades. The Siren ducked under my arms and attempted to stab me in the chest as she threw out her dagger wielding arm at me. I held out my hand, calling the water to me. I could feel the pull in my core as my water power came out, gathering the ocean for me. With a strong push forward, a wall of water appeared before my hand and slammed into the Siren, shoving her away from me. I was decently strong with my water power, enough to make use of it when I needed to – and I needed to.

The Siren twisted around to me in the water and screamed. The sound that came from her was like nothing I had ever heard before. It pierced my head, like long needles inserted through my ears. My hands clamped down on my ears without thinking, dissolving the wall of water that had protected me.

The Siren took advantage. Shooting through the water at me, she landed a kick to my stomach, which I had regrettably left open for her. I doubled over. A satisfied smile crept across her face.

Bitch.

I pulled myself up through the pain and with a quick flick of my knife I threw it. She didn't see it coming. With a sick *clunk*, it found its home. The Siren's scream died on her lips as she slowly fell in the water, my knife still sticking out of her chest.

I smiled and nodded, still catching my breath.

That was when I saw him.

In the distance a figure was in the water, watching the battle unfold. I couldn't see any details to his face, but the moment that I laid eyes on him it felt like I was zapped by a dozen eels. Without a thought to what was going on around me, I turned from the fight. Something in me knew him. Something from a dream.

Is that...

It can't be...

I swam for the stranger, needing to see, needing to know – was it him? *Could it be?* My heart beat hard in my chest. I found myself hoping, really hoping and yet knowing that the chances were astronomical. But as soon as I got closer to him, he disappeared.

I twisted in the water, searching, hoping – but nothing. My heart sank.

Where did he go?

I didn't get a chance to answer that question when the sharp tip of a blade was pressed against my back.

"Well, hello there," a Siren hissed into my ear. I put my hands up, knowing that if that blade pierced my suit that would be the end for me.

15
JETT

I SAW THE SWARM. It was the same size as the one that had attacked us earlier that day. I couldn't believe it. We had fallen for the decoy! Midira had sent an earlier wave to take out some of the strength of Triton knowing that there would be less fighters remaining for the next wave. She didn't know that *we* had taken out her first wave, but she accomplished her task anyway. Some of the strength defending the city *was* gone. I sat in the rock cropping and watched as the Siren swarm descended on the group of guards.

They fought with great heart and skill, but they were no match for the sheer numbers that the Sirens sent in wave two. When the fight fell out of my sight, behind the dome, I decided to slowly and carefully move to a better position to keep an eye on it. I didn't know what the Siren's endgame was; but, if there was a way that I could help stop them without being seen I would do it.

The Mer guards were being killed off one by one, but that wasn't what I was watching. There was one fight in particular that had caught my attention. Off to the side, a young mermaid with blonde hair had taken on a couple of Sirens, alone without the support or back up of the other guards. In fact, she looked as if she was on her own.

I watched, with much interest, as she used her skill with daggers and water to overpower the one she fought. I smiled when she killed the Siren. *Nicely done.*

Then she turned to me.

It was like a lightning bolt struck me right there in the water. I couldn't see her eyes, but in that moment I saw something in her, something that I had been aching to find as long I could remember.

Laya?

I couldn't move, I just floated there, silent and still. But when she shot toward me, I was caught off guard and suddenly did something that I had never done in my life.

I panicked.

I flashed away instinctively, back to the rock cropping and safety. *Safety?* What was I scared of? That it would really be her? That it wouldn't be her? I wasn't sure. All I knew was that I wanted to find out with every fiber of my being, but I was terrified of the answer.

I had been hoping for her to be real. Wishing it. I wanted it more than I cared to acknowledge. But, it was a dream, a fantasy. It *wasn't real* and neither was she. At least that's what I thought. But then, when I looked out from the rock cropping, I saw her face.

Her blonde hair billowed out behind her in the water. Her blue eyes were fierce and wide with hope as she searched the water for me.

My heart stopped. Her face, her hair, her eyes…I knew them all. I loved them all, at least I did in my dreams. She was the one I had been dreaming of for so long.

Laya…how can it be? She's real?

I looked again and there was no doubt in my mind that it was her. *Laya.* My Laya. I had never felt so completely dumbfounded.

Should I say something?

Will she know me?

She was beautiful and graceful…and one hell of a fighter, which was probably the sexiest thing I had ever seen. Somewhere deep in my core I felt a pull. My heart skipped as a connection to the girl in front of me intensified to the point that I found myself almost coming out of my hiding place. *Almost.*

But, suddenly her eyes grew wide and a jolt of adrenaline hit my veins when I saw why.

A Siren peeked out from over her shoulder and grinned like a cat, pressing her poisoned blade against Laya's back.

Shit…

16
KYLAYA

"WHAT DO YOU WANT?" I asked in an angry even tone. The Siren had her knife digging into my lower back. I knew that it wouldn't go through my guard suit unless she withdrew it and stabbed through hard. Still, I didn't like the sensation of having something that deadly pressed against me.

"*What* do I want?" she asked and laughed.

"What's so funny?" I asked, trying to figure out how to get out of her grasp. *Keep her talking. Buy time.*

The Siren leaned down close to me and whispered in my ear, "I want *you*."

"What?" I uttered.

"You," she answered again and pressed the knife into me a little harder.

"What do you want with *me*?" I asked, still not sure I was hearing her right.

"Oh, sweetie, you are a popular girl. You have some very powerful people looking for you," she answered.

"The Queen?" I asked, not really believing my ears.

"Among others," she answered. I tried to move, but she reached around my neck and pushed the knife against the tender skin under my chin.

"Ah. Ah," she said shaking her head. "I wouldn't do that if I were you."

"Listen, you can take me, but my father will *never* negotiate with Sirens to get me back. You are wasting your time," I explained. It was true, he told me himself. Mer didn't negotiate with Sirens.

"Oh, my dear, we don't plan on giving you back," she answered. "Let's go."

She pushed the knife into my back a little further, and I raised my hands in response. A roar sounded and Reqet blasted a wall of water at the Siren, throwing her off of me. A blade flashed in the water, heading straight for her. She swung an arm out and knocked the knife off course.

"Go!" Reqet shouted as he was taken from behind by two Sirens who had seen the fight.

I reached for the knife on my leg and was hit over the head. Another Siren had entered the fight. She grabbed onto my arm, and tried to pull the knife out of my hand as she screamed in my ear

I flipped around in the water, releasing her grip, and landing a hard kick to her gut. She was stopped for a moment but then glared and kept coming. I summoned water, feeling the familiar pull in my core and tingle along my spine as my powers came out. My anger fueled my power in a way I had never seen before as a whirlpool appeared in front of me. Even though she was a water creature like myself, she wouldn't enter a whirlpool, they could tear you apart. The one that I had conjured was no different as I watched it spin with hurricane force, ripping and tearing that the water around it.

I didn't see the last Siren coming for me until it was too late. With lightning speed, she plunged her knife down toward me from above. I dodged her assault, but it was the scream, again, that broke my concentration. It was as if the sound penetrated even my powers, as it dissolved my whirlpool. My heart punched my chest as I kept my eyes on the two Sirens who were now, most certainly, going to gang up on me.

Why didn't I listen to Reqet?

The first Siren twirled her blade in her long fingers, and I threw out my hand, pushing her back with a water wall. She hardly moved. I twisted out of the way as the other came at me with her knife.

"We need her alive!" the first Siren yelled to the second one.

"We don't need her in one piece though," the second yelled back taking out a smaller knife that wasn't tipped in poison.

I narrowed my eyes on her. There was no way that I was going to go easily, and no way that I was going in small pieces either. I reached down and grabbed a second dagger from my side. I was running out of blades to fight them off, but there was one skill that I knew they wouldn't count on. My speed.

The Sirens stood on either side of me. I turned my head between the two of them, watching carefully and waiting for my chance. It came with a bloody scream from a Siren that fell to one of the Elite. Both their eyes flicked to the fight and I was off.

I summoned the water around me and pushed. I could out swim all the Elite, even Reqet. Mazz couldn't catch me either. I left the Sirens behind to their screams of anger, sailing clear over their heads and aiming for over the dome.

When I came upon the fight though, I stopped, horror struck at what I was seeing. Blood was billowing from the bodies of the Elite that had fallen to the Siren swarm as the rest fought for their lives amongst the dead. Their numbers were getting smaller and smaller, as were their chances of survival. That's when the Sirens that had been chasing me reached me.

I managed to kick off the first that latched on to my back, flipping in the water and sending her flying away from me, but I lost one of my last blades from my hand in the process. When I turned back to the other one, she tackled me from the front, sending me falling toward the city. She landed on top of me as we crashed into the hard, smooth surface of the dome. I gasped when the air was knocked from me, as the dome punched me in the back.

While I was momentarily stunned, the Siren took advantage and grabbed my hand, slamming it against the dome. As hard as I tried, my grip on the knife was broken, as my fingers were cracked on the solid surface. I watched with a heavy heart as my last weapon skidded away from me, down the dome to the seafloor. I thrashed out with my legs, but she held on tight, swinging around and straddling me. Forcing me down, she pinned me. I watched in helpless horror as she pulled a long knife from her boot.

"You think that I want to bring back a *Mer?*" she seethed. "You're all the same. Spoiled, selfish, and undeserving of all you have. You've taken everything from my people, and we are *finally* going to get what we deserve. We will rise and bring an end to the Mer and all that they love. Your time is at an end, sweetheart."

"Whatever," I scoffed, trying to keep my calm.

"You will see. You will see," she waved the knife in front of me, taunting me with it. Her brilliant violet eyes looked down at me. Siren eyes.

Only Sirens had eyes that color, and it was the only way Mer could tell when one of their own had turned. I supposed, Handsome also had violet eyes, but he was just a dream. He couldn't have been a male Siren anyway; they didn't exist. The Sirens killed their male offspring immediately after birth.

Violet eyes were feared above all in Mer. If a young mermaid developed violet eyes, no matter the age, no matter the family, she was exiled for fear of what she would become. The Mer didn't trust anyone with violet eyes. The Siren blood in them made them dangerous and a threat. It was also a death sentence for any Siren that was caught near the city.

"Don't worry, young Constantilly," she continued, flashing the blade in front of my eyes, "this knife doesn't have poison on it. I don't want to *kill* you, I just want to *play* with you for a little bit before I take you in. Queen Midira didn't say anything about you not having a couple marks on you, or missing a finger to two." The Siren smiled and ran the knife along my cheek, cutting into it. I didn't give her the satisfaction of crying out, as it pinched and stung in the salt water.

"Oh, a tough one, are you? How fun! It's going be such an honor to watch you crack and scream and beg," she said.

"Yeah, good luck with that," I growled.

She smiled and shrugged, and looked at the knife.

"You know, it's amazing the pain that you can live through. It truly is. The body is a stubborn thing. It just wants to keep going; no matter the absolute agony that it experiences," she smiled and ran the knife down my neck. I could feel the salt water bite into the cut she made as the knife trailed along my collar bone. I was seething.

"When I get my hands on you–"

The Siren cracked me across the face with the butt of the knife. I saw stars as my head tried desperately to work its way out of the fog that had descended upon me. Everything cleared when I felt the tip of the knife break through my guard suit and plunge into my leg. I screamed out.

The pain was unlike anything I had ever experienced. None of my training with the Elite had prepared me for that.

"Didn't like that one, huh?" she asked and pulled the knife out with a twist, waving it in front of me. I was kicking like mad, a desperate and angry wild animal breaking free within me. I screamed in rage at her; but, when she lifted the knife in the air again and dropped her eyes to my other leg, I went absolutely berserk. Bucking against her, I felt like a savage beast with an unwanted rider; but, no matter how much I tried to get her off of me, she somehow managed to stay on.

A smile graced her lips as she threw her weight into the knife. She drove it into my thigh and a ragged screamed escaped me as the knife was twisted, cutting through skin, muscle, and lodging in the bone. The Siren loomed in front of my eyes, enjoying the wounds she was inflicting. She smiled and pulled the knife out. A shot of agonizing pain erupted in my leg and the world started to spin.

I knew I wouldn't be able to stay conscious much longer. The pain was simply too much. If I passed out, though, I would be completely at her mercy. That was the last thing that I wanted.

Then, from somewhere in the water, a streak of pink light came. It slammed into the chest of the Siren tossing her of off me.

It only took a moment for her to gain her composure as she turned in the water, looking for the source. I moved my head slowly, and the world swam in my sight. Nothing was focusing and I was dizzy beyond anything that I had ever felt in my life.

Blood was escaping me at an alarming rate. That's when I realized that her knife must have been tipped in something that stopped blood from clotting. The water had healing powers for Mer; we healed faster in it, but I wasn't. Pink flashed again, and the Siren was hit, tossed far into the water and away from me; but I couldn't get up.

Darkness was closing in. The last thing I remembered was the scream of the Siren as a shadow descended from above.

17
JETT

NO...

A Siren had pinned Laya to the dome. *Come on, fight. Get out of there.*

I was caught between the need to stick to my duty and stay hidden, and this instinctual need to save the woman from my dreams. I sat there, horrified at what I was watching and hoping against all that she would somehow be able to get out of the Siren's grasp.

When the Siren whipped out another blade my heart froze. I clenched my jaw hard as the Siren sliced the Mer's beautiful face, Laya's face. I had to bite my lip to stop myself from shouting out. It wasn't my first time seeing a Mer killed by a Siren...but this was different.

The Siren plunged her knife into Laya's leg, and she screamed. I couldn't take it. She was being tortured, and there was no way in Hades that I was going to sit there and listen to it, doing nothing. When the Siren plunged her knife into Laya's other leg, something inside me snapped. I saw red. A need to protect woke in me with a ferocity that I was not ready for. Without thinking of the consequences, I raced through the water at the Siren.

I shot a bolt of my power at her, knocking her off of Laya. She turned to me, a wound opening up in her chest where I had hit her. Her eyes flashed violet, and I recognized them. Eyes like mine. Every time I faced off against a Siren, it bothered me that I was related to them, that I came from them.

But, I *wasn't* them.

I called my power from my core and unleashed. Flashing to her side, I appeared right in front of the Siren. My dagger strong in my hand, I plunged it into the base of her neck. Her eyes went wide and then rolled back. It was a wound meant to kill and it worked...every time.

She had seen me, so she couldn't live anyway, but there was a lot more satisfaction in that kill than any other that I had ever done. Looking over to where Laya laid, I knew she was the reason.

My gods…

She was more beautiful than in my dreams, if that was even possible. Her blonde hair had settled to the dome's surface when I flashed to her. The blood from her wounds was still coming. If I didn't move her soon, she would bleed out. I was going to have to remove her from the area. But, where could I take her?

Before I realized that I had made the decision, she was in my arms and I was streaking through the water towards the portal home. I looked down at her delicate face, and I felt my heart kick at my chest.

It is you. It has to be.

I held her tightly, pressing her to my chest as I took her to safety, hoping against all that she was going to be okay.

Hold on, Laya. I have you.

18
JETT

"WHAT THE HELL ARE YOU *DOING*?"

Jasper was running circles around me as I settled Laya into my bed, ever thankful that I had just cleaned my sheets; though, I doubted in her condition that she would care.

"Don't start with me," I snapped as I waved him away.

"What do you mean? You brought a *Mer* back to our *house;* and, I'm not supposed to question you? Have we met?" he asked, as he stood on the other side of the bed from me. I hadn't seen him that freaked out since Louise, our foster, decided she could cut his hair just as well as the barber. She was epically wrong.

Looking at the two of us, there were many similarities. We shared the same dark blonde hair, the same deep set eyes and thick brow. Jasper stood a little shorter than me, even though he was older, which he hated. He was thinner and lankier than me. Being part of The Watch was not in his job description; therefore, he wasn't as bulked up as I was. Jasper had always been the kinder, softer, and sweeter brother; while I was a stickler for the rules; and, the harder and stronger one. Jasper let his hair grow longer than mine, its dark blonde locks curled at the ends by his ears and swooped in front of his face. That would have driven me nuts, but he liked it and so did Sam.

The two of them were celebrating their fifth wedding anniversary, but really they had been together for a solid decade.

"Help me get these clothes off of her," I said as I pulled at the tear in her pants where the Siren stabbed her.

"Are you *insane*?" Jasper yelled, threading his fingers through his hair.

"We have to dress her wounds, Jass. Get a grip!" I said, shaking my head at him.

"You bring a Mer into our house, and *I'm* supposed to get a grip. Do you know what you have done?"

"Shut up! You hear me? You might be the older brother, but you sure as hell aren't acting like it. She needed help. You just wanted me to sit there and watch her get tortured by the Siren and then taken? I thought you were against all that?"

"Of course, I think you did the right thing stepping in…but why bring her *here?*"

"Where was I supposed to take her?" I asked. "I couldn't swim up to the entrance to Triton and deliver her could I? I had no choice, I had to bring her here," I stated. "Now, stop fussing and *help me.*" Jasper's jaw tightened as his eyes focused on the wounds in the Laya's legs.

"She needs to be healed," Jasper uttered. "Sam is still out from helping that car crash victim, though. He won't be strong enough to help for four days minimum. She's going to have to heal the old fashioned way," he explained.

"What do we do?" I asked.

"We need to close the wounds and dress them to keep infection from settling in," Jasper explained. I nodded and ran from the room for some clean towels to use and our emergency kit. While Jasper wasn't a healer like Sam, he had always taken an interest in helping those that were hurt. When Sam couldn't tend to someone, Jasper was often called to help.

When I got back, Jasper had ripped the girl's pants at the wound sights to get a better look at them.

"What do you think?" I asked him as I looked at them myself. The stab wounds were deep, bone deep. They had cut through muscle and would need a lot of healing. It would be painful and require her to be in bed for a while, at least until Sam was well enough to heal her.

"She'll live," Jasper said with a confident nod. "They're deep, but they will heal. She's lucky, they just missed her major veins. An inch over and she would have bled out long ago," he said. "Now, get out," he added. I stared at Jasper.

"What?"

"Get out. I'm going to change her, and you don't need to be in here," he said, going to the closet for another blanket.

"Umm," I uttered.

"Once she wakes and finds out that she was stripped, she's going to want to know who did it and why. I think I'm the better choice. Just saying," he explained holding his hands up.

"You're probably right," I admitted and slowly left the room, letting Jasper handle changing her out of her bloodied clothes. I paced the hall, nervous energy running rapidly through me.

When Jasper called me back in the room, Laya was under my covers, her head on my pillow and her hair draped across it. I looked at Jasper who was staring at her too.

"Thank you," I said to him.

He nodded. "She will heal fine. It'll just will take time," he grumbled and then turned to me. "You know this is a big deal right?"

"I know," I said with a nod.

"You know you're going to have to tell the Council."

"I know."

"And Rayna."

"I know."

"You ready for that?'

"Nope."

"You did the right thing," he said and looked at me.

"What was that?" I asked, not sure that I had actually hear him right.

"You did the right thing. I never understood how you could stand by and watch as Sirens killed innocent Mer before. It never sat right with me. While bringing her here is going to cause a shit storm of epic proportions, I admire you for doing it."

"Wow. That…that means a lot coming from you," I said, looking at my brother, who wasn't prone to exaggeration or false compliments.

"Well, it's true. Just tell me one thing," he said, drawing the blankets further up to her chin.

"What's that?"

"Why?" He asked.

"I-" I couldn't say that I had been dreaming of this girl since I was a child. He would think I was insane. "I don't know," I said shaking my head and looking at her.

"Not exactly the answer I was hoping for, but I suppose it'll do for now," he said with a smile and clapped me on the shoulder before he left the room.

I stood there and looked at Laya. What was she going to be like in real life? Would she know me? Would she be happy to see me? Would she feel the same way I did? I ran a hand through my hair and exhaled heavily.

This wasn't supposed to be a possibility. She was a dream. But when she sighed, my heart lurched; and, it started to set in that, no, she wasn't a dream. She was right there.

Laya. *My Laya.*

I had never been so scared in my life.

19
KYLAYA

I FELT THE MOAN ESCAPE my throat before I heard it. It was like my voice was coming from far away and took an age to get to my ears.

Ugh, gods. What happened?

Sharp pains erupted in my legs when I tried to get up, followed by deep, angry throbbing. Sleep clung to me stronger than ever before and for a moment, in the brightness of the room, I thought I was still asleep and in my world with Handsome.

It took only a breath for me to confirm I wasn't home. The air filled my lungs with ease, and a scent I had never experienced invaded my senses. There was no doubt in my mind that I wasn't in Mer.

Where am I?

I tried to sit up, but the room spun on me, and I was forced to settle back down in the bed, placing a hand on my head and squeezing my eyes against the ensuing pounding in my brain. A sound came from outside the room, and I realized that I wasn't alone. Immediately I reached for my weapon. My hand flashed to my thigh, where my weapons belt was.

Nothing.

My heart nearly stopped as I ran a hand along my skin. My bare skin…

Holy shit! I'm naked!

Realizing that I had been stripped, not just of my weapons, but of my guard uniform as well, I battled between utter horror and panic. My hands found my breasts, and I heaved a great sigh. I was still in my underwear. *Thanks the gods for that.*

Fear creeped forward from the all corners of the room as reality charged in. I was in a bed that wasn't mine, in a stranger's home.

What in Hades happened to me?

Everything in me told me to get out of there. I reigned in all my strength and sat up. I swung my legs slowly and painfully over the side of the bed and dropped my feet to the floor. It was cold, but smooth and clean. I wrapped the covers around myself to cover up as best as I could and went to stand. The wounds in my legs shot to life sending jabs of piercing pain through me, buckling my knees, and sending me to the floor.

I can't walk! What am I going to do?

The covers were strewn around me, as I wrestled them out of the way. I needed to see my wounds. I had to know how bad it was.

Moving the plush covers to the side, I looked down at two thick bandages that were wrapped around my thighs. Blood stains had seeped through the white dressings in each place where that damned Siren had stabbed me.

Gods…this hurts.

I reached down and gingerly rested a hand over one bandage. I could feel my heartbeat in the wound underneath and hissed at the pain. I wasn't getting out of there on foot. It took all of my strength to get back on the bed from the floor.

I was panting and the pain had caused a cold sweat to break out across my back and up my arms. I was seeing stars and the room had started to spin again. I had never experienced pain like that before. The Siren's blade wasn't poisoned, but the cuts in my legs were still extraordinarily painful anyway.

I sighed and fell back into the bed.

Shit balls.

Kidnapped and stripped of my clothes. I thought that the Siren was bad news…but *this* could be worse.

What do these people want from me?

There was nothing I could do about leaving. I wasn't going anywhere. I needed a plan; and, so, I started to take in my surroundings hoping that there would be something that I could use to help myself. The room was bright and friendly…for a prison. A pale shade of green was painted on the walls. A window was off to my right with its white curtains drawn, but light was streaming in illuminating the room in a warm glow. The sheets I was wrapped in were a dark blue soft material that, had I not been in an unknown place, I would have immensely enjoyed.

The bed took up the majority of the room as it was small. My room back home would have been three times the size of that one easily. Just a small stand up dresser, a bedside table, and a chair were in the room. A tiny closet was in the wall in the corner by the window. I got the feeling that the room belonged to a man; the colors were decidedly darker and there were no fancy or frilly decorations anywhere. Everything practical and useful.

My attention was turned away from the simple furniture in the small room when I heard footsteps approach. I quickly looked for a weapon of some kind to defend myself with. My heart was thrumming hard in my chest as the steps neared. I knew that I was pretty much at the mercy of my captor since my legs didn't work, but there was no way I was going down without a fight. There was nothing for a weapon. Not a freaking thing. So, I braced myself for the worst as the door handle turned.

In walked a tall young man, backwards, carrying a tray. His broad shoulders pulled the light blue shirt he had on tightly across his body. His dark blonde hair was longer at the top, short on the sides, and tussled in a messy array that still looked oddly good.

"Can't leave him alone for one blessed minute," he mumbled to himself in a soft low voice.

"Who are you?" I demanded. "Why am I here?" He had his back to me, but I glared at him anyway, hoping that he would fall to the power of my death stare.

"You are safe," he answered simply setting the tray on the top of the dresser. He still didn't turn to me. He was tall and strong, his shirt didn't do much to hide his trim figure and muscle definition everywhere. I knew there would be no overpowering him.

"Safe *where*?" I asked. "And, where the hell are my clothes?" I demanded, pulling the blankets up around myself further and leveling a glare in my captor's direction.

"We had to cut them off to deal with your wounds," he answered, as he arranged items on a tray. His head was down and away from me as if he didn't want to look at me.

"Who is *we*? Where *am* I? What do you want with me?" I asked, watching him carefully. He didn't *look* dangerous, but that didn't mean that he wasn't. He was tall, but he was filled out enough to not look lanky and stringy. His skin was tanned with a splatter of freckles across the tops of his strong arms. A spark of recognition lit in me, but my anger won out over it.

"You fell unconscious outside of Triton after the Siren attack. I brought you here so you could heal. The wounds were deep and needed addressing," he answered, still not turning to me.

"Where. Am. I?" I uttered through clenched teeth.

"You are…on the surface," he answered hesitantly. He turned half to me, his eyes low under his dark brow.

"The surface!" I yelled. "What in Hades are you doing bringing me to the surface?"

"I told you, you were hurt. I brought you here to *help* you."

"Why didn't you take me back to Triton? We were *right there*!" I asked. It made no sense. Why take me away from my home? Away from medical care?

"I have my reasons," he answered slowly. My blood went cold. I could only guess his reasons. I pulled the covers higher, resting them under my chin, desperately trying to get a grip on my mind so I didn't suffer a full blown panic attack. I needed to think.

"You picked the wrong girl to kidnap. I will be missed, they will come for you," I threatened, trying not to think the very worst, yet knowing that I should expect it.

"Kidnap!" the guy yelled, and turned full on me. My heart slammed against my chest as I finally figured out why he seemed familiar.

Handsome?

"I didn't *kidnap* you!" he continued as I full on stared at him, with my mouth dropped wide open. "I – you were in trouble, I *saved* you," he explained, finally looking at me straight in the eye. That was when I noticed the color of them.

Violet.

It's him. It's really him.

20
KYLAYA

HOW IS THIS POSSIBLE? HE'S REAL?

Handsome paced the room, and I just stared at him. *Am I dreaming? I have to be dreaming.*

"My name is KyLaya," I said.

"Dream stop," he uttered.

We both froze.

Silence.

Nothing was said as we both adjusted to what just happened.

"How is this possible?" I asked, the first to speak.

"I don't know," he answered and then looked at me. "It is you, isn't it?" He walked slowly to the bed as if I might disappear in front of his eyes. "Laya?" he whispered.

"Yes," I said, and tears sprang to my eyes.

"My gods," he uttered and smiled. "I never thought that…I can't believe-"

"Me neither," I said, knowing what he was getting at.

"Jett," he blurted.

"What?" I asked.

"My name is Jett," he said. "Not that I don't enjoy hearing you call me Handsome all the time," he chuckled. My heart leapt into my throat. It was him, through and through it was him. Really him.

"Jett," I said, testing it out. "Well, Jett, it is amazing to meet you, for real. I never thought that you existed outside of my dreams. I mean, I hoped, especially after-" I stopped dead in the middle of my sentence, realizing what I was just about to say.

"Yes, I know what you mean," he said and took a tentative seat on the bed next to me. My breath stilled being that close to him. I had wanted it so badly; but, now that he was really there, it was just as terrifying as it was exciting.

"I-what does this mean? Why have we been dreaming of each other?" I asked.

"What are you talking about? I've never dreamt of you!" he answered. My blood chilled, then he smiled.

"Jerk!" I laughed and pushed him before I thought better of it. Immediately, I expected a dream stop. When I made contact with him, his eyes grew big, and it was as if we both just realized that we could touch. Jett reached out for me, his hand settled gently onto mine and a burst of energy jumped through me. My eyes raised to his.

"Whoa," I said in a voice that was barely my own.

"Yeah," he said back, looking down at our hands. "It's…" he chuckled to himself, "I just never thought that this day would come."

"Me neither," I admitted.

"Laya," he uttered.

"Jett," I replied. To that a sweet grin slid up his handsome face.

"That is probably the sweetest sound I've heard from your lips," he said, his voice just above a whisper.

"What?"

"My name. My real name," he answered.

I blushed hard. The way he talked to me made my body light up. No one could make my heart thunder like that. Only him. Only ever him. He adjusted on the bed and pain bit into my legs. I hissed and stiffened.

"Geez, Laya. Sorry," he said. His brow furrowed as he looked to where the covers hid my wounds. "As much as I want to sit here with you, you'd – umm – better rest," he said, standing up. "You're wounds need time to heal. Rest is the best for that."

"Wait," I said as he walked slowly to the door.

"Yes, Laya?" he said, turning back to me.

"It's really you. Really," I said again. Needing the reassurance that I wasn't dreaming.

"It's really me. Is it really you?" he asked smiling.

"Yeah. It's me, Handsome," I answered.

"Rest. I'll be back soon," he said.

My heart wouldn't let me settle down. It was drumming hard in my chest.

Jett. His name is Jett.

I smiled and shook my head. Was this real? Would I wake up and he would be gone, like every time before? I hoped against everything that wasn't what would happen.

Jett…I like that name.

21
JETT

"WELL?" JASPER ASKED when I came out of the room.

"Well, what?" I retorted.

"Is she everything you hoped she'd be?"

"What are you getting on about?" I asked. I hadn't told him about my dreams and I didn't intend on it.

"Don't try to hide it; I know you have feelings for her. I just can't figure out how you managed to get such strong feelings in such a short time. It's like you already know her," Jasper answered.

"I – again, I don't know what you are talking about," I said, trying to deflect.

"Sure. Okay, well, when you decide to tell me what is really going on between you and the Mer girl, let me know. Just don't wait too long, cause it will be insulting," he said and sat at table, crossing his arms and watching me carefully.

Jasper had the uncanny ability to sense things in others. He could tell a person's thoughts and feelings in a way that others couldn't. Call it perception, intuition, whatever; it was really annoying when I just didn't want to talk about my feelings, and they were the only thing the guy could focus on.

"Drop it, Jasper," I warned him. He put his hands up and zipped his lips with his fingers. *Yeah right, like that's going to keep them closed. A stapler would do it...maybe.*

"What are you going to do with her?" Jasper asked.

"What do you mean 'do with her'?" I asked.

"Aren't you worried about the Council? Rayna?" Jasper asked. I nodded, not knowing how else to answer.

"It'll be fine. We'll figure it out," he said. Jasper had a place on the Council too. I had never depended on him for support in my troubles, but I was going to need his help with this. Jasper was the one with the silver tongue, not me.

"Thanks, but I think it's a good idea to keep this between the two of us for now." I said.

"You mean the three of us?" a deep voice resonated from the porch. I hadn't heard the truck pull up or the door open, but I didn't need to look to see who it was. Sam stood at the doorway to the kitchen, leaning his lumberjack frame against the wall. I rolled my eyes and threw my hands in the air at Jasper.

"You didn't seriously think I wasn't going to tell *him*, did you?" Jasper asked me with a look that just screamed 'what did you expect?'

Sam walked into the kitchen, nearly taking up the entire thing. I moved to the side, to give him his space as he sauntered to Jasper. The two of them had never hidden their affection for each other. If you didn't want to see it…don't look. That was their philosophy.

Sam bent down and placed a kiss on my brother's lips. I admit that their relationship was a mixed bag of emotion for me. It didn't have anything to do with the fact that they were both guys; it was more that it spelled the end of the life that I had become so used to.

While Jasper and Sam got married really young, they decided to continue living with their fosters until they were of age to move out, or at least until Jasper was of age. Fosters were the families that took in Mer children when they were brought to Stenen, our home town. Jasper and I were placed with the same fosters, and a family was born. Even though there was a four year spread between us, we had always got along well. I would never think of him as anything but my brother and best friend, even if it turned out that we didn't share the same blood.

The two of us headed the farm that our fosters started long ago. Louise and Brock were older when they took Jasper and I in. They were uncommonly kind people who loved us with every part of their hearts. Jasper and I had nothing but a charmed childhood. Their passing in a car accident a few years ago left a hole in our hearts that we were struggling to fill.

With their deaths, Jasper, being the older sibling, had to remain with me until I came of age to live on my own. I had finally turned nineteen and that meant that Jasper could once and for all move in with Sam. It was the end of an era for us, and, as much as I liked Sam, I was real pissy about that.

"She up yet?" Sam asked as he leaned his shoulders against the wall, looking at me with his deep violet eyes.

"She is," I answered with a nod, taking a seat next to Jasper at the table.

"How did *that* go?" he asked, looking from me to Jasper.

"Umm," Jasper uttered.

"Fine. Good," I admitted.

"What does *that* mean?" he asked, a smile pulling at the corner of his mouth. Sam had a way of asking the most aggravating questions.

"It means buzz off because he doesn't want to talk about his feelings for her," Jasper answered for me. Sam burst out laughing.

"Please. *Jett*?" Sam chuckled again.

"What's *that* supposed to mean?" I asked, crossing my arms.

"That you haven't been interested in any woman enough to ask her for a coffee let alone kidnap one and bring her here," he answered, challenging me to argue.

"I didn't *kidnap* her!"

Sam laughed. "But, I do sense something going on. Perhaps our Jettstream has finally found someone that has tickled his fancy?" Jasper laughed along with Sam. I knew they were just poking harmless fun, but they knew I hated that nickname.

"Shut up," I clapped back. Sam shook his head with a smile and walked to the door.

"Well, I would stay longer and poke fun at Jett, but I have to run up to Sturgis and get some supplies for the shed. Just wanted to stop by and see how things were going," Sam announced.

"Right," I responded. "Thanks again for all your help with the shed."

"You're family," Sam answered with a one shoulder shrug, as if it wasn't a huge favor he was doing for us.

"I'll walk you out," Jasper offered and the two of them quietly exited the house.

Jasper and I had been running things together for the last few years on the farm. We had opened up the land more, cleaning up some rather unsightly parts with ancient broken down machinery and wild shrubbery, and were growing our little farm into a business that was more lucrative than we could have ever imagined.

I couldn't take credit for the business side of things; Jasper was the one with the mind for it. I could manage the day to day; but, as far as paper work and legalities, he was the one for that. With a growing farm came more help. We had to hire from town and pay employees; it was a whole new ball game for us, but we were loving every minute.

All the new help meant more crops, more seed, and more storage needed for the bigger equipment that we needed. Sam was building a shed that would house the new tractor and combine what we had just saved up to buy. Jasper and I offered to pay him for his trouble, but he refused.

"You're family," he responded every time.

I simply don't know what I would have done without Jasper's help on the farm. He had always seemed uninterested in it; but, when our fosters died, he took up the reins better than I could have ever hoped. His easy going nature made him a lot nicer to deal with than me. That lent itself to more business arrangements and partnerships for us, which was only good for our farm and our community.

It was essential that our community flourish, and be as self-sufficient as possible. We needed the security. We were all refugees from a world that didn't want us. Being here meant living. Living in freedom without fear.

But, I had just brought home a Mer jeopardizing everything my people had built.

I opened the door to my room where Laya slept in my bed. Her blonde hair cascaded around her fair face in her sleep, like a bright golden halo. She looked peaceful and just as beautiful, if not more, than what I had seen in my dreams. My heart pulled and I took an unsteady breath in.

Why did she have to be a Mer?

In all our time together, it never occurred to me that she was Mer. Now that she was in my house I was struck with the reality that we came from warring worlds and that anything between us was going to be complicated at the very least. My heart thudded hard, and I sighed.

But…it was Laya; and, she worth fighting for.

Will she fight for me once she finds out who I am?

22
JETT

I HAD SOME ERRANDS TO RUN IN TOWN, so I left Jasper in charge of Laya with strict instructions to keep his mouth shut about who we were so we didn't scare her. He agreed with an eye roll like it was insulting for me to have to say it to him. The thing was that he had a habit of running his mouth off, so in reality…the shoe fit.

Stenen was only a five minute drive from the farm. Down the gravel road and past the little red barn and onto the highway. The road into town was marked by a giant white church that we used for meetings and gatherings of all sorts. Marriages took place there and funerals; it was a beautiful building, and one that we took pride in.

As I drove slowly into town, I passed the gas station to my right, with the flag post and giant rock in the yard in front. The Stenen sign was next to it; freshly painted that spring, it shone like a new penny. The grass was neatly cut and tended to. The houses lined the street with flowers in their beds and hanging by their doors as I drove by. Flamingos, swans, gnomes, and deer decorated the yards. There was a whimsy and fun flair to the whole town that I looked forward to every spring.

For a small community, we really took pride in keeping the town well tended. If someone fell ill or was hurt or simply too old to do it anymore, there was always someone to help them out. Always. The only real problem to living in such a tight-knit community was that everyone was also in your business - which made keeping a secret, like having a mermaid on the farm, nearly impossible. I knew that I wouldn't be able to hide Laya for long. Just how long I didn't know.

Passing the school and the curling rink, I turned onto the main road and drove up to Vyktor's. Vyktor was one of the Council members and a highly respected member of our community. He lived in the back of the post office which also served as a little convenience store. There was almost everything you could imagine in there, from bread to booze. His small store was situated between the bank and the hair shop. There were only five businesses on the street, and they were all in the same tiny house-like buildings with living quarters in the back.

The brass bell on the door rang as I walked into Vyktor's shop, announcing my presence. A wall of post office boxes filled the entrance, and I stopped to check our mail. The shop was truly unique, unlike anything that I had ever seen anywhere else. To my left, there was a fresh deli counter, sausages and cut meat were arranged carefully, along with beautiful beef and pork portions. All of it local. Fruits and vegetables in baskets shone in the afternoon light coming in through the large store windows. A head popped up from behind the counter that stood at the center of the shop.

"Well, is that Mr. Jett?" a friendly voice called to me as I closed the mailbox.

"Yes, sir," I answered with a smile, tucking my mail under my arm and entering the store. Vyktor stood behind the counter. There wasn't a kinder man around; he greeted every person that came in with the same genuine, happy greeting. His hair, now grey but not thinning, was parted neatly on the side and combed over in the same haircut and style he had since I was a kid. Though he was a smaller man, he was strong after years of hauling around merchandise. His eyes were a subdued violet, being one of the first Sirenites to come to Stenen. There wasn't a better role model for the young Sirenites in town than him. Quiet, calm, and kind - that was Vyktor. Though, if you got him laughing, you could hear him all across town. He put his whole heart into his laugh.

I crossed the solid wooden floor to the till within a couple of strides. Vyktor reached across the counter and shook my hand heartily.

"It's been awhile since I've seen you in here, Jett. Where've you been?" he asked as he placed some new candy in the display counter. As a kid, I was always begging my fosters for a little change to come and get candy from Vyktor's when we were in town. He always had the best taste in sweets.

"Been on The Watch lately a lot and stuck on the farm with the expansion," I answered as I eyed the gummy worms that he had just opened. Vyktor smiled and nodded and followed my gaze to the candy.

"You've always had a sweet tooth," he chuckled, bringing up the carton of jelly candy. "More so than your brother."

"He likes chips," I said as I took a handful of candy and shoved them in the little brown bag Vyktor handed me.

"True," he said and handed me a bag of Jasper's favorite potato chips from the shelf behind the till. I smiled, and he winked at me. I chuckled. The bell rang and small footsteps echoed through the entrance.

"Uncle Jett!" a little voice shouted. I turned and was almost bowled over as someone jumped in my arms.

"Rall!" I exclaimed as I lifted the young boy up in the air. The six year old had been paired up with me since he came to Stenen as a baby. All babies entering our community were assigned an adult Sirenite in the community to be like a big brother and role model. We watched out for them, and they were accountable to us like another parent. Rall had always called me "uncle", and I didn't mind. I adored the kid. He was smart as a whip and kind to a fault. His fosters were Rayna's parents. They were good people and were raising him with the compassion and kindness they raised Rayna with. Rall had no idea how lucky he was.

I reached into the little brown bag and pulled out three gummy worms, placing them in Rall's hands.

"Oh wow! Thanks, Uncle Jett!" Rall shouted, squeezing me in a hug that had my heart growing about three sizes.

"You spoil him you know," Rayna said as she came in the store.

"That's what uncles are for," I commented with a shrug as I tousled Rall's dark brown hair. He smiled up at me, his freckled cheeks full of candy. I laughed heartily seeing his little face light up. Rayna laughed too and patted my arm as she walked around me, leaving her hand on me until the last second.

I swallowed hard. I looked at Vyktor, and he winked at me. I paled. Rayna had been doing things like that more often; and, like an idiot, I hadn't clued in. She had always been a work partner. Someone that I could trust without hesitation on The Watch. A fighter. A colleague. But not a mate.

I cleared my throat and reached into my pocket.

"How much, Vyktor?" I asked, pulling my wallet out.

"I'll put it on your tab," he said with a wave of his hand.

"Sounds good," I said.

"She's a catch you know," Vyktor said quietly enough for just me to hear. I looked at him in surprise, totally caught off guard. I nodded once but didn't say anything as I left the store.

Damn it. Now I have Vyktor on my case to match with Rayna.

I knew very well that she was a good catch. I just didn't *want* to catch her. I guess, Laya was responsible for my lack of feelings for Rayna. Laya had been the girl of my dreams, literally and figuratively, for a long time. Now that she was real, I couldn't fathom being with anyone else. It had always been Laya and would always be.

I walked quickly to my truck, but not before I heard my name called again.

"Hey! Jett!" a deep voice shouted as I opened the door of my truck.

Franky. Damn it.

"Hey," I answered and tried to paint on a smile. The large man walked with slow purpose across the narrow street to me. He placed a hand on the hood of the truck with a thump, hard enough to flex it but not damage it. Just enough to make you cringe, and let you know that he didn't care.

Franky was one of the other members of the Council, along with Vyktor, Jasper, Rayna, me, and seven others; twelve in all. He was an ass. Bull headed, stubborn, and narcissistic. He had always been like that; ever since we were in school he'd been a jerk. That didn't stop him from having friends, though; and, he did. You can't get a position on the Council without being voted in and he had enough sway in our community to win a seat every time. Pissed me off that there were others that supported his philosophies.

Since the time he was a kid, his fosters gave him everything and demanded nothing in return. Their only request was that he take over their business when they were gone. He did that and more, making his farm the most lucrative one in the area. It wasn't the competitive side of me that hated him; it was the way he went about his business. He bullied and threatened people into selling him their land. There were even rumors of him using his Sirenite powers on one of the human locals to get his land. Something that was expressly forbidden to do.

He was as slippery as a fish, always skirting the laws enough to stay on the good side; but, we all knew he was underhanded and dirty. We just couldn't catch him.

Franky seemingly had it all. Looks. Money. Power. And, boy, did he think he was a great prize. Unfortunately, so did several of the women around the area. He had them falling at his feet, and he kicked them around as they did.

But, there was one girl that kept him at arm's length, and that was Rayna. She had no interest in him what-so-ever, not matter what he did to catch her attention. It was just one more reason I respected her so much. She had no use for him *or* his money. Plus, I loved seeing the look on his face every time she shot him down. Priceless.

"What do you want Franky?" I asked, keeping the door open and one foot on the step.

"I just wanted to tell you that I have some of my old machinery up for sale. I'm getting all new combines this summer. The old ones don't have Wi-Fi," he said and arched a brow at me with a smile. I wanted to punch him in his bleached teeth.

"We're good, thanks," I uttered and started to lift myself up into the truck. He placed a hand on my shoulder, and I came back down to the ground. I stood a good head above him, but his personality was definitely bigger than mine. He liked to bark a lot, but I knew that he would bite the moment you turned your back on him.

"You sure?" he asked again, eyeing my truck, which was several years old but still in good working condition. "You'll never be able to afford machinery like my old stuff anywhere else. You could use an upgrade. Let me help you," he said with a tilt of his rusty colored head and a used salesman smile. I dropped my leg from the truck and smiled back.

"I wouldn't take your left overs if you *gave* them to me, Franky. My farm does just fine the way it is and will continue to…without your 'generous' help." I didn't give him a chance to speak as I climbed into my seat.

The flash of anger in his eyes was brief but potent and left me feeling like I had hit a nerve, which was perfect…that was my goal. Franky wasn't just an annoying self centered guy, he was also violent. He was known for his temper, and he had been trying to get in on Siren interrogations for years. Rayna and I were vehemently against it;

we knew he only wanted to satisfy his dark side under the guise of getting information. That was not how we worked and never would be.

There was more Siren running in his veins than I cared to think of. Unfortunately, he wasn't the only one that had that problem. A small group of Frank-like Sirenites had started to form over the last couple of years, and our community was starting to see its first bit of unrest. Those of us that wanted to keep the peace, and continue to live lives that we could be proud of, kept a close eye on those that leaned a little too close to their heritage. We all lived by a strict code of ethics and rules that we had set out long ago. We never involved the police in our matters; it would have only drawn attention to our town - we dealt with offending members of our community on our own. Secrets were our business, and we kept them well. Our people respected the code we lived by; and, if they didn't, there were consequences. It was a rare job to have to deal with that, though, and I was thankful because The Watch was responsible for upholding our laws and dealing punishments

Franky watched me as I got up into my truck. His bright violet eyes flashed in anger. I didn't trust him, never did, and now I had wounded his ego. Franky didn't scare me, not physically, but he was conniving and manipulative. In a way the was more dangerous than a Siren who reacted on instinct and in the heat of the moment. Franky had patience. He would take his time getting back at you.

The door to Vyktor's opened and Franky looked from me to the woman walking out, Rayna. A sly smile slid across his lips, and I was no longer his concern. *For now.*

23
KYLAYA

I TOSSED AND TURNED, unable to get any sleep. The room was too bright. The bed was too soft. My legs beat out a constant rhythm of pain as I tried, again, to adjust myself into a comfortable position.

"Okay!" the door flew open and a man walked in, waving his arms. "You're shaking the whole house! Settle down and stop moving!"

"Who are *you*?" I screamed, pulling the covers over myself as if they would protect me from the new stranger at the end of my bed.

"Jasper. Jett's brother; and, lady, you are driving me nuts with your flipping and flopping," he shouted, his eyes wild and his breathing heavy.

"I'm sorry, but my legs are killing me. I didn't mean to disturb anyone," I quipped.

"You aren't healed yet?" he asked and crossed the room to me, throwing the blanket aside and diving for the cuts on my thighs.

"What in Hades are you *doing*?" I yelled, pushing at him as he came at me.

"Oh, calm down, you aren't my type," he answered as he reached for the bandages. "I need to have a look and see what's going on with your wounds. If you aren't healing we're going to have to come at this another way."

"What other way?" I asked, stopping my thrashing and staring at him. Something in his tone put me on edge.

He looked at me and then back down to my wounds. In a serious tone, with a grave expression, he answered, "Amputate."

"What?" I cried out. A sly smile slid across his face, and I knew that he had just said it to get a rise out of me. I pushed at him again and he laughed.

"Sorry, it was too easy, you are entirely too amped up. Calm down," he remarked.

"Easy enough for you to say, you can walk out of here any time you want," I said.

"You want to leave already? But you just got here!"

"Yes – no. I mean, I need to get back but I want to stay?" He looked at me and lifted a brow and I knew that it came out just as jumbled as I felt about being there. I needed to go but I wanted to stay. I had responsibilities back home and my dad. I ached to know how he was doing.

"Where am I? How far from home am I?" I asked again. He sighed and looked at me with a pinched lip and one brow arched.

"Well, at least you're strong enough to ask questions. I suppose that's a good thing," he chuckled, as he closed my bandages tenderly. I looked at him closer. His longer dark blonde hair fell in front of his face in a playful manner that echoed his character. He pulled the covers over my legs again, fluffing them and spreading them out so that I was comfortable. He opened the tiny closet and pulled a blanket from the top shelf. Without a word he opened it and placed it over the bed.

"It gets cool in here at night," he said kindly and moved towards the door.

"Jasper, is it?" I asked.

"Yeah?"

"How are they? My legs," I asked politely. He stepped out of the doorway and into the room again.

"They're healing, but slower than we were anticipating. We'll have to keep a close eye on them to make sure infection doesn't sink in," he said, answering the questions rolling around in my head.

"I see," I answered, looking at the roof and trying not to let my fears get the best of me. Until that point, I was so enamored with the idea that Jett was real that I hadn't really considered the situation I was in. Where was I? What was going on back home? Did the Sirens get through? Was my father okay? *Mazz is going to be going crazy!*

"You're safe here…umm – what's your name?" Jasper asked as he took a seat in the chair in the corner of the room.

"KyLaya. KyLaya Constantilly," I answered.

"Pleasure to meet you," he smiled tipping his head slightly. "I'm Jasper, and the less devastatingly handsome one is my brother Jett," Jasper explained.

"Where *am* I, Jasper?" I asked again.

"Alright," he answered and sank in his chair a little, with a defeated smirk. "I can't tell you everything, like location or anything like that; but, I'll give you something so that you can understand why we can't tell you. How's that?" he asked.

"It's a start, thank you," I said, truly grateful for any information that at point.

"Our little community is a haven for those that Mer has cast out. They would seek to destroy us if they found us; so, we keep this place a secret. That way we stay safe," Jasper answered.

"My people wouldn't harm your people," I said defensively.

"You don't know that, not really. It's not a good idea to have Mer know where we are or that we exist at all," he said, shaking his head slightly.

"Why did Jett bring me here then?"

"I don't know," Jasper shook his head and shrugged. "He's never cared one lick for a girl before. You…you are something else, Gorgeous."

"I-" I began, but a yawn cut me off; and, I realized that my body was finally settling down.

"No more questions for tonight, you sleep," Jasper said as he walked to the door. "KyLaya, you really are safe here. Okay?"

I nodded hesitantly. That was enough for him, and he left the room, closing the door quietly.

I let my head sink into the pillow, a sigh escaped my mouth as I let my eyes close.

Visions of home passed over my eyes. Sirens attacking. My father dying. Mazz being tortured. I opened my eyes and took a deep breath. Freaking out wasn't going to help them. I needed to get healthy and go home. They needed me.

As much as I knew I needed to go, my heart was rooted in that house. In Jett's house.

How could I leave him as soon as I found him? *How?*

It wasn't fair.

That frustration filtered into my dreams, giving me a very restless sleep.

24
JETT

"WHERE HAVE YOU BEEN?" Jasper asked as I came in the door. It was late, and he was grumpy and half asleep. Standing in the kitchen rubbing his eyes with his boxers on and no shirt, I was just a little surprised to see him up. Typically, he slept like the dead. He wasn't a morning person, so his attitude wasn't a surprise at that hour.

"What are you doing up so late?" I asked.

"The girl was up," he answered and pointed to my room. "Tossing and turning so loud she woke me. You know how I feel about being woken up."

"She okay?" I asked, my heart kicking at my chest at the mention of her.

"She's not healing as fast as I had hoped, but she'll get there. Sam should be able to help out in a few days, which will be great. Then she can go." He yawned big, leaned against the door frame hard, and watched me.

I nodded, relieved to hear that Laya was doing alright; though, not happy about the leaving part.

"You didn't answer my question. Where were you?" Jasper asked again, leveling his eyes at me.

"Just…driving around," I said with a shrug. Which I had been. After talking to Franky, and everything else that had gone on, I needed awhile to think.

"Why?" he asked, rubbing his face with both of his hands.

"I had some stuff on my mind that I needed to work out. That's all."

"Like what?" he asked, stepping in the room and sitting at the table.

"I don't really want to talk about it, if you don't mind," I answered and stalked across the room.

"I know you don't," he responded, scooting his chair across the floor, blocking my way to the living room with his long legs.

"What?" I grunted.

"Look, I know things with us haven't been the same since Louise and Brock died, but I'm worried about you," he shared. His brow was furrowed, and even though sleep was still clinging hard to him, I could see that he was being genuine.

"Worried? Don't be. I'm *fine*," I said, shoving his chair out of my way. He grabbed my leg, and I tumbled to the ground. "Real mature, Jass," I groaned.

"Come on. I know there's something going on with you. I won't give up until you tell me," he warned.

"Leave it be, Jasper," I threatened and went to stand. He wrapped an arm around my waist and threw me to the ground. I flashed to a stand.

"Cheater," he frowned.

"I said leave it be," I repeated.

"*Oh*...I see. Never mind," he said as he stood. A smile crossed his face, and his hands rested on his hips as he watched me.

"You see nothing. Go to bed," I said and waved him off as I walked into the living room to get ready for a really uncomfortable sleep on the couch.

"It's *her*," he said, and I stopped. I turned to him, and he lifted his brows and grinned like a cat.

"I don't know what you're talking about," I uttered, turning to the blankets that I had on the couch.

"You *like* her, don't you?" he asked, coming into the room.

"I most certainly do not; she's a *Mer*," I emphasized and shook my head, hoping that would be enough to stop the conversation.

"Sure, sure," he said nodding. "Sweet dreams, *lover boy*." I flashed around and shot a pillow in his face. He chuckled heartily and walked with a light step back to his room.

I sighed and sat heavily on the couch, falling over onto my side and breathing deeply. I closed my eyes.

Damn you, Jasper.

How did he know?

25
KYLAYA

"OUCH!" I yelled as Jett dabbed some more ointment on my wound.

"Quit being such a baby!" he scolded.

"I am *not* a baby! That hurts!" I said and slapped his hand. He looked up with a tight lip, and narrowed his eyes. He sighed loudly.

"I have to put this on you, or your wound will get infected. You want to lose your legs completely?" he asked, his violet eyes looking directly in mine. I swallowed, knowing that he was right but hating to admit it.

"Just, be *careful*," I retorted and laid back in bed. He shook his head and began the long process of removing and tending to the other wound. For three days I had been cooped up in that damn room with no one to talk to.

Jett had stayed away from me; but, I didn't understand why. Had I done something? I wanted to see him and talk to him, but he was even absent from my dreams. I was confused and mad that, having finally met the man of my dreams, he didn't want to see me. *Why?* So, when he finally showed up, I wasn't exactly excited to see him; at least, I wasn't about to let on that I was.

Without a cheerful greeting or explanation to where he had been Jett came in the room that morning. Jasper said something about Jett having to go to some meetings - maybe that kept him away. There was just no shaking the feeling that he was trying to avoid me for some reason. He didn't seem that happy to be tending to me, barely making eye contact.

He might have been gruff and rude; but, every time he was near me, my heart slammed against my throat.

"When's Jasper getting back?" I asked. Jasper had a much better bedside manner than Jett. His easy going nature and fun spirit made him a welcome distraction from the situation I was in; and, a way to escape my thoughts for the time that he was in my room. Gods knew I needed it. It was hard to tell that Jett and Jasper were brothers purely based on their personalities. For one, at the moment, Jasper had one.

"Tomorrow," Jett answered in a grumble.

"Great," I uttered, my lips tightening into a grimace.

"Don't tell me you *like* him," Jett laughed, flashing a smile that jump started my heart. He had a beautiful crooked smile. I steadied myself, shrugged and looked at the ceiling.

"He's better company than *you* right now. You've been nothing but a grump," I mumbled and pain bit into my leg. I cried out, and Jett looked up calmly.

"I'm sorry. Did that hurt?" he asked, fanning his long eyelashes at me, feigning innocence. "You *know* it did," I said through gritted teeth. He didn't say anything but looked down and continued to dress the wound. "What's the deal, Jett? You saved my life, brought me to your home and have been nothing but an ass to me. I thought…I thought that we were friends, at the very least."

"We are friends, Laya," he said, looking at my leg and not me.

"Well then, what's going on? I mean, before, when we were in the dreams, there was a connection. Something between us, you know?"

"Sure," he answered. Frustration built in me, rising from my guts, tightening my chest as it rose up my throat.

"What the hell, Jett? I thought that we had feelings for each other, but I guess that was just the fake person that you were in the dreams, huh?" I yelled. "Clearly, you are nothing like that in real life. I thought you cared about me; you said that you did. Was that a lie? Was it all a lie?" I asked.

"No," he said, finally looking up at me.

"Well, then, why are you acting like this? What did I do?"

He didn't answer.

"Look at me, dammit! What did I do?"

"I don't know! I-" he yelled back and then dropped his eyes back to the wound and started to dress it.

"*What?*" I asked.

"Nothing, you didn't do anything; it's just that you're a Mer and I'm…I'm…" he hesitated, dressing the wound as fast as he could and then stood to leave.

"What does being a Mer have to do with this?" I asked.

"My people are forbidden from having a relationship of any kind with a Mer. In fact I should have killed you the moment that you saw me, according to our law," he answered.

"Then why didn't you?" I asked, swallowing hard and not entirely sure that I wanted to know the answer. He wasn't exactly turning out to be the guy that he was in my dreams. The disappointment of that weighed heavily on me.

"Why?" he asked, looking at me.

"Yes. Why?"

"Because it was *you*," he said surprising himself, and me, with his answer. A rush ran through me at his words. He stood to leave.

"Wait," I said. He stopped and turned half way to me; his eyes peering over his shoulder.

"I…I know this is weird," I began. "I didn't think that you were real either, but you are. The fact is that whatever we had in our dreams…was in our *dreams*, not in real life. If you have someone else that you want to be with, I understand," I shared, as much as it made me want to vomit thinking of him with anyone but me.

"Someone else? I don't have *someone else*. There's only ever been you," he said, shaking his head sadly.

"Then what's going on, Jett? Please, I think I deserve some honesty," I begged.

"You're right. You do," he sighed and sat on the chair at the end of the bed. I didn't say anything but let the silence drive him to talk, and he did.

"To start, I'm sorry. I've been a jerk today. It's not your fault. It's just…when I saw you I was so excited that you were real. After all these years, you were in front of me for *real*. It was a dream come true, literally. But, then, once you were here, I started to panic. For me, contact with a Mer is forbidden. My job is to keep my people safe from the Mer and I have violated their trust by bringing you here. Again, not your fault. It's just that…" he stopped and shook his head. "I'm sorry I've made you feel that you have done something wrong. Truly, I am," he apologized.

My heart warmed and blood coursed through me hard and fast as his eyes met mine. Something in me called to him; there was no denying it. Deep down, the feelings that had been growing in my dreams for him were coming out. I looked at him and saw the young boy that I shared so much of myself with. The boy who had grown up with me, and who I felt more for than any other.

"I just…I don't know if I can trust you," he admitted.

"What?" I blurted, taken aback and insulted. After all the years we had spent together, I couldn't believe that he couldn't trust me. "How can you say that?"

"It isn't anything that you have done; it's just…*who* you are," he said and cringed, knowing that what he had said was insulting.

"*Who* I *am*? Are you kidding me? You *know* who I am. We've grown up together! I'm the one who shared in the grief of losing your foster parents. I'm the one who talked to you about problems with your brother! How can you say that you don't trust me?" I yelled.

"Because you are a *Mer*!"

"Why do you keep *saying* that? What is so bad about being a *Mer*?" I demanded.

"Our people…Mer would…" he shook his head and bit his lip as he stood, unable to finish his sentence. "Gods, I sound like such a jerk!"

"Not going to argue there!"

"It's not that easy," he muttered.

"Just spit it out for goodness sake!" I shouted.

"I brought you here because I couldn't take you to Triton. You know what color my eyes are. One look at me, and I would have been detained, arrested, or worse. You already know there's something different about me. Once you find out the truth…who I really am. Who we all are," he stopped and shook his head.

I had been thinking about it. Sirens had violet eyes, just like Jett's and Jasper's. But, at the heart of me, I didn't feel that he was a Siren. If he had been, I would have been dead or worse. No, he was something else. But what?

"Look," I began, "we have been through a lot. You can trust me. I am fiercely protective of those that have done me a service. If nothing else, you have done me the *ultimate* service and saved my life. It would be the worst kind of betrayal to put you and your people in jeopardy in any way, and that is simply not something that is in my blood to do," I said earnestly, hoping that he would believe me. I meant it. I wouldn't betray him. Even before he saved my life, I wouldn't have betrayed him.

Jett started to pace the room, clearly thinking through his next words.

"Whatever is going on here, whatever you all are, has posed no threat to me or my people. I see no reason why they would care about you or see any harm in you and yours," I added.

"Ha!" Jett blurted. "You don't know that, not really."

"I guess you are just going to have to trust me, then, because no matter how you slice it you owe me an explanation," I answered, watching the cool and calm demeanor of his melt away to reveal a nervous man that paced the floor clearly torn about something.

"I – ugh!" he grunted, grabbing his hair and then throwing out his arms. "I'm just going to say it! That's what I'm going to do! I'm going to say it and let the chips fall where they may," he shouted. I waited and watched him as he paced the room another two times working up the courage.

"Alright, here it goes," he breathed. "We are the children of Sirens."

I opened my mouth, but nothing came out. I stared at him, jaw gaping wide, stunned silent.

Wha,,,

26
KYLAYA

"THE *WHAT*?" I ASKED, once I had regained my voice.

"The children of Sirens, well, the men are," he answered and sat heavily in the chair at the end of the bed. "That wasn't as bad I thought it would be. Feels good to get that off my chest actually," he said with a small smile, looking at me. Watching me.

"You're a Siren's *child*?" I cried. I could feel the stunned and confused look of my face, everything pinching tight, trying to work through what he just said. "How is that possible? Don't they kill all their male offspring?" I asked, knowing enough history about the terrible practices of the Sirens to know that they only valued females. They usually killed their male babies by throwing them into the open ocean to be eaten by whatever predator came by or die of the elements. They really were terrible creatures, Sirens.

"Okay," Jett uttered and moved to the edge of his seat, his hands rubbing his thighs as he bit the inside of his lip.

"Have you ever heard of the Nereids?" he asked. I nodded unconvincingly. "They are the guardians of the ocean and all of its inlets. All the salt water in other words," Jett explained with a slight smile. "They are led by a woman named Thetis. A long time ago, it was brought to her attention that there were babies that were being discarded into the ocean outside of Stronghold, the Siren city. Being the compassionate woman that she was, she rescued one of those babies and brought it back to the land where the Nereids lived. It's a beautiful place that exists only for those that belong to Olympus.

"The Nereids tended to the baby and fell in love with him, but something was happening to their land - it was dying. It turned out that the presence of the baby was killing their home. They were devastated, as they loved the child dearly; and, they had made up their minds to rescue any other baby that came from the Sirens and raise it as their own. But, they now knew that they couldn't.

"Thetis met with the Naiads, the caretakers of the fresh water. Together they set up a place where the babies would be able to grow and thrive and be raised away from the power of the gods. This is that place."

"But, the Siren babies were just that, babies. How could they raise themselves if the Nereids couldn't?" I asked.

"Sorry. I'll explain. As you know, there are two kinds of Sirens. First, the ones that are born to a *Siren*, who are raised from infancy in Stronghold and have pure Siren blood running in their veins. Siren-borns are the most violent and dangerous of the Sirens. Second, the ones that are born to a *Mer*, who are raised in Titus or Triton but later turn into a Siren at an older age. The Mer-borns are viewed as dirty half breeds to the Siren-borns. They are used and abused in the worst way. Mer-borns are brought Stronghold so that the Siren-borns can practice their torture skills and weapons on live victims. Mer-borns are forced into servitude at the hands of the Siren-born. Only the most violent and cruel Mer-borns escape by becoming the horrible creatures that they serve. They live a terrible life for the most part."

"Really?" I asked, utterly stunned. I never knew that. How could I not know that? How did no one in Mer know that?

"Many years ago," Jett continued, "a single mermaid found out what was happening to the Mer-borns and started an underground network to sneak them out of Titus before they were put to death or handed over to the Sirens. She worked with the Naiads to give them a life away from the Sirens and Mer where they would be safe from all who would seek to harm them."

"Here?" I asked, finally seeing the reason for his story. Jett nodded.

"This place has become a haven for the young, rescued Mer-born Sirens and for the male Siren babies that are cast off. We are all here because of what the Sirens have done and how Mer as dealt with them."

"So…so you are a…" but I didn't know how to end that sentence. He was a what?

"Sirenite," he answered for me. "A male Siren. Our mothers were all Siren-born Sirens, the most cruel of the Sirens," he answered with a frown.

"You were brought here as babies? All of you?"

"Well, not all of us. This place was founded a long time ago. We are a growing, thriving community now. Most of the children that you see running around here are the sons and daughters of a union between a Sirenite and a Mer-born Siren. But, we are all Siren blood in one way or another."

My mind was spinning. *Male Sirens? It can't be!* Sirens were female. *All* Sirens were horrible, mean, evil creatures. I looked up at Jett. There was nothing in him that was like the Sirens that I had learned to fear. He was kind, and caring, strong and courageous. There was no evil in that, and no evil in him.

"Jasper?" I asked.

"He's my brother. Of course, even though we look alike, we don't know for sure that he's my *blood* brother, 'cause we don't know our birth mothers or fathers. Either way, we were put with the same fosters and raised together. I could never call him anything but my brother," he explained. I nodded, still unsure how to take it all in.

"Look," Jett uttered as he leaned forward in his chair, "There are some in this place that would be really mad that I told you. They want you healed and out of here. I've been in meetings and councils and…it's been a really bad couple of days keeping others away from here. Away from harming you. You are to heal and get out," he explained.

"Is that what you want? Me out of here?" I asked, not able to help myself.

"No!" he said immediately. "I mean I do want you to get healed, but I don't want you to go," he answered as a blush reddened his cheeks.

"Aww, you do like me after all," I mumbled with a smile and a tilt to my head. He chuckled under his breath, smiling as he did.

"Very funny, Laya," he retorted.

"Well, I was beginning to wonder," I admitted and a look crossed his face as if I had slapped him. I didn't intend to hurt him I was only being honest after all; but, in that moment, I realized that maybe his feelings were deeper than what he was willing to let show.

"Jett…"

"You should rest," he said as he stood to leave the room. I didn't argue as a yawn forced its way out, but I really didn't want him to leave. Jett walked quietly to the door and turned.

"I don't want you to go, Laya. I'm sorry if I ever made you feel that way."

Never in my life had I not wanted to go home. Every trip we took was too long to be away for me. I ached to sleep in my own bed, to eat food I knew, and see Mazz. That was my life. But, in that moment, for the first time in my life I found myself not wanting to go. Guilt slammed me, as I thought of what that would do to my father and Mazz. The job I had to do back home was the most important. I couldn't abandon all of that!

Something soft brushed my cheek, and I was snapped out of my train of thought and back into the room.

"Sorry, didn't mean to startle you," Jett said softly as he tucked a fuzzy blanket up around me. "Thought you looked a little cold, and I know you like to sleep with lots of blankets." I smiled and nodded, my heart thrumming hard.

I looked into his beautiful eyes and it hit me…there was a big part of me that would throw everything away to stay with him.

Holy shit balls…what is wrong with me?

27
JETT

I'M IN DEEP SHIT NOW…

In the days that I had left Jasper in charge of Laya's healing, I had to sit in on meeting after meeting, and then in front of the Council, to plead my case. I had hoped that by being honest I would be able to keep Laya at the farm to heal *and* keep my good standing in the community. The Council was my last chance at keeping her safely with me. My reputation was in the rock, at the every leasy.

"What the hell were you thinking bringing a Mer into our home?" Franky shouted at me as I sat alone, in front of the Council members. Four men and six women stared at me in shock and disgust. Usually I was in one of the male seats, along with Jass; but, I sat in front of them hoping that I could convince them to just let me heal Laya, and get her home.

"Just let him talk!" Vyktor said to Franky, waving a hand to silence him.

"There's nothing that he can say to me that will convince me that Mer stays alive!" he snapped back, shaking his head and crossing his arms. I clenched my teeth hard, and threw all my willpower into not losing my temper on him.

"She doesn't pose a threat to us. She was hurt! My conscience demanded that I intervene. I couldn't just leave her to be tortured and taken by the Sirens! Too many had been killed that day," I said. "Look, I understand the gravity of the situation; but, I do know that we can trust this girl. She's not going to bring Mer down on us."

"You aren't suggesting that you tell her who we *really* are, are you?" Franky yelled.

"I-"

"Of course not," Vyktor answered for me. "Jett's responsible for the safety of our community and upholding our laws. He *knows* the penalty for breaking one of the main laws." Franky settled down and a smirk tugged at his lips.

Banishment. Breaking our main laws meant being sent away from all that we knew, and all that we loved, to survive without help. No one had ever been banished, and it wasn't something that I wanted for myself. I had a life that I loved…a family too. I couldn't leave Jasper. But, one look at Franky, and I knew he was entirely too happy about the idea of me getting booted from my community.

"You have my word. There is no threat to our people with the Mer in my care," I stated.

The Council mumbled for a few moments; exchanging looks with each other and me. I needed a majority vote to keep Laya safe. I didn't know what I would do if they voted against me. The tingle of my powers at the tips of my fingers made me aware that it wouldn't be good if they did.

"Let's vote," Rayan said, nodding at me. "I trust Jett."

"Of course you do," Franky muttered, glaring at me. Rayna shot him a sharp look and continued.

"I vote to keep the Mer, but that she leave as soon as she is healed," Rayna finished.

"Thank you," I said to her.

"The Mer heals and goes," Vyktor said.

"Kill the Mer," Franky sneered. I bit my lips to stop from arguing with him, knowing that it wouldn't do any good. I stood silent and still, and waited out the rest of the votes.

Time had never moved so slow as I listened to every member proclaim their decision. It came down to the last vote.

Five to four for letting me keep Laya. If there was a tie, a member would be allowed to break it. We rotated members who were give this chance. Franky smiled at me. It was his turn. If the members tied, Franky got to decide Laya's fate.

"Jett, you have never steered our people wrong. You are an outstanding member of our community, and one that our young children look up to," Councilwoman Mises stated.

"Thank you," I answered.

"That being said, I was shocked to learn that you violated our trust in such a grave manner." I dropped my head and nodded. My powers buzzed in my hands and I clenched them to keep the sight of it away.

"Just vote!" Franky yelled at her. She didn't acknowledge him.

"You may keep the Mer."

"No!" Franky shouted. My gaze flashed to the Councilwoman. I didn't dare smile, no matter how much I wanted to.

"Thank you," I said and bowed to the Council, retreating from the room before Franky exploded.

I could hear his voice all the way down the hallway and into the parking lot.

Then I smiled…a lot.

Six to four.

I was allowed to keep Laya at my place. I couldn't have been more relieved.

At the time, I was just grateful that I was able to guarantee her safety until she was healed. It wasn't until I started to really talk to her that I realized how much telling her who I was meant to me. How much I wanted her to know. How much I needed her to know.

But, even with her right in front of me, I couldn't tell her, because the damned council wouldn't let me! I had never felt so torn. When the words spilled from my mouth I was both shocked and relieved. It was out. No more secrets.

I didn't regret telling her, though. As terrifying as it was to defy my laws it was nothing compared to the amazing feeling of finally saying it to her. I felt good. Really good.

Still…I am in so much trouble.

I went to the kitchen and started the kettle for some tea, something to calm my nerves; but it was taking too long. I slipped my shoes on and went out the front door. The evening was calm and warm, and still fairly bright with the summer sun. The peaceful chirps of the crickets was a familiar lullaby that should have had me nodding off, but my mind was too busy. Closing my eyes, I enjoyed the feel of the summer air on my skin. I took a cleansing breath, hoping it would help make everything clearer.

The clouds were lined up on the horizon, painted bright pink and orange as the sun lit them from underneath on its way down. I inhaled the sweet air, feeling invigorated and calmed by the familiar scent. I loved it. The prairies might not have been my natural habitat, but it was beautiful in its own subtle way. I couldn't imagine living anywhere else, a least I couldn't until...

Don't go there...

Her presence had awoken a need in me for the water that I had ignored all my life. The Siren in me called for the sea; and, even though I loved the land that I was brought up in, there was a restless place in me that never seemed to settle. I thought that there was never going to be an answer to my unsettled heart...until I saw her.

Never engage a Mer. That was the rule. Never been seen. Never be heard; and, never, under any circumstance, talk to one. There I was bringing one home.

News about Laya got out; and, even with the Council's approval to have her on the farm, I had spent the last few days trying to calm the community so that they didn't storm my house and kill her in my bed. I returned home when I figured that I had done all I could. I was exhausted and frustrated beyond measure.

I had been waiting years to tell her. Was it so bad that I, selfishly, didn't want to keep it a secret from her anymore? Yes. To me at least. Breaking the trust of my people was harder than I thought, and I struggled with it right up until the words tumbled out. I had betrayed the people that raised me, and the laws that I, myself, was in charge of upholding.

Gods...what am I doing?

28
KYLAYA

AT FIRST, THE VERY IDEA that there was a place where the offspring of the Sirens lived was terrifying. My first thought was that it would need to be *dealt* with. But that was my job talking, not my heart. I had spent time with Jasper and Jett. They were not Sirens, not by any measure.

I could see why they didn't want to tell me where I was or who they were. I got it. If it ever got out into Mer, where these people were, they would have an army from every city descend on them in a flash. They wouldn't have a chance.

The next day the sun shone brightly through the window, and I could feel something in the air that had me itching to get out of bed.

As if he had read my mind, Jett came in and announced that it was time I got my "butt in gear". I was only too happy to oblige.

"Come on now; if we don't get you moving, your muscles will seize, and then we'll really be in trouble," Jett said.

"You don't have to ask me twice," I answered, sitting up taller in the bed. I had never, not once, been stuck in bed for that long and I *hated* it. All my life I was a busy-body. Always moving, always on the go. My new position as Prime was no different in that account and I liked that. However, being forced to stop was like running at full speed into a wall. It physically hurt.

The worst was that the majority of the time, I was left alone to think. Home. Father. Mazz. My people. They were all on my mind constantly. Running around my thoughts and my dreams, spiking my pulse and sending my stomach into backflips.

Did Sirens the get in and sack the city?
Is my father okay?

How is Mazz doing?
Had there been another murder?
Who was running the city now that I wasn't there?

It was driving me nuts! I needed a distraction. The reality was that there was nothing I could do for my people.

I had to heal.

"What? You don't like hanging out in my bed?" Jett asked, as he pulled the covers back and examined my wounds.

"You need a decorator. Your room is beyond a snore-fest," I answered. He looked up at me, and I smiled.

"Funny," he deadpanned.

"You have nothing on your walls, Jett. It's been…boring," I admitted.

"Sorry, Laya, the circus hasn't been in town. And by that, I mean that Jasper's been at Sam's. Let's get you out of the snore-fest that is my room and into the kitchen…where all the action is," he joked. I laughed lightly. He didn't realize that, at that point, watching a pot boil was exciting for me.

"Come on, sad-sack," he chuckled, as he threaded his arm around my waist and pulled me to his side.

Jett was strong and steady, and I leaned against him for the support I needed as he helped me off the bed. He smelled fresh and sweet, a scent that I had never smelled before - something you wouldn't find in Triton and not from a bottle. It was as if his very skin held the aroma.

"Hello?" Jett said, interrupting my thoughts. His beautiful violet Siren eyes looked into mine.

"What?" I asked, having lost my train of thought.

"Where did you go?" he asked, looking me in the eye. Suddenly, I felt stuck again; but, in a good way. A blush burned my cheeks and my heart beat escalated. His arms were around me and I was closer to him than I had been since our dream. I swallowed and dropped my eyes.

Oh, boy. I felt so drawn to him it was scary.

"Sorry," I uttered. "What did you say?"

"Put your arm around my neck. I can lift you or you can walk. You're choice," he said.

"Walk," I said immediately. Not that I didn't want to be in his arms. I did. Maybe that was the reason that I decided I would walk on injured legs, and suffer the agony of it, instead.

I nodded and looped my arm around his neck. He helped me through the door, down the tiny hall and into the kitchen. It was my first look at his home. The place was white washed with blue trim around each door that matched the baseboards. The floor was a light golden wood; the kitchen was tiled in greys. A small wooden table was at the center of the kitchen and took up the majority of the space, as a counter ran its way around the kitchen including the sink and stove. The place was small but neat and tidy.

Every step was torture. I could feel the stabbing pain in both my legs as I tried to place as little pressure on them as possible. How he thought that I was going to be ready to walk in a couple of days was beyond me. I was starting to feel like I would never heal.

Jett gently sat me into a wooden chair and lifted my legs to move me into a more comfortable position at the dark stained, round table. It was a gesture that looked natural and well-practiced, whose tenderness warmed my heart.

"Who did you have to care for?" I asked, picking up the cup of hot brown liquid in front of me and giving it a smell.

"It's tea," he said with a smile. "Try it. I can add more sugar to make it sweeter, if you don't like it."

I took a small sip, feeling the warmth spread down my throat and coat my stomach. It was like being warmed from the inside out and was a very welcome sensation. I moaned out loud.

"No sugar then?" Jett asked, smiling out of the one side of his mouth, looking at me from the sudsy sink.

"No," I answered. "It's perfect."

"Good," he said, turning back to the soapy water and diving in. The sink was under a window that looked out the front of the house. White curtains flapped in the breeze from the open window and the sun shone through them. The air that came through was sweet and filled my lungs unlike anything I had ever experienced. It was like I was breathing for the first time.

"You didn't answer my question," I said, taking another sip of the delicious tea and enjoying the sensation of it warming me again.

"What?" Jett asked and looked over his shoulder at me.

"Who did you care for? Was it your fosters?" I guessed.

"Yes, it was. When they got older, they needed more care. Jasper and I looked after them until the accident took them. They were good people," he said with a nod, focusing on the dishes he pulled from the hot water.

"I'm sorry, Jett. I know they meant a great deal to you," I said genuinely.

"They lived a good life. They had no regrets at the end of it. Not many can say that," he answered. I nodded.

"I lost my mother and my sister," I shared, not knowing what drove me to say it.

"Oh? You never told me that," he said turning.

"I didn't? I suppose I don't like talking about it. My mother died in childbirth when I was young. She didn't make it and neither did the baby. A few years later, my older sister was kidnapped. We never heard from her again…never heard from the kidnapper either. We still have no idea where she is or if she's even alive," I said, feeling the weight of it in my chest all over again.

We were still recovering from Mother's death when KyLena was kidnapped while on a trip to Titus Prime. We had been there with my father, to see the king. KyLena and I had come along to vacation while our father worked with King Zale. She had thrown an epic tantrum, for a teenager, when Dad said that it was just me going; so, she was allowed to go too. I wasn't happy about that as it was supposed to be my first solo trip; but, KyLena had a way of worming her way into my good graces – and she did. We ended up having a really great time together, despite the age gap between us. KyLena was three years older than me.

A month into our vacation, I woke up in the night, something having disturbed my sleep. The room was dark, but I sensed something off. KyLena and I shared a room in Court, the residence for the government in Titus Prime. I instinctively looked to her bed; but, it was empty. I called out for her, but there was no response. I yelled and yelled, eventually drawing the attention of a guard.

Soon Court was lit and searches were mounted, but she wasn't found. There was no sign of a break-in to the room. No sign that there was a struggle. Nothing. It was as if she had just got up and walked out of the room on her own and disappeared. But *I know* that she would never have done that. We were close. She would have said something to me. She would have told me if something was wrong. I knew that. Something else happened.

No one believed me, though. In the end, there was no evidence of a kidnapping, so everyone thought that she just ran away…met another Mer and took off.

But not me. I will *never* believe that she just left. She was taken.

I hadn't realized that I had gone so far into my thoughts until I felt a hand brush mine. I inhaled sharply and realized that tears were on my face. Reaching up quickly, I wiped them away with my finger-tips. Jett had moved away from the sink and was sitting in the chair next to me, his warm hand on mine.

"You okay?" he asked, looking deeply into my eyes. My heart jumped, and I could feel the blush starting. His fingers trailed over my skin, softly and slowly. I never knew a touch could be igniting as I felt a tightening in my core, like a spring about to go.

Yet he was a Siren's child.

What would that mean for us? What would that mean for Mer? Where would we fit in this world? The Mer hate all that is Siren and the Sirenites fear the Mer. Where would we be able to make a life?

I was suddenly realizing that the relationship in our dreams was so much easier than any one that we might try in real life.

I pulled back my hand and cleared my throat. The battle for my heart was raging inside of me, and I just didn't know what to do with it.

"I – umm. It's been a long time since I've thought about my sister," I answered, breaking eye contact and looking down at the table.

"Of course," he said and stood. "You want another cup?" he asked.

"Sure," I answered with a grateful smile.

"Coming up," he said, scooping my mug in his hand and turning to the stove. I watched as he fussed with the tea and found myself oddly attracted to the way that he managed himself around the kitchen. His strong arms moved over the stove as his hands turned knobs and added ingredients to the brew he was making. In High Hill, I had never seen a man in the kitchens other than the chefs. Dad was the Prime, so his meals were brought to him. Mazz and Hasp had always been served their food too. It was a domestic skill that I lacked as well. Seeing Jett take complete care of himself was attractive, sexy. I could feel the ridiculous smile that etched across my face, and knew I must have looked crazy.

"What?" Jett asked as he turned around, cup in hand, and caught my expression

"What?" I asked, breaking eye contact and trying to look innocent.

"Don't give me that," he scolded and sat across from me, sliding the tea towards me. "What were you looking at? I can tell when you are lying, you know."

"I wasn't thinking about anything," I shrugged. There was no way I was going to admit to him that making tea was equivalent of foreplay for me.

"Liar," he said and leaned forward, as if proximity would release my secret. "It was about me," he stated, staring hard into my eyes. My throat was punched by my heart, and I swallowed hard to get it back where it should have been.

"What?" my voice squeaked, I inwardly groaned. *Nice cover, Ky.* "No." I said in a firm even tone that was better but clearly forced.

"It *was* me," he said with a smile and a nod. "Now…what about me?"

"Oh gods," I uttered and turned from him.

"Must be something embarrassing because you are blushing pretty hard," he teased.

"I am *not*," I argued, knowing full well that I was. He didn't contradict me, just nodded and smiled.

"It's cute," he smiled. I blushed harder. Clearing his throat he studied me. "My hair?" he asked and I wouldn't look at him. "Nope, not juicy enough." I stared out the window at the sky and crossed my arms, refusing to give him any information or be a party to his ridiculous line of questioning.

"My butt!"

"What? No!" I shouted. "I wasn't thinking of your butt!"

"So, you admit you were thinking of me!" he shouted back. I opened my mouth, ready to argue, but then closed it figuring there was really no point. I just gave him the answer.

"I am a little hurt that it wasn't my butt; I've heard that I have a pretty nice one, if I do say so myself," he said with a little pout.

"Oh, jeez," I groaned.

"So, not my butt. But it is something that was embarrassing to you…" he mumbled. His eyes dropped from mine to the tea I was sipping from.

"The *tea?*" he asked and looked up at me. *No way. There's no way that he actually guessed it.*

"What?" I asked, to make sure that I heard him right.

"Why the tea?" he asked, looking at me with a half-smile and a furrowed brow.

"Tea? What tea?" I asked with a shrug and a smile. He lifted an eye brow at me, and I dropped my shoulders. "Fine," I relented. "I've just never been around a guy that can…"

"Make tea?" he asked, his brow furrowed and his lips cocked to the side.

"No! Well, yes, kind of. I mean, all the men that I'm around don't do that kind of stuff. I'm not sure if they even know how to or would be able to if they had to," I answered.

"Okay, I get that, but why are you embarrassed?" he asked as his voice trailed off. I didn't say anything, but I could tell that he figured it out from the smile that burst onto his face. "Oh," he smiled, "I get it now."

"Whatever," I said, trying to distract from the embarrassment I was feeling. "I think it's nice that you can fend for yourself, and you know how to take care of yourself," I said, trying to justify it without it sounding like a turn on.

"Thanks," he smiled, and a warm chuckle came from him. He turned; a big smile graced his face and showed just how handsome he really was. My heart gave a solid thump in my chest and heat raced to my cheeks. I looked away, still not used to the reaction my body had to a guy that I found infinitely attractive.

I was only nineteen, but my focus had always been academia, not a mate. Mazz and I had been intended since I could remember, so I had no reason to look at other guys. My schooling was private. My chambers were located away from everyone else. Everything about my life was sheltered from the outside world especially after KyLena was taken. The only men in my life were the ones that my father trusted above all and that was extended to Mazz and Hasp only. I didn't have other guys to look at until just recently when I started training with the Elite, but even then I wasn't interested. What was the point of looking for something you already had? I had a future with Mazz already planned out. No one else could light a candle to him.

But, when I looked at Jett, I could feel something that I had never thought was meant for me. Something that overshadowed every plan, every thought that I had about my future with Mazz.

And that was downright terrifying.

29
KYLAYA

"AND YOU HAVEN'T TRIED TO RUN for the hills, yet?" Jasper asked me.

He had arrived back home that night and came to see how I was managing with his brother. To say the least, he was happy when I said that we were getting along, but he was the most shocked that Jett told me what he really was.

"No. I'm fine. A little weirded out that there has been this whole society, that belong to Mer, who have existed in secrecy for so long. It seems…wrong," I shared as I dug into the cupcakes that he brought for me. We were sitting on my bed, crossed legged, chowing down on the delicious treats that he brought from town for me.

"What seems so wrong about it?" Jasper asked stuffing a chocolate cupcake in his mouth, almost whole.

"I don't know. I understand why the secrecy exists, I mean, there are many that wouldn't ask questions before they killed anyone with blood relation to a Siren; but, it just seems sad that you don't get to be a part of the sea. It's such a huge part of who we are," I shared.

"Who said we don't get to be in the ocean?" Jasper asked through a mouthful of cake.

"Wh – well no one. I just assumed that since you lived on land that you didn't get to be in the ocean much…or at all really," I admitted.

"Just like a Mer," Jasper said, shaking his head and clicking his tongue at me.

"And just what exactly is that supposed to mean?" I asked, crossing my arms.

"That you think everyone is living in misery just because they aren't in Mer," Jett answered from the door. "Come on, lazy bones, time to get some fresh air." I looked from Jett to Jasper, and he smiled.

"We thought you could use a nice walk outside. It's a beautiful day. The sun is shining and the birds are singing," Jasper chimed.

"Birds? Real ones?" I asked, my spirits raised. I had never seen a real bird before. Jasper laughed, and Jett shook his head.

"Yes, real ones. The fake ones are in the shop," Jett teased. I swung out a hand and swatted him as he got close.

"I've never seen a bird," I said, looking seriously at him. His tone changed.

"What? Never?" Jett asked.

"There aren't a lot of birds in the depths of the ocean," I answered sarcastically.

"Well, there are plenty outside," Jasper answered and swung off the bed. "You ready, Gorgeous?"

I sat up tall and summoned my strength. I was going to need it. My body was weak from not using it, and my legs were still really sore; but, I wanted to get stronger, and this was really the only way that was going to happen. I let Jasper and Jett grasp me around the waist and lift me off the bed as I held on around their necks.

"Geez, you're as light a feather," Jasper gasped. "Have you eaten since you got here? Jett, you're not starving her are you?"

"Certainly not," Jett replied. "But, he's right, we need to get your weight up."

"But I-"

"You are too thin, Gorgeous," Jasper interrupted. "We will get you some food after our walk."

"I-"

"No arguments. Jass is right," Jett interrupted.

Jasper leaned in and whispered in my ear, "I have more cupcakes stashed in my room." I laughed lightly. *I could agree to more of those!* Jasper let me go and pulled some clothes from a bag, setting them on the bed for me to change into.

"Where did you get these?" I asked, looking between the brothers. Jasper mumbled something about an awkward shopping trip to a place called Sturgis.

"It's going to take me years to counter the rumors I started getting you these things," he said as he handed me some black yoga pants that stretched easily over my bandages, and a "bunny hug".

I laughed, "A bunny hug?"

"A hoodie. A sweater," Jasper answered. I nodded and thanked him.

"I do appreciate it, but-"

"What?" Jett asked, turning to me. "Not your size?"

"No. You weirdly got that right, it's just…I don't want to put on clean clothes when I'm so…" I looked at the two of them and hoped that they would fill in the blanks. I hadn't showered in days, and I still had blood on my skin from my wounds. I desperately wanted to wash the grime from my body.

"Ah," Jett nodded. "Well, you aren't strong enough to stand in the shower, but we could draw you a warm bath."

"That's a good idea, your wounds could use a soak too. We have some stuff that we can put in the water that will help the healing along," Jasper added with a nod.

"That sounds divine," I answered as Jett steered me towards the bathroom.

After convincing them that I would be able to get myself into the bath on my own, they left the bathroom. Jasper had drawn an amazing bath, complete with wonderfully scented salts that he put in the water for my wounds. Jett got some towels for me and helped me remove the bandages.

"If you need anything, just call," Jett said and closed the door.

I had no intention of doing that. I could strip myself, *thank you*.

The bathroom was small, but quaint. It had some frilly white curtains in the window that let in the sunlight. The walls were a light shade of green blue and reminded me of the sea. Just like the rest of the house, the bathroom was tidy and neat. Feeling a familiar pull, I eyed the tub of water. Even that little bit of water had my Mer side calling out to it. I was missing the sea, but there was nothing I could do about that.

Drawing the long shirt that Jett had given me to sleep in over my head, I sat gingerly on the edge of the tub. I bit my lips hard as I lifted my legs over the side of the tub and slowly lowered myself into the welcoming water. The pain was enough for me to see stars, but I was determined to do it on my own. If I couldn't clean myself, I was a damned invalid and that just wouldn't work for me. I moaned as the water filled in over my body, washing away the grime that had built up across my skin since I had come to Jett's. It was the most incredible feeling. I sighed long and low and leaned back in the tub.

I could feel the water in my wounds; but, the initial sting only let me know that the water was doing its job, cleansing away the remnants of the Siren's blade. After that, they didn't hurt. I closed my eyes and cleared my mind as best as I could. I needed a break from my reality. I needed a moment to recoup. I needed….

Jett.

What? No! *Well, maybe.*

I opened my eyes. For years I had wanted him in my life for real. Now that he was right in front of me, the attraction I felt for him was beyond anything my dreams even hinted at. The connection we had was undeniable. I felt it whenever we were in the same room. But, how could a Mer and a Sirenite be together? Our worlds could not have been more at odds.

A shiver ran up my spine. Moving my hands in the water, I was surprised to find it cold.

What?

How long have I been in here?

The guys had been nice enough to let me come in and freshen up before our walk. I didn't want to spend the whole day in the tub. Reaching for the ledge, I pulled my body up as much as I could to the top of it. I tried to sit on the edge of the tub so that I could lift my legs over, but it was wet and slippery. When I leaned on my hand to shift my butt to the ledge, my hand slipped off the tub throwing me completely off balance and sending me crashing down. My ribs slammed onto the ledge and a great splash sounded in the room.

My side burst in pain and I knew I had probably bruised my ribs if not worse, which made pulling myself out of the tub nearly impossible.

I was stuck.

30
JETT

"YOU OKAY?" I called from the bathroom door. I'd been sitting in the kitchen, reading, when I heard a cry and a splash. I flashed to the door and knocked. No answer came.

"Laya!" I shouted and banged on the door.

"Don't come in here!" she yelled back. I could hear the panic in her voice.

"Are you okay?" I asked, leaning closer to the door, as if that would give me a clue as to what was going on.

"I'm fine!" she shouted.

I didn't think it through; I just did what I would do to Jasper if I thought that he needed my help. It wasn't until I was already in the room that I realized that she wasn't wearing anything.

"Get out!" she screamed, pulling the shower curtain closed in a blink. *Oh, shit! Oops!* I spun around, ready to exit the room as fast as I could, and then it dawned on me.

"You can't get out can you?" I asked slowly, my back facing toward the tub.

The splash. The cry. She had fallen into the tub and was stuck. Knowing her, she was too proud to ask for help. I had to place my hand over my mouth to keep form laughing out loud. I knew I really shouldn't be seeing it as something humorous, but it was really funny.

"I'm fine," she answered in a small voice.

"Really?" I asked. "You sure about that?" I crossed my arms, turned, and leaned against the sink.

"Damn it, Jett, you know I'm not!" she yelled at me, and I chuckled.

I reached over and grabbed the towel that we set out for her. Pulling back the curtain the smallest bit - and being a gentleman and not looking - I threaded my arm through.

"Here. Wrap yourself up as best as you can. Tell me when you're covered, and I'll get you out," I said, handing her the towel. She took it from me without another word, and I stood back from the tub and waited.

"Okay," she said quietly and pulled back the curtain. She was a tangle of limbs in the now empty tub. Long, lean limbs that were perfection on a level I was not prepared for. Her blonde hair hung around her head, damp and dripping. Her skin was glowing, having been revived by the water. The stubborn set to her jaw as she raised her head and looked at me made a sly smile creep across my lips.

"You are a mess," I chuckled. *Damn, hot, sexy mess.*

"Just help me, please," she demanded and reached out to me. I could have made her wait longer. I could have been a complete jerk about the whole situation; but, when she reached for me, I instinctively leaned down and wrapped an arm around her. Her eyes met mine, and I started to lose my concentration. Her body was warm and soft against me as I pulled her further into my arms.

"At least you smell better," I teased, trying to snap myself out of the connection I felt to her. She slapped me on the back as I put my other arm under her legs, slowly and carefully.

"Ready?" I asked her. She nodded once, and I stood. She gasped and hissed in my arms as I carried her back to my room and placed her gently on the bed.

"Thank you," she said slowly, as she adjusted the towel around herself.

"You're welcome," I said and turned to go.

"Jett?"

"Yeah?" I stopped and turned back toward her, trying very hard to look her in the eye and not take advantage of her towel situation, no matter how much I wanted to.

"I can't...I mean..." she looked around the room and back to me. She rolled her eyes and sighed. "I need help getting dressed," she admitted.

"Oh," I uttered and cleared my throat. "Okay, what do you need me to do?"

"I need help getting the pants on; I can't reach my feet to put them on," she said. Her face was bright pink, and I was sure mine was too. She fitted the sweater on over the towel while I grabbed her pants that Jasper bought her and kneeled on the floor in front of her. I gently threaded her feet through the legs of the pants. I looked up to see her lips firmly clamped between her teeth, and her eyes closed as she breathed steady, even breaths.

She grabbed the top of her pants when I raised them to the point where she could reach but she didn't pull them higher. Instead, she opened her eyes and looked at me.

"I'll go," I said, standing.

"No," she said, thinking, "I need you to hold me up so I can pull my pants up."

I froze and stared at her, not sure that I heard her right.

"Umm. What?" I asked again, watching her. Laya's face went bright pink, and she smiled despite the awkwardness of it all. It was a lovely, goofy smile that came from the sheer ridiculousness of the situation, and I loved it. I loved her smile.

I walked over slowly and reached for her.

"Try not to enjoy this too much, okay?" she said, with her face next to mine.

"I make no promises," I uttered, to which she playfully shoved at me. Chuckling, I lifted her off the bed, holding her tight under her arms, and looking dramatically away as she pulled her pants up. When she was done, I lowered her slowly down to the bed.

I pulled back and rested my hands on my hips. "Well, I don't know about you, but that was a first for me." I said, and realized that I was blushing too. *Damn it!*

"Uh, yeah. I don't usually have people to pull my pants up for me," she answered with a nod. Then she looked up at me, and something in my chest jumped. I felt the now familiar pull to her - that was getting stronger by the day. I found myself wanting to kiss her so badly it almost hurt.

Whoa.

I was not ready for the torrent of sensations that went with that. I felt my core coil as if it were getting ready for something…big. I cleared my throat and took a step back.

An unnatural laugh passed across my lips, and I ran a hand through my hair trying to break whatever had passed between us.

Listening to whatever was going through me was a bad idea. A really bad one. No matter how amazing the feel of her lips on mine was, or the touch of her skin…

"Thanks," she said, breaking through my thought bubble and bringing me back to reality. I looked at her again and knew that no matter how many times I would try to convince myself that she was bad news…there was no contending with how I felt for her.

And that was a *huge* problem.

"My pleasure," I said with an honesty that startled me, but put a smile on her face. I left while she finished getting ready, which she assured me that she could do without my help. I admit I was fine with that; if I had to hold her again, touch her again, I didn't know if I would be able to stop myself from kissing her.

Damn, she looked good in that towel, though.

31
KYLAYA

IN THE SAFETY OF JETT'S STRONG EMBRACE, I was led slowly outside. The warm, fresh air hit me *hard*. I had never breathed like that before. I had never smelled anything like that before. Sweet and new and absolutely divine. I inhaled it like it was the last life giving breaths I would ever have.

"You like that, huh?" Jett asked, a deep chuckle escaping his lips. I hadn't realized that I had closed my eyes and a smile had creeped out.

"It's like nothing I have ever experienced. Wonderful," I answered, taking in another deep breath. Jett's brow was slightly furrowed against the bright sun; but, when he tilted his head down and looked in my eyes, something passed between the two of us. I was so drawn to him - my pulse was racing out of control, and I immediately wanted to be closer to him even though I was already in his arms. He cleared his throat and smiled at me. I returned it, looking away and breaking the spell that had descended over us.

"Thank you," I whispered.

"For what?" he asked.

"For this. I needed it."

"Anytime. You're always welcome here," he said as pink darkened his cheeks. It was so sweet I wanted to kiss him right there. His full lips begged for mine.

"Your home is so pretty, truly," I pondered as I looked out at the bright field of yellow grass and away from his beautiful face. The sun-spun crop swayed in the wind like a sea of gold and reminded me of home. Puffs of white clouds moved lazily in the light blue sky, as a couple of little birds trilled above us. I gasped and laughed as they flew over.

Across from Jett's house there was a large structure that was just being built. The building looked like a wooden skeleton, golden yellow and gleaming in the sun. I could smell a distinct wood scent drifting to me. In Triton, we used wood that we got from places we had ties with on land. It was one of the advances that we had on Titus; they still built with all sea material in keeping with the age of their city. I always liked the smell of freshly cut wood; it was the smell of building something new, something better. It was progress.

Between the new build and the house, there was a wide garden and a row of trees. The garden was just starting to sprout plants of all shapes and sizes. I could smell the perfume of the green leaves from where we were and wanted to taste them for myself. Our food at home was grown in standing planters that took up less soil, water and space. They were a great source of food for our people and delicious to boot. I imagined that Jett's garden would taste just as good.

A rumbling sounded from far off and all eyes turned to the cloud of dust that was making its way down the gravel road to the house.

"Sam's back!" Jasper yelled, a huge smile spreading across his boyish face. Sure enough a black truck pulled up to the house and a tall, strong man stepped from it. Jasper ran over and hugged him tightly. Jasper had told me about his husband, but that was the first time I had ever seen him.

"Sam, this is KyLaya," Jasper introduced. I stuck out a hand to shake his as the other was still wrapped around Jett. Sam was taller than both Jett and Jasper; he looked like someone that would have fit into the Elite easily, his strong build screamed soldier; but, it was his eyes that took me in. They were those of a healer. I could see it the moment he looked at me. In that second I thought of my father and my heart ached. Sam's eyes were a dark violet compared to Jett and Jasper, and his chocolate brown hair was cut close to his head, just visible under the cap he wore. He had a strong chin with a dimple in it and angular features with a few days growth of facial hair. Sam's curious eyes went from me to Jett and back again; a smile lit his kind face as he grasped my hand in a warm shake.

"Very pleased to meet you, KyLaya," he said in a warm voice.

"We were just getting her outside for a bit," Jasper explained.

"Good idea, the air is sure to do you well," Sam commented with a grin. "I am starving," Sam said, looking again from Jett to me. "How about we have lunch outside today? You want to help me prep?" Sam asked Jasper, already turning to the house, not waiting for an answer.

"Coming!" Jasper shouted and, with a shrug sent our way, followed his husband inside.

I looked at Jett. "Was that strange to you? Or just me?"

"I'm used to Sam having moments like that," he admitted, adjusting his grip around my waist. "Want to take a walk around the garden? That should be enough exercise for you for today, I would think. By then Sam and Jass will have lunch ready," Jett asked, his stunning violet eyes on me again.

"Yeah. That would be nice," I answered, swallowing the rising pressure in my chest. I felt Jett's hand on my ribs as he braced me against him and a shot of electricity burst in my core. My heart thudded hard in my chest, and I started to worry that he was going to feel it.

Calm down, damn it!

"Umm, where are all the other Sirenites?" I asked as we very slowly walked around the garden. I tried not to look at Jett, instead I focused my attention on an orange butterfly that flitted around the garden.

"They live in Stenen; it's the closest little town to us. We are one of the farming families. Our grain is sold and that helps to run the farm and the town as a whole. We all contribute in one way or another to the success of our little community," he answered.

"How does that work when you have so many people? Does everyone have to stay here? What about jobs, kids, a future?" I asked. I had so many questions.

"Whoa!" he laughed. "Well, first of all…not all of us stay here. There are many that grow up and leave. We don't look that different from the humans; and, we don't act it, so we blend in well. Those of us that choose to stay can either take up a trade that serves the community or become part of The Watch."

"What's The Watch?"

"A group of us that venture into Mer and try to take out the Sirens. It's what I was doing the night we met."

"What?"

"For a long time now, we have been keeping your city safe from the Sirens. Haven't you wondered why you haven't seen a Siren in so many years?" he asked.

"Well, yes, but we assumed that they just lost interest in us and were more focused on Titus," I answered.

"Nope, not even close. But, to be fair, it's not like we advertise that we're there," he admitted.

"Why do you do it?" I asked, stopping and looking at him.

I was stunned. For a group of people who hated Mer and Sirens almost equally, why would they risk their lives protecting us?

"We love our community, but we don't want others to be forced into having to join it. If we can stop the Sirens from gaining numbers, we will. Without access to Titus Prime, we stay with Triton and protect it. *No one* should have to go through what our people have. We fight to keep others from the same fate as us."

"Even though you hate the Mer?" I asked.

"We don't *hate* the Mer," he said with a half-smile and a shake of his head. "We fear them."

"Fear us? Why?"

"Because they fear the Sirens so much that they wouldn't hesitate killing all of us just because of the blood that runs in our veins," he answered. I opened my mouth to argue, but I shut it as the weight of his statement hit me.

He was right.

No one would take the time to get to know them. The Mer would come in and destroy the Sirenites and everything that they had built without question and without trial. Until that point, I had never been ashamed of my people. But...I was.

"You okay?" he asked, looking deep in my eyes.

"Huh?" I answered, breaking away from my thoughts. "Yeah. Sorry. You've just given me a lot to think about."

"Oh, sorry,"

"No, don't be," I said, looking at him in earnest.

We walked on in silence for a few minutes. The weight of what he had said heavy on me.

"Want to see something fun?" Jett asked, distracting me from my thoughts.

"Sure, yes, please," I agreed.

"Well, a long time ago, we found out that some of us have some special skills. Being the offspring of Sirens have made us...different," he hinted.

"How?"

He raised a hand and pink light zapped from it, hitting a tree and severing a limb from it. I jumped back, my leg buckled, and I went down. A set of strong arms, tightened around me before I hit the ground.

"Geez, Laya. Sorry. I should have warned you," Jett uttered as he pulled me back to my feet. "You okay?" he asked, as he steadied me. His hands were tight on my arms and I was pressed against his chest to steady myself.

"Yeah, fine," I answered, not being able to look him in the eye now that I was against him. My heart was thundering and I was blushing hard; but, it wasn't any of that that had my attention. It was the feel of his heart against my hands that had stolen my thoughts. It was pounding just as hard as mine was.

I couldn't stop myself. I looked up at him, and his eyes turned down to meet mine.

Jett lifted a hand to brush a hair from my face, gently grazing my cheek as he went and sending a tingling sensation through me. My eyes took in his face from his deep set eyes to his strong jaw. I reached up and drew a line from the nape of his neck to his shoulder with my thumb as I grasped him around the neck, steadying myself. The feel of his smooth skin sent a pulse of butterflies through me. Jett bit his lip and closed his eyes as my hand ran down his shoulder to his chest, where I could feel every beat of his heart through his shirt.

His eyes opened, revealing a brilliant violet that I had never seen before. They flicked to my lips as Jett moved in closer. I could feel the heat from his body on mine. Goose bumps broke out across my skin at his touch, as he cupped my cheek in his hand. It was the dream all over again, but this time...this time is was real.

Nothing was said as our connection drew us together. Our eyes stayed locked on each other as he bent down, closing the distance between us. I could almost feel his lips on mine as my eyes closed.

"Lunch!"

"*No!*" Sam yelled at Jasper.

We moved away from each other with a start, as if we were just caught doing something that we weren't supposed to be doing, and whatever spell we had been under was gone. He cleared his throat, and I shook my head. *Dream stopper.*

"Let me help you," Jett offered and bent down, gently gathering me up in his arms and carrying me to the table. My heart sank. I knew I wanted that connection, that fire, with Jett; but, until that moment, I wasn't aware just how much. My body ached being that close to him and then being torn away.

Damn it, I wanted to kiss him.

When Jett put me down, he didn't look at me; his jaw was tight and his eyes serious. Sam took one look at Jett and swatted Jasper in the arm.

"Ow!" Jasper gasped, clasping his arm with his hand and staring in wide eyed surprise at Sam. Jett walked back into the house without a word to us.

"I told you it was too soon," Sam whispered to Jasper.

"Sorry," Jasper whispered back. The door to the house slammed as Jett went inside.

What just happened?

Sam placed a plate of sandwiches in front of me. Jasper put down a pitcher of iced tea, at least that's what he said it was. Sam was clearly not happy with Jasper, but a look and a nudge from Jasper had Sam grinning despite himself, which I found just too cute. I watched the two of them for a moment and could see the deeper connection they had. There was unspoken chemistry, an easiness in the way they were together and a trust that extended into every word they said. I watched them as they moved around each other, exchanging a smile, a laugh, a kiss, and suddenly I ached to have that. That undeniable and inescapable chemistry.

"Hey, Gorgeous, you okay?" Jasper asked as he took a long swig of his drink.

"Gorgeous?" Sam commented with a pout that looked almost comical on a man of his stature.

"Oh relax. You know I think you're hot," Jasper retorted. Sam nodded, appeased for the moment. Jasper turned his eyes back on me. "You okay?"

"No," I answered automatically and regretted it by the look on Jasper's face. "I mean, I'm fine, I just…" How could I tell them that I was a little jealous of what they had?

"Yes?" Jasper looked at me, and I knew I wasn't going to get off easily; so, I just went for it.

"I just admire what you two have, that's all," I said with a sigh and a smile. Jasper and Sam looked at each other and then me.

"You don't have someone back home?" Sam asked and Jasper leveled his eyes on him.

"I…" *how do I explain Mazz?* "Not like you have each other, no."

"Oh," Jasper uttered and looked away.

"I have a…an engagement, I suppose. That's something right?" I asked, looking at the two of them.

"Of course!" Jasper answered excitedly. "Who's the lucky guy - or gal?"

"Oh, umm, his name is Mazz. He's been my best friend since we were children," I answered.

"And then you fell in love! That's so romantic!" Jasper beamed, and I swallowed hard, not looking at him.

"Not exactly. We've always known that we would be married, as it kind of comes with the territory of our families and our jobs. He's more like a brother to me than anything," I shared.

"Do you love him?" Sam asked to the chagrin of Jasper.

"I do, very much, but not like you two love each other," I said rather pathetically.

"Is that what you want? To be married to someone you don't really love?" Sam asked, and Jasper kicked him under the table. Sam kicked him back and glared at him. They were not being subtle.

"It's fine. I mean, I could do a lot worse than Mazz. He's a wonderful person and again my best friend. But, yeah, I don't know if I could ever love him the way that I should. The way you guys do," I added.

The breeze picked up, and I started to shiver slightly. Jasper and Sam turned the topic away from me and my pathetic love life, thankfully. They started talking about something to do with a crop they were growing. I wrapped my arms around myself and took another bite of one of the sandwiches that Sam had made.

The screen-door slammed and Jett came walking out of the house. I looked down at my plate. I didn't trust myself around him anymore. The connection and attraction to him was stronger than ever. He had been *the one* for so long. Finding out that he had Siren blood complicated things for sure. But, it didn't change how I felt about him. Not a bit.

That scared me.

It wasn't until I felt a weight gently placed on my shoulders that I realized that he had drawn near. A familiar soft sensation nuzzled my neck and I knew he had brought the blanket from the bed that I liked so much. He tucked it around my neck and sat next to me at the table. Sam and Jasper stopped talking and watched Jett with intrigue.

"Thought you might be cold," he said with a sweet smile.

"I was," I said, feeling the heat back in my cheeks, "thank you." Jett nodded once and started to fill his plate. I grabbed the blanket in my hands and pulled it higher on my neck, the warmth of it wrapping around me, sheltering me from the cool summer breeze.

Jasper and Sam had completely stopped talking and were just staring at Jett…and me. Jett took a bite of his sandwich and looked up at the two of them.

"What are you two staring at?" he asked waving his sandwich at them.

"Nothing!" Sam answered with a shrug.

"Nope," Jasper answered and tried to hide a smile.

It was becoming increasingly obvious that they had hopes of something happening between me and Jett. Obviously, my being a Mer didn't matter to them. I wondered if it mattered at all to Jett anymore, since he told me that they were Sirenites.

"You warm enough?" Jett asked me, pausing mid sandwich.

"Yes," I said, a goofy smile sliding across my face. "You know you aren't getting this blanket back right?"

"Oh, we'll see about that. It's my favorite too, you know," he teased.

"I'll fight you for it."

"No offense, but you're in no positon to fight me," he chuckled.

"When I'm all healed."

He looked me up and down and a grin tipped his lips. "That could be fun."

"Fun for me, embarrassing for you." I leaned over to him, "I'm going to kick your butt."

Jett let out a whole hearted laugh. The corners of his eyes wrinkled and his smile lines deepened. Like a smack in the face, I was struck with how gorgeous he was. If I wasn't an invalid I would have tackled him right there and kissed him until he begged for mercy.

Gods…where did that come from?

Was this what it was like to fall for someone? Losing control of your thoughts, of your body? I felt like I was in a free fall with no way of pulling myself out.

And it was freaking amazing…

32
JETT

I WAS NEAR READY TO STRING JASPER UP by his ears at the end of lunch. He had never been a subtle person; but, really, couldn't he keep his little smirks to himself for once?

When lunch was over, I helped KyLaya back to her room. Threading an arm under her small frame I helped her up as she attempted to walk back to the house on her own two feet. Every step was painful and was echoed in the pinch of her face and her laboured breathing. I tried to take as much weight off her legs as I could for her as she refused to let me carry her again. We were still a ways away from the steps when a divot in the ground found Laya's foot. She tripped, crying out at the pain and surprise of it. I caught her before she hit the ground, placing her safely into my arms again.

"I'll take it from here," I said and lifted her off the ground. Her hands circled around my neck, and I could feel my core tightening. A rush of heat ignited in my chest and ran through me hot and fast. Just the feel of her skin on mine was enough to pull a desire from me I had never felt before. It took everything in me not to press her to me and just kiss her. Kiss her good.

When her eyes lifted to mine, I was nearly undone. I looked up and focused on the house. Counted each step up to the door. The cracks in the paint of the door frame. The dust that had settled into the corner of the deck. Anything to keep my mind off of the pleasure I felt having her in my arms.

Delicate and light, she was a small thing; but, I knew she was strong. I had seen her fight. She was fierce and agile and could take on the Sirens with the best of Triton's guard. The role of the invalid was not something that came naturally to her, and I could see the frustration of it brewing just underneath the surface every time her body failed her.

I swallowed hard as I laid her gently down on my bed and pulled the covers over her soft skin. Her eyes didn't leave mine, but she didn't say anything. My heart stammered out an unfamiliar beat against my ribs, and I cleared my throat. Never, I mean *never*, had someone had that effect on me. It was unsettling and invigorating at the same time. Sweet torture. The way she looked at me. The way her heart fluttered when she was in my arms. The way her cheeks blushed when I looked at her. Everything about her…

I shook my head.

Snap out of it. Mer. Sirenite. It can't work.
But it's Laya. Laya!

That argument had been raging inside me since I realized what she was and how impossible of a situation we had put ourselves in. My heart didn't agree though. Not. One. Bit. Every time I saw her, every time I thought of her, my heart reached for her; clawing at my ribs like the fool thing didn't know it belonged to me.

My heart kicked my chest as I laid her soft blanket over her.

Before I touched the door, she was asleep. I smiled as I walked into the kitchen, but it dropped right off my face when I saw Sam and Jasper enter the kitchen carrying the dishes from our lunch.

"You two. Outside," I stated and walked to the door. They just stood there and looked at me. "Now!" I ordered.

"You think we're in trouble?" Jasper asked Sam.

"I think so," he answered. They placed their dishes and food on the counter and walked through the door in front of me.

Taking a seat together on the bench on the deck, they looked at me, eyes wide, feigning innocence. I started to pace, as I did when I needed to think clearly about what I needed to say.

"I know what you two are up to, and you need to *stop*," I demanded.

"What are you talking about?" Jasper asked, as if he didn't know.

"Don't give me that. I'm not an idiot," I answered.

"What is it that you are accusing us of here?" Sam asked, leaning forward, placing his elbows on his knees and lacing his fingers together.

"Of meddling where you shouldn't be!" I replied.

"And where is that?" Sam asked.

"In my love life, damn it!" I yelled. "You think I can't see the side glances and the nudges that you're giving each other every time I look at or talk to Laya," I asked them.

"We don't mean anything by it; we're just hoping-"

"Hoping for what, Jass?" I shouted, cutting off Jasper.

"That you might have finally found someone," Jasper answered.

"I – it's not that easy and you know it! She's a -" I cut myself off, waving a hand and shaking my head. "A relationship between us could spell death for all of us!"

"Oh, please. KyLaya isn't dangerous," Sam interjected.

"Plus, she likes you, too," Jasper added.

"She – she what?" I asked, thrown out of my anger and into more dangerous territory, intrigue.

Jasper and Sam smiled knowingly. "It's so obvious that she's into you," Jasper said.

"No. No she's – she can't be," I said shaking my head.

"Why not?" Sam asked.

"Look. So what if she is? So what if I am? She's a *Mer* and I'm a *Sirenite*. It can't work. Can it? No. No," I said with a wave of my hand, trying hard to convince them, and myself, that it was impossible; no matter how much I wanted it.

"She's special, Jett," Jasper shared. "You can feel it. I know you can. Sam can see it. We all know there's something more going on here, a reason, a plan, fate. Whatever it is. She was brought here for you. You've been waiting for her. Why are you fighting it?"

"I don't believe in fate," I uttered. *Yes, I did.* It was hard not to when the girl you had been dreaming of was now in your house, in your bed…

Sam leaned back and looked at Jasper. Jasper leveled a look at me, and I knew I was in for it. "What is going on with you? I know you have a stubborn streak, but this is something else," he said a little too loud for my liking.

"Just leave it," I said and turned to go for a walk.

"You're a coward!" Jasper shouted at me. That made me stop. *He didn't just call me a coward…*

I turned around slowly and glared at my brother. "What did you just say?" I asked slowly.

"Umm, you sure you know what you're doing?" Sam uttered, looking at Jasper with a furrowed brow. Sam knew damned well what I was capable of and while I had never turned my powers against my family, Jasper was walking a thin line. Jasper didn't glance at Sam, but kept his eyes on me.

"You heard me, Jett. You're a coward. A girl comes along that you might actually feel something for, and you run scared. What is your life going to be like if you don't let someone in for once? You are going to end up *alone*! You know that! *Alone*, Jett! Grow some balls and do something about it for a change!" Jasper yelled.

I could feel my power snap to life with the flare of anger that ignited in me. Jasper never talked to me like that. Never.

"You want to start being the older and wiser older brother *now*?" I yelled, challenging his right to give me a lecture. "Where has that guy been? Huh? You've been too tied up in your own relationship to give two shits about my life! Where were you when Louise and Brock died? I'll tell you! With *Sam*! You weren't here! You didn't deal with the funerals, the paperwork, the graves - you didn't do anything but show up on the day of the ceremony! Don't act like you know me or what's best for me. You don't know *shit*!" I yelled as anger and sadness warred inside me, bringing the threat of tears to my eyes. I swallowed hard and pushed them back.

"Oh, that's right, poor Jett, everything bad happens to Jett. He has such a hard life," Jasper mocked.

"Shut up, Jass! Just shut up!"

"I know I wasn't there for you. You think that was easy for me to realize? That I wasn't there for my little brother when he needed me the most? That I was a selfish jerk that wallowed in my own grief so deep that I forgot that you were in there with me? You think I like being *that* guy? Huh? That I don't feel guilt every day for that?"

"You never said anything to me," I uttered, coming down slightly.

"I didn't know how. I still don't really know how to. You aren't always the easiest person to talk to you know."

"I – yeah, fine," I conceded. He wasn't lying.

"Look, I might not have been there for you *then*, but I'm here *now*; and, I'm not going anywhere! So, until you get your head out of your ass, I'm going to keep spelling it out for you. SHE'S THE ONE FOR YOU, you moron!"

"She's can't be!"

"Why the hell not?" he yelled back.

"Because…"

"Why? What is the problem?"

"I'm terrified!" I bellowed, finally letting it out. I walked to the deck and slammed down into the chair across from them as Jasper slowly sank down next to Sam. Sam's eyes were as big as plates. I ran my hands through my hair and held my head.

What hell, just tell them already.

"I haven't felt anything for anyone…ever. I just assumed that I didn't work that way and that was that. I had my chances; but, no matter how many times I tried, nothing came of it. I couldn't fall. Four days with her, and I feel like I'm being pulled apart and put back together in a completely different way. Just her presence in the house…it's scary. Damned scary," I admitted.

"Love is a scary thing," Sam commented.

"I'm not in love," I grumbled.

"Really?" Sam asked.

"Really. I can't be. It's too soon. Too much," I said as my heart punched me in the throat, as if I had just betrayed it. Maybe I had.

"Some say it happens at first sight, you know," Jasper said, looking at Sam.

Ah, damn. I walked right into that one.

I knew that was the way that they felt about each other. While most of us had grown up in and around Stenen, Sam had moved away with his fosters when he was really young. They came back when he was a teenager, and that was when he met Jasper. According to them, time stood still, the planets aligned and unicorns were brought back to life. One look, and they both fell…hard. Literally, that first day, all Jasper could talk about was Sam. Sam this and Sam that. He didn't shut up about Sam for months. They both have said that they fell the first time they laid eyes on each other. It was like coming home, they said.

Was that the way I felt with KyLaya? The answer scared the shit out of me.

Yes.

The fact that I had been dreaming of her since I was a kid was terrifying in a completely different way. Was Jasper right? Were we fated to be together?

What if we were? What if we were put here together for a reason? What would that mean? Are our feelings genuine, or a product of something that we couldn't see?

Did it matter when I couldn't get my mind off of her? When all I wanted was to reach out and touch her. To hold her.

Ah damn…I'm in so much trouble.

33
KYLAYA

I WOKE TO THE REVVING OF AN ENGINE outside the house. Lights shone through the windows and deep voices shouted in the yard.

"Where are you?" a man called.

"Yeah, come on out here so we can see your little Mer ass in person," another yelled with a laugh.

My blood ran cold. I didn't dare look out the window as a light flashed past it again. I winced against the pain in my legs as I pulled them quietly and carefully over the edge of the bed, instinctively readying myself for a fight. I had regained a little movement in them, but not enough to stand on my own just yet. My heart nearly gave out when the door opened and a shadow filled the frame.

I almost melted into a relieved puddle when Jett walked in. He crossed to over to me quietly, crouching down in front of me and placing his hands on either side of my legs. He wasn't wearing a shirt, just sweat pants, as if he had just been woken from his sleep. I couldn't help but run my eyes over the planes and valleys of his chest and abs. Even with all the noise from outside, I wanted to reach out and touch him, to feel what his smooth skin felt like under my finger-tips.

"Listen to me very carefully," he whispered and looked in my eyes. "*Do not* leave this room, no matter what you hear. Do you understand me?"

"What's going on?" I asked, jumping as the vehicle revved its engine loudly.

"These guys are from town. They're drunk and are looking for…you," he admitted.

"Me?" I echoed, pointing to myself as my voice went high.

"I told you that there would be some in town that wouldn't like a Mer being here. I'm going out to talk to them. Just stay here, out of sight. Okay?" he instructed, his jaw tight as the men shouted and thumped on the house.

"But – "

"Laya. Out of sight. Got it?" he insisted again, placing his hands on my cheeks and looking seriously in my eyes.

"Okay. Yes," I nodded. He sighed with relief. His eyes searched mine and with a nod he stood.

"Keep this door closed." With that he shut the door. I could hear the front screen door slam as he left the house and went around the front of the house and into the back yard. Alone.

Jasper had gone home with Sam. There was just Jett and me at the house. From what I could hear, there were at least four men outside. My heart was in my throat when I heard Jett's voice. I moved around to the other side of the bed, slowly and quietly. Leaning over, I pulled over the curtain a fraction to see what was going on.

"Okay, guys. It's time to go home," Jett announced, walking over to the truck that was parked in the yard. "I think you've had enough fun for the night." He approached the five - there were *five* - men.

"Shut up, Jett," one of them spat. "We know you're holding a Mer wench in there. Bring her out!"

"We can't have her running back home and telling everyone where we are!" another yelled.

"Well, as wonderful of an argument you are making for our lovely community, I will *not* be bringing her out here tonight," Jett replied. "So, go home gentlemen. Sleep it off." Jett turned to leave but one of the men, wearing a red shirt and cowboy hat, reached out and landed a hand on Jett's shoulder. Jett frowned and turned his head to look at the man.

"We're not leaving without her," Cowboy Hat said.

"Davy, I *strongly* urge you to go," Jett said sternly to the man in the cowboy hat.

"And I *strongly* urge you to screw yourself," Davy said smacking Jett in the face. Jett's lips tightened into a thin line and his jaw thrummed.

I bit my lips to keep from shouting out the window.

Asshat! If you hurt him, I will come straight through this wall at you.

"We know you're in there!" Davy yelled at the house. My hands balled as two of the other men started to walk towards my window. My temper flared. I wanted to go out and kick some ass, but the dull ache in my legs made me very aware that I was completely incapable of doing that. A stab of fear punched me in the gut knowing that if they got in the house, I was next to helpless.

"Okay, that's enough," Jett said. "Get off my property. *Now*." It wasn't a question. It was an order and the five men turned to him. My heart skipped a beat, not knowing what they would do.

They laughed. My jaw clenched so hard I could have cracked a tooth.

One walked up to Jett and stood toe to toe with him.

"Make us," he said and spat in Jett's face. Jett tilted his head back and a half smile tipped his lip.

Punch him, Jett.

"Damn, Hank, you really shouldn't have done that," Jett answered lifting his foot and bringing it down hard on the man's knee. I could hear the pop from my room as the man's kneecap was hit right out of joint. He howled and fell to the ground.

I can't say that I didn't enjoy that just a little bit. Where I come from, you simply don't do the kind of thing that man did. I was vibrating I was so angry.

Jett's assault put the others into gear and they all ran at Jett. I couldn't tear my eyes away from the awful sight in front of me as four grown men took on Jett.

Davy ran at him first, swinging out at Jett's head. Jett quickly ducked his punch and shoved Davy past him, using Davy's momentum to send him off. Davy fell head first in a heap some distance away from Jett and was promptly knocked out.

The second one just full out tackled Jett, sending them both to the ground.

"Get him, Barry!" one of the others shouted. But, Barry didn't get the chance. Jett flipped over, grappling with him until he was on top of Barry's back. Jett reached around Barry's throat with his arm and choked him. His strong arm flexed under Barry's chin, bringing the blood to Barry's face and bloating it. The other one took advantage of Jett's position and distraction and punched Jett straight in the head, which didn't affect him at all. Instead, Jett threw a punch back, landing it in the other man's jewels and dropping him to the ground.

It was the last man standing that had Jett's attention when he pressed a knife against Jett's throat.

"Let him go," the forth man ordered. Jett released the choke hold he had on Barry, who flopped to the ground, coughing and choking. The knife man dug the sharp tip into Jett's throat and Jett stood up.

Shit! Shit!

"Go get her," the knife man said.

"You sure about this Brendan?" Barry asked in a ragged voice, as he rolled to a sitting positon.

"I said get her," Brendan yelled. I watched in horror as he pulled the knife back and cracked it against the back of Jett's head. Jett fell in a heap on the ground and didn't move.

"No!" I squeaked through my hands as I looked out the window. In a moment the door to my room was thrown open and Barry stormed in. Grabbing my arms, he yanked me from the bed. I tried to fight him off, but I was still so weak. I couldn't walk, so he dragged me along as I tried to kick out, bite, scratch and pinch as best as I could.

I landed hard on my knees next to Jett and quickly scrambled over to him; the ground scratched at my bare legs under the shirt Jett leant me to sleep. I reached for him, but my hair was ripped at, snapping my head back and eliciting a cry from me.

"You think you can just come here and take what we have worked so hard for?" Brendan yelled, slurring slightly as he spoke.

"I'm not here to take anything, you idiot!" I shouted.

"Lies!" Brendan shouted, yanking my hair again. "All Mer are liars!"

"I'm not lying!" I yelled. My hair was released and I fell to the ground. My head throbbed and my heart was racing. But, it was the sight of Jett that chilled me.

"Jett brought a Mer into our home. What are we going to do with *him*?" Hank asked, still holding his knee from when Jett had kicked it.

"The same as her, only we'll have some *fun* with her first," Brendan answered with a smile that made my blood run cold. His eyes slithered up my legs. I grabbed the shirt and yanked it down as far as it would go to cover myself.

"The Council's not going to like that, Brendan," the last man said.

"Screw the Council, Trevor! They've allowed this to go on too long! They're blind! If *we* don't get rid of the threat, no one will!"

"You think that the Mer are so bad? Are you really so different than those that you fear? You came here for blood. How is that any better than the Mer you hate?" I shouted at Brendan, glaring at him and seething with a rage that I desperately wish I had the strength to execute.

"Shut up, Mer wench," Brendan yelled and smacked me across the face. I was knocked over, my head bouncing off the grass. I had been hit before and I knew how to take one. My guard training came with plenty of bruises, none of which my father was happy to see on my face; but, it was good practice on how to avoid getting stunned in a fight. Thanks to my training, I saw the slap coming from a mile away. I had a couple of tricks up my sleeves.

I laid on the ground where I fell and sobbed into the grass. Holding my face for effect until one of them came over to me. When Hank reached for me, I grabbed his hand in mine and pulled him over my shoulder, flipping him on his back and knocking the wind out of him. In the same movement I reached for the knife on his belt and drew it to his neck. By the time that he could react, I had the tip pinching his throat.

"Get out of here," I demanded.

"You think that we're just going to let you be? We know-"

"You know *nothing* about me - just as I know next to nothing about your kind, other than you would kill an innocent woman for nothing other than what kind of blood runs in her veins. How does that make you any better than the Mer you so fear? Huh?" I asked them.

"You think we want to listen to a lecture from *you*?" Trevor spat.

"No," I answered. "But, I also don't think that you want to see your friend bleed out in front of you either." I pushed the knife harder against Hank's neck. He uttered a couple of less than kind things at me but stayed still.

"You don't have the nerve, sweetheart," Brendan challenged. I laughed.

"Really?" I answered. I flipped the knife in my hand and drove it into the hand that Hank had resting on the ground. He howled as the blade sailed cleanly through.

"You bitch!" he yelled.

"Oh, calm down. You'll be fine," I scolded him and placed the knife back against his throat. I lifted a brow at Brendan. "Leave!" I shouted.

"Do what she says! I need my hands!" Hank whimpered.

"This ain't over, bitch," Brendan threatened.

"Yes, it is," I answered.

But I didn't get to celebrate my victory long. I was too slow when I saw the look on Brendan's face change. I was hit over the head from behind and knocked to the ground. The knife was kicked away from me and the world spun as I rolled to my back.

"That was a really stupid move, Mer. And you will pay for it," Davy said, leaning over me.

The next sensation I had was a hard hit to my stomach and then another, and then another…

34
JETT

THE WORLD WAS A CLOUDY MESS when I opened my eyes. Things slowly started to clear up in front of me as I rolled from my back to my stomach on the cold grass. Four figures came into focus. Four men.

Gathered together, they stood in a circle. It took me a moment too long to realize what they were doing. Stomping and kicking, they hollered and cheered. Then, through their bodies I saw what was on the ground.

Laya.

Surrounding her, the four men stood over her…kicking her. Brendan was standing to the side, slipping off his belt with a smile on his face. A ball of raging heat lit in my core as my powers called out. Instantly, I felt awake and charged with a power that extended beyond anything I had ever felt before.

Laya's face was a mess of blood and dirt, her body flopping freely, as they landed kick after kick to her. Standing, I could feel my power humming in my core, intense and ready. Pink light glowed beneath my skin as my blood ignited. I could feel the pressure build in me as I brought my powers out to play.

I pulled hard and threw out a hand. Pink light blasted from it and tore into Barry as he pulled back a leg to kick Laya again. A hole burned into his chest and he fell in a heap to the side. The others turned to me, their eyes wide and mouths open. Whether they had forgotten that I had powers or they seriously thought that I wouldn't use them on their sorry asses, they were going to pay for what they had done.

I could hear their shouts of warning and fear; but, all I could see was Laya's unconscious body on the ground, and that fueled my rage that much more. When they ran for their truck I ran for it too. Streaking through the air in a pink bolt of light, I was in front of them before they knew it. Standing between them and their escape vehicle, I rested a hand on the hood, letting my powers flow into the truck. The hood melted and it set on fire.

I watched the flames of the truck reflected in their eyes as they stood there, stunned and frightened. Pink flame lit up my hands, and I turned to them.

They ran, grasping, pulling and tripping over each other as I whipped out a strand of pink energy at them. My powers snapped in the air and wrapped around Davy's legs. He fell face first into the ground. I could hear the sound of his nose break as his face smashed off the road. I pulled the whip of energy, and it cut into his skin, burning and searing it. He screamed hard and long.

Hank ran for the road. I flashed in front of him. His eyes flew open when I appeared. I could see the apology on his lips before it came out, and that just pissed me off that much more. I punched him square in the gut and then head butted him in the head. He dropped to the ground, and I placed a finger on the back of his neck as I walked past him, releasing my power into his skin. Zapping him and watching him vibrate under my touch.

Trevor and Brendan were left. I launched a bolt of light at Trevor and brought him down. He laid in an unconscious heap in the road, steam rising from his clothes. Then I turned to Brendan. Who I had left for last.

I looked at Brendan who held a knife toward me, as if that would do anything. A slick sheen of sweat had broken out over his forehead; it gleamed in the fire light from his flaming truck. I didn't say anything to him as he watched me with a wary, frightful gaze. I wanted him to be scared. I wanted him to know he was just barely going to survive what I would do to him. To know that there was nothing that he could do to stop it from happening. I narrowed my gaze at him.

"Now, Jett, be reasonable. She's just a damned *Mer*!" he pleaded. I said nothing as pink flames flashed up my arms and across my shoulders.

"You son of a bitch! You'll pay for this!" he bellowed. Then he threw the knife straight at my chest. Without a thought, I reached out and caught the knife before it touched my skin. Brendan's eyes grew about three sizes as I tossed the blade over my shoulder. I summoned my power and unleashed because there was no way in Hades that I was going to let him walk out of there. A great ball of zapping energy shot straight for him, searing a raging burn into his chest and arms as it exploded against him.

Should have left when I told you to.

Flashing to Laya, I gently lifted her head off the ground and placed it in my hands.

"Laya?" I whispered as I ran a hand over her cheek. Her bruised and bloodied cheek. She didn't answer. Not even a flicker of her eyelashes. *Shit.* A roaring down the road told me that Jasper was on his way.

Sam's great black truck thundered up the yard and came to a slamming halt right beside the abandoned smoldering truck of the crew that had come.

"We're here! Are you okay?" Jasper yelled through the window before he could even get out. The truck wasn't in park yet before he was out the door and at my side.

"What happened?" He asked as he looked at the bodies of the men that I had taken out. He bent down beside me and Laya.

"They came for her," I answered.

"Let's get her inside. Sam?" Jasper called.

"I'm here; get her in the room. I'll see to her this time. I have the energy," he said, checking the pulse on a couple of the men.

I picked her up carefully in my arms and carried her back inside. One of Jasper's unique Sirenite gifts was sensing danger and distress. Since we were kids, if I was hurt or in trouble, he knew. He must have sensed the fight and came.

In the house, Jasper ran and got a bowl of warm water and a cloth to clean some of the dirt from her skin. Her face was a mess of red scratches and mud; grass was in her hair, caked in the blood that was coming from a cut on her scalp.

"Gods," Jasper uttered as I placed her in the bed and sat next to her.

"They were drunk. Came to kill her," I told them. Jasper and Sam both stopped and looked at me.

"*What?*" Jasper asked just above a whisper.

"Said that they were tired of the Council's soft approach, and they wanted to take things into their own hands," I huffed.

"Things are getting out of hand. That's not what our people are about. What's wrong with these guys?" Sam asked.

"I don't know, but they were out for blood," I answered.

"I suppose they got what they deserved then," Jasper replied.

"They deserved worse. I held back. I could have killed them, Jass. With a smile," I answered, knowing it was true. They were alive, but I didn't want them coming back ever again. There was only one way to drive that message home. Near death experiences have that effect.

Sam pulled up his sleeves and walked to the other side of the bed. He reached out over Laya's unconscious body. Keeping a space between Laya's skin and his, he ran his hand up and down her body. His eyes closed and his brow furrowed as his concentration mounted. A pale pink light shone from his hands as his power ignited in them and sank below Laya's skin.

"Come," Jasper whispered, gathering my arm in his hand. "He likes to be left alone to heal. He'll do all he can for her. That's a guarantee," he added. I nodded hesitantly, not wanting to leave Laya, and yet knowing that her best chance at healing was Sam's powers. Getting off the bed slowly, I watched Laya's face until Jasper closed the door.

"You okay?" Jasper asked as I sat at the table in the kitchen.

"No. I'm not," I answered.

"You need Sam? I can go get him right now!" Jasper exclaimed.

"No! It's nothing that Sam can help with. I'm mad, Jasper. Really mad," I told him and slammed a hand on the table. "They didn't just want to kill her, Jass. They wanted to...do things to her too."

"*No*," he said in a stunned whisper, sitting slowly at the table.

"Yeah," I sighed, placing my hands roughly on the table, not able to calm myself enough to sit just yet.

"Geez," he uttered. "Did they? I mean...did they?" he asked.

"No, at least I don't think so. When I woke up they were kicking her. Four of them. The fifth was taking off his belt," I told him, clenching my jaw and biting the inside of my mouth to try to calm myself. I would never get over the sight of her helpless on the ground like that.

"If I wouldn't have woken up," I couldn't finish the thought. What would they have done to her?

"Don't do that to yourself, Jett. You did wake up. You stopped them," Jasper said. He sighed and leaned back in his chair with a shake of his head. "Poor girl, like she hasn't been through enough," he uttered. I nodded.

"She's going to hate us," I said, scrubbing my face with my hands and sitting slowly into a chair at the table.

"What? Why?"

"Those were *our* people that did that to her. You think that she's going to be happy to still be here with us after that?" I asked.

"I think you have no idea what you are talking about, Jett," Jasper said. "KyLaya's no idiot. She knows that those guys are *not* us. She isn't going to blame you for their actions. Nor will she hold all the Sirenites accountable for their behavior."

"You think?" I asked, hopeful that he might be right.

"I *know*," Jasper emphasized.

I stood and started to pace the kitchen. Jasper watched me, as he usually did when I was in a mood. *What those guys did...*

I could feel the power in my veins ignite just thinking about it. Laya on the ground, lifeless. What was it about her that made me want to protect her so much?

"What are you so afraid of?" Jasper asked me.

"Huh?"

"You. KyLaya. There's something there. What are you afraid of?"

"I – look I...it can't work!" I admitted rubbing my hands over my face.

"Why not? You two...it fits. Don't ask me how I know, but I do. I'm never wrong about this stuff," he boasted. I looked at him and as much as I wanted to argue with him, I couldn't. He was always right about couples around town, even set up a few of them. They were all happy, really happy.

"You're my brother," he continued. "I want to see you happy. You've always been a miserable sod. This is your chance to bring a little life into your world. For goodness sake...take it!" Jasper implored.

At that moment, Sam came out of the room. I stood up and walked to him.

"How is she? She going to be okay?" I asked, trying to get the answer from his expression.

"She's going to be okay," Sam answered, and I grasped his arm with a relieved smile.

"Thank the gods," I sighed happily.

"She's a fighter, that's for sure. I could feel her battling to live. She's quite the girl."

"Thank you, Sam. For everything," I said with a grateful smile.

"She's asking for you," Sam said quietly.

"What? She's awake?" I stammered.

"I told you, the girl's a fighter. Go," he said with a nod at the door. I looked at Jasper, and he tilted his smile and lifted his brow. I nodded.

My heart climbed into my throat as I walked through the door. There she sat, propped up by pillows, in my bed, looking really beat up and yet stunning at the same time. In that moment I was consumed by the swelling in my heart. The fear I had of losing her. The anger for what they had done to her. The look on her face when I walked in the room spelled out everything as a sweet smile played on her perfect lips.

Pink flashed and I was at her side. Her face in my hands and her divine eyes on mine.

I let go of all my reservations in that moment. Shut my mind off and for once just did what my heart wanted…

…and kissed her.

35
KYLAYA

JETT'S SOFT LIPS TOUCHED MINE and my heart nearly jumped out of my chest. A rush burst from my core, rolling and racing through my veins and across my skin. It was as if my body had been waiting for this moment to wake up. I had never felt anything like that.

I reached out and wrapped my hand softly around his neck and pulled him harder against me. A low sound crept across his lips as we deepened the kiss. My heart was beating out a rhythm I didn't know; but, that I knew I never wanted to stop.

When he pulled back, his eyes looked into mine, and I felt like I was seeing him for the first time. That we were seeing each other for the first time all over again. He planted a soft kiss on my forehead, and I closed my eyes.

"I have been waiting a long time to do that," he said. A sheepish smile playing across his full lips.

"I've been waiting for you to do that for a long time," I laughed.

He leaned down and kissed me again. It was everything that I had hoped for and more. Every sensation that I had in my dreams was echoed in that kiss and amplified. Soft, slow, and sweet.

"How are you feeling?" Jett asked, breaking away from me. His thumb ran delicately down my cheek as his brow furrowed at the injuries on my face.

"Umm, sore," I answered with a nod. "But, other than that, I will survive."

"I'm so sorry, Laya," Jett apologized.

"It's not your fault. You did everything you could. You saved me," I said, placing my hands on his sad face and bringing his eyes up to meet mine. "Again."

He shook his head, looking down at the bed.

"What is it?" I asked.

"You can't stay here anymore," he answered.

"What? You're kicking me out?" I blurted.

"No. Not like that. It's just – it's not safe for you here anymore. I didn't know that there was such unrest in our community. Such anger. I knew people wouldn't be happy, but not that they were willing to kill."

"But-"

"No. I will not keep you here where you are not safe. You must go home," Jett determined. Jasper walked into the room to the horror on my face.

"What did you do?" Jasper accused Jett, walked to my side, and took my hand.

"He's kicking me out," I uttered, still in shock.

"You're *what?*" Jasper shouted.

"I'm not kicking her out! It's not safe for her here, not with people trying to kill her. She has to go home where she'll be safe," Jett explained.

"Oh," Jasper mumbled and looked at me.

"Not you too," I groaned.

"I don't want you to go, Gorgeous. But, he's not wrong. It isn't safe for you here anymore. Besides, you're all healed," Jasper reasoned.

"What?" I gasped. I threw aside the covers and lifted the bandages on my legs. The wounds underneath were sealed up, healed to perfection. Two angry scars remained where I had been stabbed and some bruising from where I had been kicked, but other than that I was healed. I moved my legs just to test them and, sure enough, no pain. A smile stretched across my face and joy lit inside me at the ability to move again. But a look from Jett and my smile faded. How could I leave now? When things were just…starting.

"I don't want to go," I whispered looking at Jett. He took my hand, and my heart punched me hard.

"I'll give you guys a minute," Jasper said and left the room, closing the door.

I gazed at Jett, who was watching me. "I don't know what this is, but I'm not ready to give it up," I explained. "I've never felt…" I sighed, dropping and shaking my head.

"Me neither," Jett offered. I lifted my head and smiled at him.

"I find that hard to believe," I uttered. Jett was hot, there was no mistaking that. His features were strong and angular, giving him a stern look most of the time; but, it was his eyes that captured me the most. There was kindness and warmth in them. His hands were strong, with long fingers and lithe arms; and, I wanted them around me more than I wanted to admit. There was no denying my attraction to him.

"You can ask Jasper about my dating history, and he will sum it up in one word for you…pathetic," Jett chuckled. "Just never found anyone I wanted."

I swallowed hard as his eyes met mine. Did that mean that he wanted me? I didn't have to ask as he leaned over, placing a warm kiss on my lips. This time, there was fire behind it. The tentativeness of our first kiss was gone and something else woke.

Need.

Desire.

Lust.

His fingers wrapped around my neck as he pulled me harder against him. I could feel his heart beat hard against my chest and that only drew me to him more. Reaching up I slipped a hand across the back of his neck, feeling his thick dark blonde hair between my fingers as I grasped him tighter. He moaned, and I smiled into his lips.

I got up on my knees and threw a leg around him, sitting in his lap and bringing myself even with his face. His hands trailed my back and down to my waist as he pulled me closer. I have never wanted someone so much. My heart was hammering in my chest, desperate with desire.

He pulled back from me, a pink blush on his cheeks, and leaned his head against mine.

"Whoa," he uttered. "I…umm…there's a good chance that I will get lost in you, Laya." His violet eyes met mine, and I was held in them. I knew, in that moment, that there was a good chance that I would get lost in him too.

I touched his cheek and there was a flash that lit the room in blinding light.

Then, the room disappeared.

Spinning around, I saw the place of my dreams. I was facing Handsome. The boy I had known since I was a little girl. The boy with the violet eyes that a part of me loved deeply.

It was Jett. He smiled back at me sweetly and took me into his arms. In that moment I knew, without a doubt, I was meant to find him. I was meant to love him.

A flash of light lit again, and I was back.

We sat there for a moment and just stared at each other, as if what we had just seen couldn't have been real…and yet it was.

Then, at precisely the same time, we launched at each other. In that moment, two parts of my life collided in a way I never thought was possible. Jett's lips were on mine, hot and passionate. Conquering my skin, his hands ran over me. He trailed a line of sweet kisses down my neck to my shoulder. I was lost to the feel of him.

The sheets were tossed aside as Jett moved onto the bed with me. Leaning me down on the bed, his weight settled on me, carefully. My hands ran up his back, feeling his muscles flex and coil under his smooth skin. His hands found the bottom of my shirt and my heart spiked a bolt of energy through me. My skin felt alive and new as I felt the warmth of his skin against mine.

"Jett come quick!" Jasper yelled as he burst through the door.

Jett flashed around, blocking me from being seen. Jasper came to a dead stop looking at Jett and me, tangled up in the bed together, obviously in the middle of something.

"Finally!" he shouted. Jett grabbed a pillow and chucked it at Jasper. He smiled and gave us a thumbs up; and, then turned and closed door.

Jett and I looked at each other. The fire slowly dying out between us as an awkward laugh tumbled from our lips. Jett leaned over and placed another kiss on my lips. It was so hard not to keep that kiss going. I felt myself needing him, wanting him more than I had wanted anything.

"What do you think it is?" I asked him.

"It better be damned good, I'm just sayin'," Jett grumbled. I wrapped my arms around him from behind and rested my head across the back of his shoulder. Jett took a deep breath and squeezed my arms with his hand.

"Ugh, damn Jasper," Jett cursed as he slowly lifted himself off the bed, looking back at me and shaking his head. "Stay here," he said and left the room, but not without landing another hot kiss on my lips. *Damn, the boy could kiss.*

The door closed, and I sat there for a moment in the wake of the kissing session we just had. My heart was starting to come back to normal when I realized that I was told to stay in that room like a child.

What am I doing? Like hell, I'm staying here.

I swung my legs off the bed, my feet hitting the floor a little harder than I would have liked. I stood on weak legs but there was no pain in them anymore. Whatever Sam had done did the trick, and I was healed. Grabbing my favorite blanket off the bed, I walked unsteadily to the door and out into the kitchen.

In the yard was an orange truck. Sam, Jett and Jasper were gathered around the back of it, a pretty young woman about my age was with them. I didn't see any others and nothing screamed danger to me, so I summoned some strength and walked out the door to the deck.

The night air was cool, but it wasn't the breeze that caused me to wrap my arms around myself to get the chill off; it was the body in the back of the truck.

The body with the symbol of the gods revealed on his collarbone and his neck sliced open to the bone. Just like Mistress Hol.

Not again…

36
JETT

"WHERE DID YOU FIND HIM?" I asked Rayna as she stood serious and silent at my side.

"In his shop," she answered.

"Damn it," Jasper cursed. "Who would want to kill Vyktor? Everyone loves him."

"I don't know," I uttered. It just didn't make any sense. Vyktor was liked by everyone, literally everyone.

I turned from the truck with a heavy heart, and my eyes slammed into Laya's. She stood on the deck, a blanket draped around her shoulders and her bare legs showing below. My heart stuttered just looking at her, and immediately I was drawn to her.

"What are you doing out here!" I scolded, running to her side. Laya raised her eyes to mine.

"The mark," she said.

"What?"

"On his collarbone," she clarified.

"What are you talking about?" I stammered. Jasper flipped the blanket off of Vyktor revealing what looked like a symbol of some kind just under his collarbone.

"Whoa," I uttered, going over to look at it closer. "You ever seen anything like this?" I asked Rayna. She shook her head. I looked at Jasper, and he did the same

"Wait…how did you…" *she couldn't have done this…no. She was with me the whole time.* Laya looked at me, and I could tell she knew what I was pondering. Her brows furrowed and her lips tightened to a thin line, and she descended the steps and walked toward us.

"No, I didn't *kill him*," she stated and smacked my chest. "There was a murder just like this at home right before the Siren attack. They had broken into our archives and killed our keeper there. She had a mark just like this one," she explained, flinging the blanket from her shoulders and leaning into Vyktor to look closer. Her movements were strong and agile, and I was finally getting to see the real Laya. Damned if it wasn't sexy as hell.

"Two murders, in exactly the same way and both with markings like that?" Sam laid out. "Anyone else wondering what the hell is going on?"

"It's the mark of the gods. Mistress Hol, the vault keeper, taught that to me long ago. The gods mark those that are under their protection or service so that other gods will not interfere with them or harm them," Laya explained. "I just don't know what service that Mistress Hol would have been doing for the gods in the vault all these years. She had a family and everything."

"Anyone else's head spinning?" Jasper asked. We stood in silence. No one knew what to do, what to say, or what any of it meant.

"What now?" Laya asked.

"Well, it's not going to be hard for others to draw a line to the Mer in town. Just saying," Rayna said, looking at Laya.

"What?" Laya exclaimed. "I would never do such a thing! Besides, it's not like I could have just got up and killed someone; I haven't been able to even walk!" Laya exclaimed, crossing her arms defiantly across her chest.

"You look fine to me, and you will to the rest of the town too. They will come up with some kind of answer, you can be certain of that. Your Mer powers helped you do it. You've been lying to Jett and Jasper. You put them under an evil Mer spell. You can fly…who knows the explanations that they will come up with to pin this on you," Rayna said.

"Okay, whoa. Laya didn't do this," I interceded.

"No offense, Jett, but your word isn't going to mean much. No one is happy with you right now for even bringing her. Now there's been a death. Plus, you seriously injured several of our community and killed one. You see where I'm going with this?" Rayna answered back.

"How did you know about that?" I asked.

"Sam called me. Who do you think cleaned up the mess?" she asked, pointing to where the body of Brendan had been and the truck they brought. It was all gone.

"They were going to rape and then kill her, Rayna! Was I supposed to just sit back and let that happen? I thought that we stood for more than that!"

"*We* do, but that doesn't mean that everyone else does, Jett. Franky-"

"Ah, hell, Franky," Jasper uttered, throwing his hands in the air.

"Franky can go to Hades, Rayna," Sam spat. "You know he's an ass," he finished, tossing in his two cents.

"I know. I know," she agreed. "But, whether we like it or not, he has a following of people that aren't happy with how things are. They want revenge for the wrong doings of the past. He's got them all fired up and angry. Anger is a strong emotion and one that easily sways people to do things they normally wouldn't," she said.

"Those guys that were here tonight?" I uttered, placing my hands on my hips, finally seeing where she was going with this.

"Some of the strongest supporters of Franky's," she answered, nodding gravely.

"Well," Jasper huffed, "I can guess who put the idea in their tiny brains to come out here then. Got them to do his dirty work while keeping his hands pearly white and guilt free."

"So what are you saying, Rayna?" I asked, starting to pace back and forth beside the truck, trying to dampen the fire of rage growing in my core.

"I'm saying that you might want to lay low for a while. Leave town while I sort all this out," she offered.

"That ass-wipe isn't going to drive me from my home!" I barked at her.

"Don't you throw that damned temper my way, Jett! I'm trying to help you!" Rayna bit back. I threw my arms in the air and walked away, back towards the house. Rayna huffed and shook her head at me.

"I'm Rayna, by the way," she said and extended a hand to Laya. Laya smiled and grasped her hand back.

"KyLaya Constantilly," she replied and shook Rayna's hand. Rayna shook it and looked at Laya with wide eyes. *Constantilly*?

"I'm sorry, what did you say your name was?" Rayna asked, stepping closer to Laya, still holding her hand.

"KyLaya? Constantilly?" she answered, stepping back from Rayna and pulling her hand from Rayna's grasp.

"Jett!" Rayna called, keeping her eyes on Laya.

"Yeah, I heard," I said, coming back to Laya and Rayna. I looked at Laya. How had I not asked her what her name was? I was slapped in the face with the realization that Laya and I had a lot to talk about now that the dream stoppers were a thing of the past.

"My last name is Constantilly?" Laya answered and looked at me. "My family has been ruling Triton for centuries. It was why I was out with the guards that night. I am Triton's Prime."

I knew that my jaw hit the floor hard but nothing came out. Trust Jasper to have the opposite reaction.

"Look at that, Jett! You picked yourself a royal mate!" Jasper shouted.

"I-" I stuttered. Looking from Laya to Rayna, I knew that this was going to be a huge slap in the face for Rayna, and I was right. She gave a solemn nod and turned toward her truck door.

"Wait, Rayna," I called to her and ran up to the truck.

"It's *fine*, Jett," she answered, pulling the door to her truck open and placing her foot on the guard.

"I'm sorry," I said, and meant it.

"Please, just *don't*. Okay?" she answered, a look of anger and pain crossing her face. "I should have figured it out a long time ago that you weren't interested. I guess I was just hoping that you would come around. I'm just not the one for you…obviously." She looked over at Laya. I hung my head.

I never wanted to hurt Rayna. I respected her too much, and she was my closest friend. The door to the house slammed shut, and I knew, without looking, that Laya had gone back inside. I could hear a whispered argument start between Jasper and Sam from the back of the truck.

"I hope you find what you are looking for," Rayna said as she pulled herself into the cabin of the truck. "Just do as I say and let me sort this out, okay. Lay low." She closed the door and started it up. Sam shut the gate of the box and Rayna slowly pulled out of the yard.

I turned to Jasper.

Holding up his hands in defense he started to back away from me, "I'm sorry! I wasn't thinking. It just came out!"

"Do you have *any* filter what-so-ever?" I hollered. He shrugged.

"There's a good possibility that…no I don't," he answered. I flashed pink and was in front of him.

"If you screwed this up for me and Laya…" I threatened.

"She's *fine*," Sam answered with a wave of his hand.

"How do you know?" I asked, and he looked at me as if I was asking the stupidest question on earth. Sam had the ability to heal and a very strong ability to sense things in others. Their feelings, emotions, and sometimes even thoughts - Sam understood them all.

"Go talk to her," Jasper encouraged, and I glared at him. "Or not…your choice," he yelped.

I stalked away from the two of them and went inside. Laya was sitting at the kitchen table. Her eyes were off in the distance; I wasn't sure she even knew I had entered the room.

"Hey," I uttered as I pulled a chair out next to her. She turned her blue eyes to mine slowly.

"She's in love with you, isn't she?" she asked.

"Yes," I said, opting for total honesty instead of deflection. "But it has never been reciprocated."

"She's beautiful and seems like a good person, Jett. Why-" she stopped herself, and shook her head.

"Why don't I return her affection?" I asked, trying to help her out. "Yes."

"I don't know, to be honest. I just have never felt that thing you're supposed to feel with her. Do you know what I'm talking about?" I asked, watching her closely. A smile lifted the corner of her lips and she nodded.

"I'm engaged," she uttered.

"What?" I blurted loudly. A pain shot right through me, more intense than anything I had ever felt. In that moment, I wanted to run and hide from the world…or destroy it, I couldn't tell. But Laya reached over to me and grasped my hand, and I was suddenly grounded again. She looked into my eyes, and I was caught in them.

"From the time we were kids, Mazz and I have been promised to each other. He's been my best friend since I can remember, but…that's it. He's my *friend*," she emphasized and I started to relax…slightly.

"But, you're engaged!" I said standing and starting to pace the floor.

"I'm not in love with him, Jett," I said, shaking my head. "I love him, I always will; but, there is nothing romantic about it. For either of us."

"You can't be serious! No man could resist you," I blurted and then turned from her as I realized how that sounded.

"Look, I didn't want to keep it a secret from you. I didn't think it was right to keep going and not tell you."

"Not sure how to take that, to be honest. What are we then?" I asked, not knowing where the nerve came from. Maybe hurt. How could she be engaged?

"We are *unexpected*," she said hesitantly, "but there has always been a part of me that has waited for you," she said looking at me. "I had always hoped, but in reality I was faced with a world without you in it. I had to move forward and treat what we had as what it was…a dream. Now, I can't. You are real and that changes everything, Jett. *Everything*. I don't know how this will work, but I know that I have to try. We…this thing between us was meant to be. Surely, you feel it too," she said quietly.

I wanted to say 'yes'. That there was a part of me that had been in love with her from the time I was a young boy, but how could I? She was promised to someone else! Sure, there was something between us, something big. An attraction. An understanding. A connection that had always been there…waiting.

"I…I – yes I feel it," I said.

Suddenly, I was scared. Really scared. What did all this mean? Why me? Why us? I stood and started to pace.

"Jett?" Laya called out to me, but I was barely hearing her. "Hey! You okay?"

"It's all so fast; and, yet, not at the same time. You were just a dream a few days ago and now you are more real to me than anything in my life. To go from not having feelings for anyone to…gods my heart around you. You are more than anything I could have imagined or hoped for. But, I can't ignore the fact that we are Mer and Sirenite. We come from very different worlds. What is that going to mean for us? What if everything that we feel is a product of the dreams? That it isn't really us?" I admitted, spewing everything that I was fearing out at her as it came to me.

"I know," she agreed nodding. "I have the same questions you do. I fell for the guy in my dreams, who was kind and sweet and made my heart beat hard in my chest. But in reality, you're a bit of a jerk. So, what I'm feeling for you now is all my own, I suppose," she said with a straight face, at least it started that way, until a smile cracked her tight lip.

"Nice, Laya," I uttered and sat next to her.

"I think that we just have to take this one day at a time," Laya said, brushing her hand over my shoulder. "Obviously, there is a reason that we've been brought together. We just need to figure out what that is and why. Along the way…we'll figure out where our feelings are. I trust my heart. Do you trust yours?" she asked.

"Yes," I answered. She leaned over and placed a kiss lightly on my lips. I looked at her with astonishment. She was so…logical about it. I was about to lose my freaking mind, and she managed to calm me in less than a minute.

"Now…that was impressive and damned sexy," I said, leaning in and kissing her back.

"I know…get used to it," she said and laughed lightly.

I reached for her hand and drew it into mine.

"It's been a day," she said with a sigh. I could really see the darkness under her eyes starting to creep out and a bruise was beginning to form around her mouth from the beating that she had taken. She must have been exhausted.

"Go to bed, Laya. We'll talk more in the morning," I urged. She nodded reluctantly. I walked her to her door and opened it for her. She popped up on her toes and kissed me lightly on the cheek.

"Good night, Jett," she said and walked into my room.

I smiled like a fool and walked back to my seat. I leaned back in the kitchen chair and crossed my arms.

I wasn't ready to let her out of my life. Not now. Maybe not ever. But how could I keep her there if it was dangerous for her?

Did I really have a choice if she was engaged to some Mer?

37
JETT

JASPER AND SAM DECIDED that it was best to stay at the house. Not knowing what could be lying in wait for them at Sam's if they were to leave, they made the bed for their stay. Sam had lots of clothes and supplies for himself at our place anyway, having spent just as much time at our home as his own. They were heading to bed as I started to make up the couch for myself.

"She's going to have to go tomorrow. You know that right?" Sam asked.

"I know. I don't want her to stay if it's dangerous for her," I answered. *But, I don't want her to leave either.*

"It's not going to be safe for you here either," Jasper added. "I don't want something to happen to you. Those guys that came here, they have friends. Franky for one."

"I'm not afraid of Franky," I said with a shake of my head.

"Maybe you should be. Look at what he did to KyLaya. He has a way of getting what he wants, Jett. You can't deny that," Jasper replied.

"You're right about that," I admitted. As much as I wasn't afraid of Franky, I knew that there were others to consider. He came after Laya. As much as I didn't want to think of it, a part of me worried that it was a way for him to hurt me. Who else would he hurt just to get at me? Rall? Sam? Rayna? Jasper?

"We'll figure it out," Sam said and threaded his arms around Jasper.

"Whatever we do will have to wait for morning now, anyway," I said to the two of them.

"You know we will support whatever you decide," Jasper said and I nodded. "Good," he responded.

They said good night and went to bed.

I wasn't going to get any sleep. My mind was a mess. I tossed and turned on the small lumpy couch. Banging on the pillows and cushions in an attempt to make things bearable; or, maybe I was just needing to get some aggression out. I couldn't stop thinking about Laya. Her skin. Her eyes.

"Jett?" That sweet soft voice floated over to me from the kitchen. I sat up on the couch and turned to the sound of it.

There she stood, in the entrance to the living-room. In my t-shirt.

Only my t-shirt.

It was long on her, coming down almost to her knees; but, it was doing things to me that I was not prepared for.

"Umm…yeah?" I asked, trying to keep myself in check and not stare at her until my eyes fell out of my head.

"I…I couldn't sleep, and I heard you," she said.

"Sorry. This couch is old. I'll settle down so you can rest," I apologized and started to lay back down.

"No, that's not what I meant," she replied and stepped further into the room.

"Oh?" I swallowed hard. My heart played in my chest like a basketball.

"Can we talk?"

"Sure." I moved over so there was a place for her to sit next to me. I was suddenly aware of how much skin I was showing, but more so how much she was. My shirt laid on the rocking chair across the room from me where I had tossed it in frustration. I wondered if I should have been getting it or not.

"I…umm…I need to thank you, again, for saving me," she began. "The night that the Sirens attacked I would have been taken if not for you. I don't know what that would have meant for me; but, if Midira is the one that is wanting me, I can't imagine that it would have been any good. I was too out of it when I got here to thank you properly for what you did for me."

"Oh. You know you don't have to thank me, Laya."

"Yes, I do. Because of me, you are in trouble with your people; and, now someone has died just like back home. I can't help but feel like I brought that with me somehow. You have a really good thing going here, and I am ruining it for you. You did me a kindness, a huge kindness; and, I feel like you are being punished for it," she said and stood up from the couch.

"What? How – that is so far off-"

"Is it?" she interrupted. "Did you have a peaceful life before?"

"Yes, but-"

"Did you have a community that respected you and trusted you?"

"Yes, but-"

"Were you wanted for murder?"

"No, but-"

"Well, seems to me that all the bad things that have happened in your life recently happened after I got here!" she said, her voice raising as she gestured wildly with her hands.

"Laya, this is *not* your fault," I insisted, but she huffed and turned from me.

"I'm going."

"What?"

"I-"

I flashed to her, becoming fully formed right in front of her eyes as I grasped her chin in my fingers. "You're not going anywhere," I said and blocked her way out of the room.

"You can't stop me," she said with a determination that I took as a challenge.

"You think so?" I asked, and she nodded proudly.

"Very well. If you can get out of this room, you can go," I offered. The corner of her lip tipped up and a seriousness set into her jaw. She was in fighter mode; I could see the moment it switched on, and it was sexy as hell. She pulled her hair back, tying it up and squared herself to me.

She was just in my shirt and her underwear, so I knew I could take her easily; she wouldn't risk showing extra skin. She walked up slowly and carefully, watching me closely. I didn't budge but enjoyed seeing her body move the way it could when it was all healed. The strength in her was returning, and I was finally getting a look at who she really was.

I liked it. *A lot.*

She made a playful lunge and tried to fake me out, but it didn't work. I grabbed her around the waist and tossed her back into the room. She landed on her feet and a smile came out.

"Nice try," I teased, crossing my arms over my chest.

"It wasn't, but I'm glad *you* thought so," she answered. She paused a moment and then ran at me. When I tried to reach for her again, she slid under my arms. She would have gotten past me if I hadn't turned and whipped out a foot, tripping her, and bringing her to the ground. I stooped, grabbing her hand and hauling her to her feet again, making sure that she was well into the room.

"Okay, *that* was a good try," I admitted.

"It was *better*," she said with a shrug. She got up and readied for another pass. This time I stiffened and waited for her to run at me, but she didn't. Laya dropped out of fight mode and walked toward me slowly, her eyes not leaving mine. Her legs were on full display under my shirt, and I couldn't help my glance from wandering down them.

When she got to me, she placed her warm hands on my bare chest and pushed lightly. Playfully. A smile pulled at my mouth. I pushed her back, but she ducked under my arms, and I was thrown off balance. In a blink, she was behind me; and, with a solid kick to my back, I was on the floor. She had the open door that she wanted.

Smiling triumphantly, she turned to walk through, but I was up and flashed to her.

"Are you really going to make me say it?" I asked. Her eyes were wide and a blush filled out across her cheeks as she looked back at me.

"Say what?" she asked, gazing back up at me. I dipped my head down, even with hers and drew close enough to almost feel her lips against mine. Her breath caught in her throat, and I could see her pulse spike.

"That I have no intention of letting you walk out that door without me," I whispered against her lips.

We stood there, barely a breath between us, locked in a gaze that held us both. Suddenly, Laya leaned in and placed her lips on mine. My heart pounded inside me as we pulled each other closer and deepened that kiss.

Gods, I had never felt anything like that before. I was a mess of sensation, all of it good. So freaking good. She ignited a need and a want in me that I never knew existed. When her hands trailed up my chest, a hunger opened in me that just about consumed me. I brought my arms around her and lifted her off the ground, carrying her to the couch. She wrapped her legs around me as we fell onto the cushions.

Her lips were soft and warm and played against mine with a rhythm that was years in the making. I felt a tight coiling deep within me as a rush of blood filled my veins and ignited my senses. My hands took in her skin, racing up her legs to her waist, feeling her sweet skin under me.

I had never felt an attraction to someone like that before. I couldn't get enough of her. I wanted her more than anything, and I was having a really hard time managing it. I looked down at Laya laying on the couch, her shoulder exposed as my shirt slipped off of it. I trailed kisses down her neck to her bare skin, eliciting a gasp and moan from her. The sound of her awoke a side of me I didn't know was there, this animal urge to devour her, protect her. It was all consuming.

Her skin called to me, and I was pulled in again. Her eyes met mine, and I was almost undone.

My gods, Laya. What have you done to me?

38
KYLAYA

I WANTED HIM.

There was no mistaking that he wanted me too. I could see it in his eyes and the way his body moved against mine. The hunger, the need, matched mine and was exciting and scary beyond anything I could have dreamed. But as much as I wanted to see where it would go, I knew we were moving fast. Too fast. I sat up and away from him when he pulled back and took a breath.

Things were good – I mean, things were *really* good between us - but, as much fun as that promised to be, we didn't really know each other and there were things about our races that could pose a problem. What would happen in a Sirenite and Mer union? Was it even possible for us to build a life together?

I sat up and away from Jett, who sat up and away from me. I smiled and stood up. This was all so new to me. I really had no idea what I was doing, but retreating was the best course of action I could come up with. Jett reached for my hand when I turned to walk back to my room and pulled me back to the couch. This time closer to him.

"Where do you think you're going?"

"Back to my room," I answered.

"Boy, you really know how to make a boy feel like a piece of meat," he chuckled.

"What? That's not what I meant – I don't think of you that way," I answered.

"I know, Laya. Relax. This is new to me too. Don't go. Stay," he said, lacing his fingers in mine.

"Okay," I said with a smile.

"We need to talk," he said.

"You sound entirely too serious," I replied, settling in next to him.

"Dream stoppers have kept a lot from us. I think it's time to meet the other side of each other. The sides that have been kept a secret all these years. I want to know more about you, everything about you, actually. I'm not really ready for the night to end." Jett pulled a blanket over my knees to keep me warm. It was so sweet and just what I was needing - a connection beyond the physical one I felt for him. Though, *damn*, our physical connection was fire in my veins.

Jett leaned down and whispered in my ear, "Just being near you is driving me nuts. So, you better start talking," he teased, as he trailed a finger across my shoulder before pulling the shirt up and over it. I grinned as my heart thundered.

"What do you want to know?" I asked as my eyes trailed across his bare sculpted chest.

"All of it," he said, leaning back and putting his hands behind his head as he watched me. His long sculpted arms flexed and I just about lost my train of thought.

"That's a lot…and it's boring," I laughed.

"Not to me, Laya. Get started," he said and nudged me with his knee.

"Alright," I laughed lightly and leaned against the other side of the couch.

We didn't stay in those positions for long. Gravitating to each other, we ended up curled up in each other's arms, fingers laced together, small tender kisses exchanged, and chatting for hours.

We stayed up most of the night talking about everything and nothing. I learned more about his family and his upbringing. He learned about my job and home. Everything that we had been forbidden to talk about in the past. It was amazing and so interesting to hear more about the guy that I thought I knew so well.

All the core stuff was there. His integrity, passion, kindness, and pride in his community, none of that changed; but, it was all the other stuff that fully formed who he was in my mind. The more he talked, the deeper I fell for him. A steady fall into a place I had never been before and never thought I would go. In one night, we learned more about each other than some couples learn in a year or two. We knew who we each were at the core of all things, but to hear him talk about his heritage was heart-warming. He wanted to know all about my role in Triton and what life was like there for me. My parents, my sister, my life in general were all open to him.

I felt more connected to Jett than ever before.

"You seriously have never seen a movie?" he asked me.

"We don't have movies in Mer! We *read*," I answered.

"We are going to a movie. You're missing out," he determined.

"I'd really like that," I answered with a smile. Jett ran his hand up and down my leg. At first it was exhilarating; but, after a while it was comforting. A way to keep a connection with me.

Suddenly, he stopped.

I looked up at him and his eyes were glowing. I waved a hand in front of him and he didn't respond.

"Jett?" I whispered, waving my hand in front of his eyes again. Nothing. I placed a hand gently on his cheek and light lit the room. I was shot out of the little farm house and into the dream world that I knew so well.

In front of me were two men. I knew right away that one was Jett, but the other seemed familiar, though I couldn't figure out why. They were deep in conversation. Before I could hear what they were saying, they turned to me, their eyes glowing; and, I was pulled away. Thrown out of the dream, I could feel myself travelling back to my body for the first time.

When I opened my eyes, I was on the couch.

Alone.

39
JETT

ONE SECOND I WAS TALKING TO LAYA and the next I was dreaming. I didn't think that I had fallen asleep, but more like I was taken out of reality and pushed into a place I knew just about as well as reality.

In front of me was a man that was really familiar but that I had never seen before. I couldn't understand the feeling I had looking at him, as if I had always known him; and, yet I couldn't recall ever meeting him. Tall and strong, with dark features and pale blue eyes. He looked regal and powerful.

"I'm sorry to pull you away from her, but the time has come," he said to me.

"Time? What time?" I asked.

"He has come for you. We have done what we can to keep you two safe, but he was smarter and stronger than we thought," he said.

"Who? *Who* are you talking about?"

"You will see soon enough," he answered. "There is only so much I can tell you, as we are forbidden from giving more than a warning and guidance. Trust your instincts, my boy. They will serve you very well. They were one of our gifts after all," he said with a smile.

"Gifts? Who are you? How are you here? This is Laya's and my place," I asked, watching him carefully.

"I wish I could tell you, but I am forbidden. You will figure it out. I have faith in you, Jett." With that I was shot out of the dream and back home.

I woke up, not on the couch with Laya, but out on the deck laid out across the bench. The sky was dark. It was still night, though I had no concept of how much time had passed. I stood on shaky legs and looked out at the night sky. *What the hell just happened?*

I leaned my hands on the rail around the deck and took a deep breath. The evening air was clear and clean, as always. There was nothing like it in my opinion. Normally, it would help to clear my head but not this time. When I opened my eyes a set of headlights coming down the road stole my attention and had my power humming in my veins.

If Franky's friends had come for another fight, they were going to get one. I'd blast the truck before they could get their doors open.

When the vehicle turned slowly into the farm, I readied myself, pulling my power out and letting it dance across my hands. But when I recognized the truck, I calmed down…a bit.

What on earth is she doing here at this time?

Shaking off the remnants of the weird dream, I descended the steps to greet our visitor. My bare feet hit the cool grass as a woman with shoulder length salt and pepper hair bounded out of the beat up old green truck and walked with purpose to me.

"Pearl Wasche!" I exclaimed. "It has been a long time, my friend."

"Jett, it is good to see you," she replied and wrapped me in a warm hug.

"What can I do for you? This is kind of late for a social call. Is everything okay at camp?" Pearl ran a camp at Crystal Lake and we provided all her food and supplies, for free.

Pearl Wasche was the original Mer that started to save Mer-born Sirens from death sentences in Titus Prime and being taken by the Sirens back to their city of Stronghold. Her younger sister was turned when Pearl was young, and it had been her mission to keep as many Mer-born Sirens from suffering the same fate as her sister did. She was a wonderful person and, like most around town, I adored her. Her work for the Mer-borns was crucial in the development of our town and the fosters that raised the Sirenites as babies. My foster was one of the first that Pearl had saved. Louise would talk about Pearl a lot in the house with such affection.

After Pearl was banished from Titus Prime, she moved close to us, to a community that loved and supported her. We would often volunteer at her camp to help get it ready for the campers each summer. She ran a tight ship and was the most popular destination for kids in our area. All except for our own children in Stenen as their violet eyes would draw unwanted attention. We stayed to ourselves. In return, she offered time for just our families to enjoy the lake for free each summer. It was the highlight of the whole summer, and the entire community came out and enjoyed the safety of the waters of Crystal Lake.

But to see her drive up to my farm in the middle of the night was disturbing as that could never mean anything good.

"Well, I think we both know that I'm not here about supplies for the camp at two in the morning, Jett," she said with a knowing smile.

"Okay, what's up?"

"I have had a visitor from Triton," she answered.

"What? How"

The door to her truck opened and a guy got out. He was dressed impeccably well, his dark hair styled perfectly. He was tall and thin, with an air of importance to him. He walked straight over to me and with two hands, shoved me.

"Where is she!" he yelled.

"Whoa!" I shouted, totally taken a-back. Pearl rushed over and placed a hand on the guy's shoulder. He shrugged her off.

"What have you done to her?" he yelled.

"Who is this guy?" I asked Pearl, not acknowledging the shouting man in front of me. If he touched me again, he would be leaving with scorched hands, though.

"He's looking for-"

"Mazz!" a scream ignited from the house as the door flew open. Laya flew into the arms of the angry guy.

"Ky! Thank the gods," he uttered, squeezing her tight. *Mazz...her fiancé.* My heart hit the ground so hard I thought it might have stopped on impact. Laya's hands were on his face and her smile was ear to ear. He kissed her on the forehead, and I thought I might throw up...or punch him.

"I'm okay! I'm okay!" she repeated as he looked her over.

"Where have you been? We've been worried sick! Dad's had the Elite out every night and all day looking for you. We've sent parties to Titus Prime and Aquious searching. What happened?" Mazz asked her.

"How is Dad? Did the Sirens get in?" Laya asked.

"He's fine, at least he's not worse. I understand that you punched the doctor?"

"He wanted to cut open my father's head, Mazz! Then he tried to stab me. He had it coming long before that, though," she answered. A smile cocked the side of my mouth. She punched a doctor. *Awesome.*

"We have someone new watching him. He's in good hands, I assure you," Mazz answered.

"Thank you," she sighed.

"To answer your other question, the Sirens didn't get in. The city is safe. It would like its Prime back, though," he said looking straight at her.

"How did you find me?" Laya asked him.

Mazz looked at Pearl who shrugged and waved a hand.

"Okay, don't freak, but I've been working with Pearl for a while," he answered.

"What? Pearl? As in Pearl *Wasche*? The Siren Smuggler?" Laya shouted.

"Just Pearl is fine," Pearl smiled and waved to Laya. Laya's mouth gaped open as she turned back to the guy. He shrugged and smiled.

"You? A Hasp. Working with a Siren smuggler," Laya interjected. "Your father is going to *kill you*, you know that?" Laya said.

"Well, no offense to my father, but I have hidden it from him and everyone else for a couple of years now; so, I think I'm okay," he said crossing his arms proudly.

"Pearl, is this true? You've been working with the Mer?" I asked, looking at her in awe.

"Jett, there will come a time when we will need the strength of both the Sirenites and the Mer working together. Mazz is a good man. He has kept my secrets for a long time now. I trust him, fully," she said. I looked at Mazz; and, as much as it pained me, if Pearl said he could be trusted then he could be. She was an unbelievably good judge of character.

"When I found out that you were gone and that there was a Siren attack I had to do something. Dad sent scouts to Titus and Aquious, and I went to Pearl. It just took me awhile to get out of the city. Things have been on lock down and High Hill is in an uproar. I finally got out tonight and came straight here," he explained.

"News has travelled even to me that you were caring for a Mer, Jett," Pearl added. "When Mazz came looking for KyLaya, I knew right away it was her."

"I'm so happy you are safe!" Mazz gushed and hugged Laya tightly again.

I couldn't take looking at Laya in another's arms for one more second. Clenching my hands at my sides, I stalked back to the house.

"Jett, wait!" Laya shouted. "Don't go."

"What?" I said, turning and crossing my arms so tightly across my chest I thought I might break a rib.

Laya ran to me and threaded her fingers in mine, releasing the iron grip I had on myself. She smiled at me and pulled me over to Mazz.

"Mazz, this is Jett. He saved me from the Sirens," she said. Mazz looked at our hands and then back at me. Laya smiled at him, watching him closely.

"I see," he said, a frown tipping his lips down.

Damn, the guy loved Laya. Really loved her. And she had no idea. I reached out a hand for his and he took it.

"It's good to meet you," I said, shaking his hand and trying to sound believable for her sake.

"Thank you for saving my girl," he said, making sure that I got the "my girl" part.

"My pleasure," I answered, holding Laya's hand tighter. No way was I letting the competition stick around. "Thanks for checking on her, but as you can see she's fine."

"I don't see that, actually," he answered. "We need to talk," he said turning back to Laya and effectively dismissing me.

"Okay," Laya answered and released my hand. I could feel my muscles tighten as they turned away from me and walked towards the garden.

"Whoa, Jett the smitten kitten," Pearl teased when they were out of earshot. "Never thought I would see the day." She walked slowly, standing by my side.

"Me neither. Why'd you have to bring him here?" I asked, knowing how childish that sounded. If I had any confidence in my relationship with Laya, this guy shouldn't matter; but, the truth was…I wasn't sure where her heart was with him. I knew where mine was with her. And watching them together only confirmed how I felt about her.

In that moment I was flooded with jealous anger that I just didn't know what to do with – and I hated it. I turned away from them, not able to watch her so close to another guy that she had such a close relationship with.

That's when I smelled it…smoke.

"You smell that?" I asked Pearl. She nodded and her brow furrowed. I looked back at the house, expecting to see smoke coming from it, but there was nothing. Walking around the yard, off in the distance, I could see where it was coming from. A glow lit up the dark night sky.

Oh, no…

Stenen was on fire.

40
JETT

I FLASHED WITHOUT STOPPING to tell Jasper or Laya where I was going. I couldn't take great distances in one flash, so I took short ones, making it to town in less than a minute.

I arrived to see Vyktor's shop up in flames. Long red tendrils of flame reached for the night sky, flicking and waving in the evening air.

Damn it!

I ran for the door, hoping to get his dog out - he loved that thing. I pulled water from the pipes and blasted back the flames as best as I could until I got to this residence at the back of the store. Crying and whining in his crate was his floppy grey hair mutt. I opened the door and he jumped into my arms. A beam fell across the path that I had made, blocking me from getting out the same way. I looked around, finding the only path left. The window.

Summoning my strength I ran at the glass and jumped through, holding the dog tightly against my chest. I landed in t a crouch, the grey mop of a dog still in my arms. He looked up at me and licked my face.

"You're welcome," I said to him. Putting him on the ground, I walked back around to the front of the building. Vyktor's dog following at my feet. The fire flamed bright, and I was forced back into the street. An explosion and crash from inside sounded, and I knew there was no going back in. The building, and anyone left inside, was lost.

What a loss for the town.

That's when I realized that it was eerily quiet. Silent in fact.

I looked around and realized that I was the only one on the street.

"Where is everyone?" I asked the dog.

A fire like that surely would have drawn some attention by that stage. But there wasn't one person around. I flashed around town trying to find someone, anyone, to help me put out the fire, but there was no one around. Not one soul.

I had just flashed back to main-street when I saw someone crumpled on the ground in the middle of the road. Laying lifeless, I flashed to them and turned them gently toward me

My heart stopped.

Rayna.

"Rayna," I urged loudly. She was barely conscious. A soft moan came from her as I tried to get her to open her eyes. There were burnt patches on her clothes and deep gashes on her face and neck. She was bleeding a lot. *My gods, what happened to you?* Her eyes opened but she didn't speak.

"What happened? Where is everyone?" I asked, trying to get her to focus on me. She coughed slightly, her eyes roaming as if they didn't see me.

"He took them," she answered, her lips wavering as she spoke. I had never seen her so scared - the girl was fearless.

"Who? Who, Rayna?" I demanded, trying to get an answer from her.

"The man in black. He came in the night. I heard screaming. A fire was burning. Anyone that fought…killed. Turned to ash," she uttered.

"Where is he?" I asked.

"I'm sorry. I failed," she said. Her head dropped back and she was gone.

Damn it, Rayna! I lowered my head down to hers. *Be at peace my friend.*

That was when I noticed the mark of the gods on her collarbone, gleaming bright as if it was lit from beneath her skin.

Why would the gods have marked Rayna?

I closed my eyes and pulled her close, mourning her loss in my very core and feeling the heaviness of the anger that came with it. Gently, I set her on the ground. I didn't have time to process what that mark meant, when the dog started to growl. Looking up, a towering figure stood before me. A man in black.

Vyktor's dog snarled and barked, his fur standing on end.

The man took a step toward me and I stood, knowing that my next move might be my last. If he could kill an entire town he was dangerous beyond measure.

"Who are you?" I yelled, watching him closely. He was much taller than me, unlike any man I had ever seen, standing seven feet tall at least. His skin was darkly tanned, his hair black as night. Icy blue eyes stood out like beams in the night under his thick dark brow. He wore a long black leather trench coat with the collar up high around his ears, and pants to match. No shirt. Heavy boots thudded against the ground as he took a step towards me. He looked like a cross between a biker and a pirate, but radiated a power that was far beyond either of those. An ancient power.

"I said, who are you?" I yelled, pink flashing into my palms.

He didn't speak but was in front of me before I could flash away. I choked on a gasp as his hand wrapped around my throat. The man lifted me off the ground. I grabbed for his arm and poured my energy into him. I didn't know if it hurt as much as it surprised him, but he dropped me. I flashed around landing a kick to his chest which threw him back a couple of steps. He turned, unfazed and rushed me. I flashed out of his way and landed a punch to his face.

He stood and grasped his jaw, a grin spread out across his face.

"Not bad," he complimented in a smooth voice.

"Who are you? Where are my people?"

"I'm not here to explain myself to you, boy," he answered, walking in a slow circle around me. It was an intimidation tactic, and it wasn't working on me. I started to walk the same circle opposite of him. He smiled. "You're different than the rest."

"I won't ask again. Who are you?" I shouted.

"I'm a little hurt that you can't figure that out for yourself," he replied.

"Should I know someone that would murder and kidnap an entire town for fun?" I asked, keeping an eye on him closely.

"You should know a *god* when you see one," the man proclaimed.

"What does a *god* want with my people?" I said, unimpressed.

"I'm looking for someone," he answered.

"All you had to do was *ask*, you know," I said through clenched teeth.

"Not much fun for me that way," he said with a shrug and a grin.

"What did you do with them? Where are they?"

"They are mine now. I needed some fodder and *fun*," he said with a smile. My insides lit in rage thinking about all the innocent lives he took, Vyktor, Rayna, and Rall, and what he would do to them.

"Son of a bitch," I growled. He just shrugged.

"It's all part of the gig, kid," he answered spreading his arms wide.

I was done talking.

Pink lit across my hands and I flashed to him. This time, though, my punch didn't land. He flashed out of the way in a cloud of red smoke. When I turned a fist smacked into my face, sending me to the ground. I flipped over and braced myself against the ground. He turned and shrugged off his large jacket.

"You know, I haven't sparred in ages. This is going to be fun," he said, lifting his hands and signaling me to come at him. He was having too much fun, and that was pissing me off more.

Summoning my strength I shot a bolt of pink light at him. He dove out of the way into a flawless roll and came up unharmed with a smile on his face. I shot three more times, watching the way he rolled and how he maneuvered. The last shot I aimed at him and then blasted again to his side. This one landed its mark, searing into his ribs and stopping his roll.

He stood up slowly. His icy blue eyes narrowed on his bloodied skin and the burn that had gone through flesh and muscle, right to the bone.

How is he still standing?

"Damn…that hurts, kid," he winced. A concentrated look filled his face as his eyes closed and his brow furrowed. His lips tightened and his muscles flexed and right there before my eyes, the wound I had dealt healed, leaving no mark behind. He turned to me and opened his eyes. They were orbs of light and my heart stopped.

"How…"

"God," he said and pointed to himself.

"What god would do this to a group of innocent people?" I asked and then it hit me. "Ares?"

"Close. Deimos, Ares's son, at your service," he said and bowed.

"Was I really supposed to guess that?" I asked, tilting my head. Deimos's eyes narrowed and he glared at me. I guess not knowing that he was Ares's son was an insult. I didn't get the chance to say anything else though, before he flashed to me, slamming his hand to my chest.

A searing pain radiated from the point of contact and I cried out. The world spun as liquid fire ran through my veins. I felt like I was being burned from the inside out.

When he dropped me to the ground, I expected that to be the end. Knowing now that he had to be the one that killed Vyktor, Rayna, and the woman in Mer that Laya liked so much, I knew there was nothing on the other side of his touch but death.

But, where I expected to find death, there was life.

Deimos looked at me and narrowed his gaze as he poured more into his hand, more into the burn. I cried out as the pain scorched my skin, burning and melting it to the bone. But, still, I didn't die.

Deimos removed his hand and stood, huffing over me, "It's you. Finally," he said. His eyes were light as he looked down at me. "Damn, I really wanted to kill you," he said. I couldn't move. The pain was too much, I was having trouble focusing as the world around me started to spin. I knew I was starting to pass out.

That's when a voice shot the pain right out of me and a chill settled into my chest.

"Jett!"

Laya…no…

41
KYLAYA

"WHAT'S GOING ON WITH YOU and that guy, Ky?" Mazz asked me as soon as we were out of earshot of Jett and Pearl.

"Whoa, cutting right to the point huh? No *how are you feeling* or *when are you coming home*?" I asked placing my hands on my hips and frowning at him.

"I can see that you are just *fine*. From the looks of things, I'm going to guess that you aren't sure when you want to come home and resume your leadership over one of the greatest cities in Mer - all because some guy makes goo goo eyes at you!" he whispered in a harsh voice.

"What has as gotten into you, Mazz?" I asked, truly thrown back at the way he was acting. "I thought that you would be happy for me."

"Happy? How could I be happy for you? You're throwing away everything that you have worked for your entire life! You're throwing *us* away, Ky!"

"I am *not*!" I countered, insulted that he would say that. "Look, I know that this isn't exactly how you thought you would find me, and I can see that being a shock, but there is something going on with Jett that I can't explain."

"You *can't* or you *won't*. You know, I thought that we were closer than this. I thought that we were team," he said.

"We are a team!"

Mazz took a step back and placed a hand over his mouth, closing his eyes. When he opened them, he let out a frustrated roar. He placed his hands on my arms and looked in my eyes.

"I love you, Ky," he said.

"I love you too, Mazz," I answered. He shook his head sadly.

"No…I *love* you," he corrected quietly. I staggered back from him, my mouth dropped open. I looked at him then, really looked at him.

"What? How – how long? Why didn't you tell me?" I stammered.

"I didn't know, not until you disappeared. I suppose I started having feelings for you months ago and never realized it."

"But – you – I…" I didn't know what to say to him. I loved him, loved him very much, but not in the way that he was now seeking from me. My heart was breaking. *Why now? Why at all?* Jett was the one. He was. I knew it. I had always known it, I supposed. It was just that, until now, he wasn't real.

Shit balls, now what do I do?

"How…how do you feel about that, Ky?" Mazz asked, looking hopefully at me. I glanced back to where Jett was, but he was gone.

"I – I can't answer that right now. I'm sorry." Mazz dropped his head and nodded. "I'm so sorry, Mazz," I said as tears started coming for me. Gods, he was my brother. I didn't want to hurt him. I tried to reach for him, but he backed away from me. It was like a punch to the throat and I actually choked.

"I just…need time," he said.

"Mazz…"

"Don't, Ky. It's fine. I don't know what I was thinking. You have always made it clear that you didn't have any other feelings for me. I fooled myself into thinking that your heart had changed like mine."

I cried. Let it all pour out. It was killing me to see him hurt – and it was infinitely worse that I was the reason.

A slam from the house sounded. Jett must have gone in. At least, that's what I assumed, but it was Jasper that jumped down the steps and ran towards me.

"Where's Jett?" he asked in a furious breath and then stopped dead when he saw Mazz. "Whoa. Hi, I'm Jasper," he said smiling from ear to ear and reaching for Mazz's hand. Mazz looked at me and then at Jasper and reached for his hand.

"Mazz Hasp," he introduced. Jasper held his hand a second too long.

"Wow, baby soft," Jasper uttered when they released hands.

"Jasper," I interrupted his staring at Mazz. "Jett?"

"Right! Where is he?"

"I don't know," I admitted turning to where he had been talking to Pearl.

"He's gone, Jasper!" Pearl shouted.

"Where?" Jasper asked.

"Town!" she pointed to the horizon where a glow was lit. "Fire."

"He's in trouble. We have to go. Now," Jasper said and ran for Sam's truck. Sam barrelled out of the house, half dressed, threading his head through a t-shirt, keys ringing in his hands.

"I'm coming!" I shouted as I ran for Sam's truck.

"Quickly!" Sam shouted, and then stopped short when he saw Mazz. "Who's that?"

"My…fiancé," I uttered as I climbed into the back of the truck.

"Not for nothing, but well done," he smirked. "Jett's not going to like that guy."

"Nope," Jasper chimed.

I watched as Mazz climbed into the truck with Pearl and we were all speeding down the road towards Stenen and whatever mess Jett had gotten himself into.

"Holy Hades, Vyktor's!" Jasper shouted as we drove into town. Sam pulled up to a building on the main street which was completely up in flames.

"Geez," I uttered. "How did this happen?" The truck squealed to a stop, slamming me and Jasper forward. "What is it?" I called forward to Sam. But, looking through the front, I saw.

A body.

We all ran from the truck to the person on the ground. *Please, not Jett. Please.* Rolling the person over, we were all relieved and saddened at the same time. It was Rayna.

"She's still alive, but just barely. I can hardly make out a heartbeat but it's there," Sam said.

"We have to get her out of the street," I said to him, looking at the burning building and knowing being that close wasn't safe.

"Here! Put her in my truck. There are blankets in the back that I was taking to camp!" Pearl shouted. Sam lifted her from the ground and into the truck on his own, which impressed me since Rayna was built like a boxer. I turned from them and my eyes drifted down the street. In the light from another building on fire, I could see a figure hunched on the ground and immediately, my fear got the best of me.

"Jett!" I cried and took off running, pouring my Mer speed into every step. But when the figure stood and turned to me, I knew I had made a mistake. It wasn't Jett it was someone else. A shot of red power blasted from the figure. My Elite training kicked in and I instinctively dodged the attack, but it landed a target behind me.

"Sam!" Jasper cried. I threw my hands to my face as I watched Sam fall to the ground from the back of the truck. Jasper fell down beside him. My eyes flashed to the source of the power.

The man took a purposeful stride to me. He was clad in leather, his eyes shone silver in the evening light like cat eyes. Tall and strong, he was easily over six feet tall, if not more. His coat was blood red, his hair echoing the dark hues.

"What do you want? Where's Jett?" I yelled at him.

"He's fine…for now. He'll be coming with us. You, however, really should have stayed home tonight, sweet heart. I guess it's my luck you came out," he said, licking his lips as his eyes roamed my body. A chill ran down my spine like an ice cube sliding down my skin.

"What do you want?" I asked, looking around for Jett, hoping that he was okay.

"Doesn't matter now. You are a pretty little bonus we didn't expect. How nice, two birds with one flame filled stone!" he smiled.

"Me?"

"Midira's been looking for you. Her Sirens weren't getting the job done, so she called in a favor. I'm the favor. I almost had you in Triton, too; but, my pesky brother got in the way, damn Eros. He's not here to save your sweet butt this time, though. You're all mine," he replied and took another step toward me.

Eros?

My dream! It wasn't a dream, someone really did come to my room! I looked at the man in front of me and knew that what I saw, what I heard was real. And that meant that he was the one that tried to kill me back home.

"Phobos?" I asked.

"Very good!" he said nodding. "Most can't tell me and Deimos, apart."

"Eros told me that you had come. Why?" I asked, backing away slightly.

"Now, if I told you that, it would spoil the fun for us wouldn't it," he chuckled darkly.

"Where's Jett?" I asked again.

"Well, now, here's a little piece of serendipity. My brother's been looking for him, and here we find the two of you together! Isn't that nice? So convenient for us," he teased.

"What have you done with him?"

"Me? Nothing! But, my brother…he's a different story, sweetheart."

Out of the corner of my eye I caught movement. Two more figures were in the street down from me, debris littering the road in their path.

"Jett!" I called and ran. Phobos didn't move, but watched as I took off from him and closed in on where Jett laid on that ground.

Folded up in the fetal position, Jett didn't move as I fell to his side.

"Jett?" I placed my hand on his face and he didn't respond.

"What did you do to him?" I screamed at the man that stood by Jett's body.

"We were just talking," he said and laughed. Phobos walked over and stood beside the other man and that's when I understood. Deimos, Ares's other son, had been fighting Jett.

Gods! Literal gods!

"Why are you doing this?" I cried, as I trailed a hand down Jett's face. He looked rough, with a cut on his lip and a bruise forming around his eye.

"Why? 'Cause, it's fun," Phobos answered, which made Deimos laugh. A rage burned in my gut and I felt the pull of my power snapping to life in my core.

"Leave us alone," I said in a straight, even tone as I stood, moving in front of Jett to protect him - with what I had no idea.

"Not going to happen, sweetheart," Deimos answered. There was movement by my feet and my heart leapt - Jett was waking.

Thank the gods…but not these particular ones.

"I'm not leaving him," I said, planting my feet and getting ready for a fight that I knew damned well I was going to lose.

"Very well," Phobos said and shot a bolt of light toward me. It was faster than anything I had ever seen. All I could do was throw my hands up and hope it killed me quickly.

A glow emitted from my palms, as if the very presence of Phobos's power awakened something in me. I felt a rush from within, a sensation that I had never experienced before, and I watched in stunned confusion as the red light bounced off of my hands. As if they had created a shield, his power rebounded and shot right back at Phobos. He had no time to react. Standing there, disbelief written across his face, he took the full force of the hit that was meant for me.

It collided with his chest in a great red explosion, throwing him back through a building on the other side of the street. Deimos turned and watched as his brother soared past him and out of sight. We all watched as, with a great groan and crack, the building collapsed onto Phobos.

I looked at my hands in utter shock. *What? How?* Deimos turned slowly toward me.

"How?" Deimos demanded. Looking back toward where his brother laid buried in the house, a raging battle cry cut through the night air as Deimos summoned his power. He turned his icy gaze at me and shot his hands out. A ball of red energy burst from his palms and flew with great speed toward me. I raised my hands and the power bounced off me again, but unlike Phobos, Deimos dodged the rebound.

Pearl and Mazz, who had been tending to Sam and Rayna with Jasper, came at a dead run to help.

Showing more training than I ever gave him credit for, Mazz came along side Deimos, swung a fist through the air and made contact with Deimos's face. Deimos twisted out of Mazz's reach, as he tried to punch him again, and flashed red disappearing into a cloud of red smoke. Mazz threaded his hands through the blood red mist, but came up empty handed.

"What the-" he uttered. Then, Deimos reappeared right in front Mazz. Before I could give any warning, Deimos reared back and kicked Mazz square in the chest. Mazz flew into the air, back down the street and slammed into the truck, his head bouncing off of the door. *Damn it!*

"Mazz!" I cried.

Pearl flipped a knife into her hand from her pocket. Swinging low with a foot, she tried to trip Deimos as she stretched out an arm to slice Deimos's leg. She managed to cut a thin line through his pants. He cried out in pain and turned. With a sick *smack*, he back handed her with such force she was sent flying towards Mazz. She landed next to him at the truck.

I whimpered. Deimos turned his eyes on me. My heart was in my throat as he drew nearer.

"What are you?" he shouted at me and red haze lifted from his hands. He came at me with such speed I couldn't have moved out of the way if I wanted to. And I really wanted to. His hands were just about around my neck when they were shot away from me by pink flame.

Deimos and I both turned to see where it came from.

My heart lurched when I saw a weak Jett, standing in the street his power glowing in his hands. A stream of pink sparked and he was by my side.

"Get away from her!" he growled at Deimos. Jett placed himself in front of me.

"Oh, I don't think so. She's coming with *me*," Deimos said, running his eyes up and down my body. All of a sudden I felt more like prey than a person. It flipped the switch on my guard side and I punched him in the face.

Deimos stumbled back, holding his cheek. He looked just about as shocked as Jett did, who turned to me with eyes wide.

"What?" I asked.

"We will discuss how hot that was later," Jett answered with his crooked smile that made my heart thunder in my chest.

Deimos was not impressed and a red haze started to rise in billowing clouds from his skin. I could feel the power in the air as his temper flared.

Oh, crap. Don't punch a god. Lesson learned.

Jett flashed to him, but as he did, Phobos stormed from the rubble of the building I had shot him into and tackled Jett to the ground. The two of them squared off as Deimos made his way to me.

"Run, Laya!" Jett shouted.

But I couldn't.

Something inside me demanded that I stay. Something inside me…woke up.

Red lit across Deimos's skin, gliding up his arms and across his shoulders as the power within him mounted higher. I could feel the energy in him surging and flowing with his anger. So strong, I was drawn to it.

Suddenly, I could see the power within him. Like rivers of blue sparkling liquid running in his veins. It wasn't blood, it was something else…and I wanted it. Without knowing what I was doing, I reached up and placed my hands on his face. A shock wave burst from us at my touch, so strong that it extinguished the fires in the burning buildings.

His eyes stretched open and his mouth gaped. A part of me was revealed that had never been there before, the part of me that craved, needed…power.

I pulled.

Red haze left his skin and seeped into mine as his power entered me. I felt alive and light and strong and I wanted more. Much more.

Deimos's eyes stared in wide horror at me as I pulled again. He screamed. But nothing dampened the feeling of his power within me. No matter what came from his mouth, I wouldn't stop.

Before the last remnants of his power came to me, I was thrown to the ground.

Immediately the world spun and came back to normal.

Dark. Dank. Normal.

I found myself aching to feel what I had just felt again.

More. More!

I knew that I had just found a drug I never knew existed. Without understanding what it was. Without knowing where I could get more, I was suddenly and strongly addicted.

My very core called out to the power running in his veins and the high that came with it.

42
JETT

PHOBOS SHOT FROM THE BUILDING, through the air, straight at me. Wrapping his arms around my waist, he tackled me, throwing me from Laya and leaving her helplessly facing off against Deimos. It wasn't that I thought she couldn't fight. I knew she could, but he was a damned god!

I sprang from the ground and flashed back to Laya, but before I made it to her, Phobos grabbed me right out of the flash and tossed me back down the street.

"Okay, now you're just pissing me off," I growled at him.

"Come at me, pretty boy," Phobos grinned.

"Gladly, smart ass," I said with a smirk. I didn't know what Laya had done to him, or how she had repelled his power, but it had to have left him weakened, and I was going to take advantage of it.

I squared on him and summoned my power to my hands. Pink electric haze lit in my palms, building and pulsing as I pulled it from my core. Phobos raised a hand and red haze seeped from it, a family trait I guessed. A squeal from Laya caught my attention as I watched Deimos lift her off the ground by her throat. That was the opportunity that Phobos had waited for. Aiming his power at me, he shot. It collided with my shoulder, searing and burning as the haze bit through my skin.

Ah, shit, that hurts!

I buried the pain as best as I could and focused on the god in front of me. Flashing closer to him, I shot out with my power. He dodged by dropping into a graceful roll, and swept a foot out for me. I jumped, escaping his attempt at a take down. Then, as if my power read my mind, a pink blade appeared in my hand. It was the first time that my powers had taken the form of a weapon. Reacting out of instinct and training, I whipped it at him as I landed. It soared through the air and sliced deep into his side, with skin cut away to reveal the bone beneath.

He turned his head, the wound not registering on his face. It was as if he felt no pain. I stood there and watched as his stone cold eyes dropped to the lesion. He placed a hand on the deep cut, then brought it up even with his eyes. Blood ran down his fingers as he examined them, as if he had never seen his own blood before. Then, he smiled and licked it.

No, gross, don't do that. I grimaced and tried not to think about how disgusting that was.

"You're sick, you know that?" I called to him. He shrugged.

"The scent of blood in the morning-" but I didn't give him a chance to finish, I shot him with a bolt of my power, sending him falling back and effectively shutting him up. I flashed to his side and a dagger in pink flashed into my hand, just the weapon to finish the job.

"You think you are going to win?" Phobos laughed.

"Looks to me like it," I nodded.

Phobos laughed and shook his head. "This is only the beginning, pretty boy."

Red haze exploded from where he laid on the ground. I coughed and stumbled back, waving my arms out in front of me, swiping the dagger through the blood red mist. *Nothing.*

When it dissipated, he was gone.

"Damn it!" I swore, turning and looking around. But there was no trace of Ares's son anywhere. That was when I saw her.

Deimos had Laya. His powers were swirling around them and…going into her.

I stood in stunned silence and watched as Laya pulled Deimos's powers from him. His eyes bulged and his mouth opened in a silent scream. Red haze left him and absorbed into her. Losing all color, his skin looked half dead, as she took from him all that made him a god. I had never seen anything like that before. I had never heard anything like that before.

Her face was a mixture of pain and pleasure as she drew from him. Suddenly her eyes went red and I knew that couldn't be good. If she kept going, she was going to kill him, I could feel it. Not that I particularly cared if he died, I was more worried about what it would do to Laya, if she absorbed all of his power.

Not wasting another second, I ran at her. Grabbing her around the waist, I pulled her from Deimos and we fell to the gravel street. A wave of power unleashed from where she touched him, blowing a gust of wind down the road, lifting the dirt and dust into a whirlwind cloud. Deimos fell to the ground in an unconscious heap.

"Laya!" I shouted and shook her. Her eyes were closed and she was barely breathing. "Come on," I urged. "Come *on*!"

Her eyes fluttered and my heart spiked. "Thank the gods," I uttered and held her close.

"What happened?" she moaned, pulling back and looking at me. When I looked in her eyes my heart chilled. Silver. Her eyes were silver.

What the?

She blinked and the color was gone. I looked at her harder. *Did I really just see that?*

"Jett? You're okay!" she gushed and threw her arms around me.

"I'm fine. Are *you* okay?" I asked, placing my hands on her face and examining her.

"I'm great!" she said with a smile that was not natural in a situation like the one that we were in. A groan caught our attention as Deimos regained consciousness and stumbled to a stand. I guided Laya behind me and stood, pulling my powers and narrowing my eyes on him. If he wanted a fight he was going to get one.

"Leave!" I shouted at him as my power slid down my arm and out my palm creating a long sword in my hand. Laya came around beside me, red haze lifting off of her body as she watched Deimos.

"You think that you have won, but you will see…this is only the beginning. We know who you are now…," he threatened. "We *will* be back. That's a promise."

"Yeah, well, feel free not to keep it," Laya interjected, lifting her palm and watching the red haze swirl around in it. She smiled at him.

A burst of crimson smoke exploded where he stood and he was gone.

Laya turned to me.

"Did we seriously just take on a couple of gods and *win*?" she asked me, looking at her hands.

"It seems that way, for the moment anyway," I answered. She leaned her head against my chest and I pulled her into a tight embrace.

"We'll figure it out," I said to her as a protective urge flared within me. "I promise."

43
KYLAYA

THE POWER THAT RAN INSIDE ME was still coursing my veins. I could feel it in me, racing and firing in my veins. The strength of it was intoxicating and I knew that there would never be anything like that for me, not until I got more. And I wanted more. But I turned my attention away from the call of the power of Deimos to Jett.

There was a moment, before Jett pulled me from Deimos that I was almost lost to the power within him. I couldn't stop myself and I knew that. I would have taken it all. Like a starving vampire, I had no control over this thirst I suddenly had.

What did that mean? *What am I?*

Jett drew an arm around me and suddenly his lips were on mine. Everything disappeared in that moment and my thirst turned from Deimos to Jett immediately, but it wasn't his power I sought, it was something else.

"You scared me," he said against my lips as he pulled back.

"Likewise, mister," I answered.

"We're going to have to talk about this new talent you have," he said with a half-smile. Though I could see, from the furrow in his brow, he wasn't teasing. He wanted information, or at least an explanation. I wouldn't be able to give him one. I had no idea where all that came from or why.

"We'll talk…but later," I answered and pulled away, unsure of what to say to him. A groan sounded from the truck.

Mazz…

With all that had happened I had completely forgotten about him. I ran to the truck where he had been tossed. Mazz was just coming to. He was bloodied up from a cut on his forehead, but otherwise, luckily unharmed. Pearl had a gash on her cheek, but she would recover too. We dodged a bullet with them both, it could have been so much worse.

"Laya?" Mazz grumbled.

"I'm here," I said gently and placed a hand on his chest. He grasped my hand and smiled, happy that I was alive. My heart hurt, knowing that I would have to choose between the man that I had loved since I was a child and the man that was closer than a brother to me.

Gods, why me?

44
JETT

I LOOKED AROUND FOR JASPER. When I saw him, he was hunched over a figure in the street.

Gods, not Sam.

I ran to Jasper, who was crying over Sam.

"Jass?" I said hesitantly. Sam was white as a ghost and there was a giant gash across his chest.

"No…" I uttered, looking at the man that I thought of as another brother. He couldn't be…

"Sam?" I uttered and knelt down beside him. "Is he?"

"He's alive, but barely," Jasper uttered quietly, wiping at his running nose and holding Sam's head in his lap. He placed a gentle kiss on Sam's head and I could just about feel the heaviness of my brother's heart in that moment.

"Fear not, your friend will live," a voice echoed from all around us. Jasper and I turned our heads to the voice.

A man, who stood the same height as Deimos and Phobos approached us. I stood as my power lit my hands.

"Stay where you are!" I yelled at him.

"Relax, I'm not here to hurt anyone. I came to help actually, but I see that I am a little late for that," he said, placing his hands on his hips and shaking his head. His blonde hair shone with a light of its own, as did his startling light blue eyes. With only jeans on, there was no missing the muscular frame he was sporting. He wasn't even wearing shoes.

"Who are you?" I asked, standing in front of Sam and Jasper and looking for Laya. Laya was standing in front of Mazz and Pearl, her eyes wide as she watched the man walk toward me.

"My name is-"

"Eros?" Laya called out and ran to my side, looking at that man closer. "It *is* you!"

"Hello, KyLaya. I wasn't sure that you would have recognized me," he answered with a smile, taking her hand and kissing the top of it. I grabbed Laya's other hand and pulled her back to my side before the guy got any ideas of kissing her anywhere else.

"How do you know him?" I asked her, getting her to peel her eyes off the half-naked male model and look at me.

"We met back home. He saved me from Phobos when he came to Triton to find me," she answered, looking back to Eros, as if he were a god or a dream.

"And stop glaring at him, Jett," she whispered to me. I grabbed her in a one armed hug and pulled her to my side. She poked me in the ribs and eyed me.

"Okay, so who are you, exactly?" I asked him.

"Sorry," he chimed. "I'm Eros, son of Ares-"

My powers flared across my hands.

"Whoa!" Eros said, raising his hands. "Let me finish! Ares and *Aphrodite*. My mother is Aphrodite," he yelled staring at me. I glared at him and he shrugged. "I take after *her* side of the family," he jested. I didn't want to believe him, since Ares's other sons had been sadistic assholes, but, looking at him, I could see that he was telling the truth. Deimos and Phobos looked like warriors and fighters with a penchant for gore, where Eros looked like an easy going guy with a flare for chiseled features and high end jeans.

"It's okay, Jett," Laya said softly, meeting my eyes. "He saved me. He's fine. We can trust him," she said and looked at him. "Well, we can trust that he isn't going to kill us right now. Beyond that I can't say."

"Ouch," Eros uttered.

"What do you want?" I asked him, grasping Laya's hand in mine, ready to pull her out of harm's way.

"Like I said, I came to help," he said looking around. His eyes fell on Sam and without stopping to ask or say what he was doing, he went over and knelt at Sam's side. Jasper gasped and flinched as he came closer.

"It's okay. I won't harm him," Eros said in a smooth kind tone. Jasper nodded and move aside, letting Eros have more room to maneuver around Sam. I looked down at Laya and she gazed back at me. I could see from the down turn in her lip and her furrowed brow that she was worried. I was too. We really didn't know anything about the guy.

"Stand back, this is going to be bright," Eros said so quietly that we almost didn't hear him.

He wasn't kidding.

It was like the sun itself decided to visit Stenen. I pulled Laya to my chest, squeezing her tightly to me, and dropped my head down to hers. Even through my closed eyes and my arm, I could see light. It shone through flesh and bone.

When at last the light died out, it took a moment to be able to see again in the darkness of the street.

"Sam!" I heard Jasper cry and then the sound of gravel crunching. I scrubbed at my eyes with my palms to try to clear them quicker. When they did, I saw my brother on top of Sam, planting a steamy kiss on him. I cleared my throat and looked away. Laya was smiling big and wiping a tear from her cheek.

"Softie," I teased as I whispered in her ear.

"I'm so happy he's okay. Jasper would have been lost. They love each other so much," she said in awe and in that moment I realized something. For the first time in my life, I had the opportunity to have what Jasper had. Someone to die for. Someone to live for. Someone to give everything for.

I drew Laya up into my arms and kissed her hard.

"What was that for?" she asked as her smile turned from the guys to me.

"I-"

"Well, not to interrupt, but I think that there are a few things that I should be discussing with you folks," Eros said interrupting what I was going to say to Laya.

What *was* I going to say to her? *I love you?* My pulse shot through me as I realized that it was coming out of my mouth.

What in Hades are you thinking, Jett? You can't say that to her! You'll scare her right back to Mer.

Plus, I don't love her.

Yes. you do.

"To be continued?" Laya asked, looking widely as me with her big blues.

"Yeah, sure," I answered, with a nod.

Great. Just what the hell am I going to tell her?

45
KYLAYA

"WELL, I DON'T KNOW ABOUT YOU, but I can think of better places to have a conversation in," Eros announced. Then, with a wave of his hands, the street and town disappeared.

I was speechless as I looked around Jett's house. Rayna was on the couch in the living room and Jasper and Sam were in his room. Sam was breathing easy and resting in bed, Rayna's color was back in her cheeks and she was sound asleep. The rest of us were in clean clothes, sitting around the kitchen table with cups of tea. It was like we had been home for hours.

"What the-" I muttered looking around at the stunned faces of everyone else. Around the table sat Jett, Mazz, myself, a relaxed looking Eros, and Pearl.

"How?" I questioned, looking at my new clean clothes and into the cup of tea in front of me.

"I thought we would be more comfortable here," Eros answered with a shrug. "This is your house, *right?*" he yelled, staring hard at Jett.

"Yes! Yes, but-"

"Oh good, I was worried for second there. The look on your faces had me convinced I got the wrong house," Eros explained.

"What is going *on?*" Jett asked, pushing away his cup of tea with a frustrated look.

"Right, you deserve an explanation and I will give you as much as I can, as it seems that the time has come. Deimos and Phobos are the sons of Ares. The gods of terror and horror," he started.

"Yeah, nice guys," I scoffed.

"Try growing up in the same house as them, sweetheart," Eros answered back. I frowned, not the happiest of homes I would imagine.

"Anyway, the two of them have been joined at the hip since we were kids and they feed off each other's energy and hate. So, when the two of them started to lurk around Mer it peaked my interest. What was their concern with the Mer? You basically aren't even on the radar for the gods, I mean you are a pretty peaceful lot."

"They were there for me," I answered and Eros nodded.

"But, I still couldn't figure out why. So, I went to my mother, Aphrodite. She's got influence all over the world, in pretty much every life, so she generally knows what's going on. Now, my brothers are also her children, but I have always been a little, okay a lot, closer to my mother than they have. They run along the same lines as Father. Anyway, I found out that Mother had been keeping a secret from me. She was protecting someone in Mer. When I told her that Deimos and Phobos were sniffing around she turned white. She sent me to watch them and protect you."

"She didn't tell you why she was protecting me?"

"No," he answered with a shake of his head. "I was able to stop them from getting to you that one day, but when I returned to tell my mother, she was gone."

"Gone?" Mazz asked. "What do you mean gone?"

"Kidnapped!" he answered.

"Who could kidnap a goddess?" I asked.

"Ares. I know he did it. He's up to something. My brothers have been extra active lately and they only ever act on his command. He took her, I just know it," Eros answered, his expression dark.

"What does this have to do with Jett?" I asked.

"Well, I'm not sure. After my brothers left Mer, I followed them here and right to you. I never thought that they would kill your people or take them. I'm so sorry," he said looking at Jett.

"Thank you," he answered with a frown.

"Here's the thing," Eros said, leaning across the table and looking Jett and me in the eyes. "Ares wants you for something. Whatever it is that he needs from you, I can just about guarantee that it's not good. The last thing that my mother asked me to do was watch out for you, and that's what I intend to do."

I looked at Jett and he looked back at me.

"What now?" I asked him. He leaned over and placed a kiss on my forehead.

"No clue," he answered and I laughed.

What do you do after a god tells you that the god of war is after you?

"What does this mean for Ky?" Mazz asked Eros. "She has a city to lead and people who depend on her."

"I'm sorry, but returning to Triton is out of the question at the moment. Ares has followers everywhere. There are too many people there and I would have no clue who to trust with her. Are you confident that she would be completely safe there from Ares?" Eros said looking at Mazz. Mazz frowned. "Didn't think so."

"How do we get out of this mess?" Jett asked. "There must be someone that can tell us what we are wanted for and what we can do."

"Well, possibly. My mother wasn't the only one that knew about you two. There would have been others, the ones that know past, present, and future. The Fates."

"The Fates?" I asked.

"Yes. They will know why Ares is interested in you and why my mother was protecting you. If you can talk to them, you will get your answers," he said.

"How do we contact them?" Jett asked.

"Well, it's not as easy as picking up the phone or mailing a letter. You have to go to them and their home changes all the time. They never stay in the same place," Eros answered.

"Where are they now?" I asked.

"They are at the bottom of the Marianas Trench, I believe," he said.

"The *bottom*?" I stressed. Even our people didn't venture to the bottom of that chasm. There were creatures there that even we dared not waken.

"What is it?" Jett asked.

"It's a dangerous journey to say the least," I answered.

Jett looked at Eros, "Is there really no other way?"

"None that I can think of, but I will keep trying to find out what I can. The Fates are our best bet to find out Ares plans and why Aphrodite was protecting you."

"I guess that means that we are taking a trip," I said to Jett. He nodded solemnly.

"Well, you aren't going to just go to the deepest part of the ocean on your own. I'm coming too," Mazz said.

"I can protect her just fine," Jett said back to Mazz with a tight jaw.

"How do I know that?" Mazz retorted. Jett held out a hand and pink zapped between his fingers. Mazz didn't bat an eye, "Pretty," he deadpanned. Jett's jaw tightened.

"Okay, that's enough you two," I ordered.

"There is the issue of your guardians," Eros said.

"What about them? Deimos and Phobos killed them," Jett answered, still trying to stare down Mazz.

"They did, but the powers of a guardians are always passed on to another. Someone that the guardian trusted and knew would do the job," Eros said.

"Really? Who would that be?" I asked.

"Rayna," Jett answered.

"What?" I stuttered.

"When I saw her in the road, there was the same symbol on her chest as Vyktor had. It was glowing," he recalled.

"That's the warning that there is a danger to those that you are protecting," Eros explained.

"But, she brought Vyktor to us when he died. If she was a guardian then why would she have done that?" Jett asked.

"Habit? Concern? Disbelief in what she was given? Who knows. You'll have to ask her. All I know is that with the mark comes knowledge and power. She would have been driven to go back to deal with the source of the warning. That's when she would have come upon Deimos and Phobos. Being new at her job, she wouldn't have been strong enough or skilled in her powers enough to really have a chance. She's very lucky she lived," Eros explained.

"So you are telling me that Rayna is my guardian?" Jett asked.

"Yep. And he's yours," Eros said looking at Mazz and then to me.

"What?" I blurted.

"Ugh, yeah," Mazz said blushing. "I didn't really get a chance to talk to you about that after Mistress Hol's death. I woke up with this the day after you disappeared," he said, pulling back his shirt and showing the same mark as Vyktor.

"Whoa," I uttered, looking at the mark of the gods on my best friend.

"You guys are going to have to stick close to KyLaya and Jett. Those marks only work when you are in the same area. They also cloak KyLaya and Jett from being sensed by the gods, which makes them harder to find. Once Ares killed the guardians, he was able to sense out your powers easier," Eros explained.

"I'm not one for wanting a babysitter around, thanks," Jett replied.

"Don't want to babysit your butt, anyway," Mazz responded.

"Well, whatever you do with your butts is your business, and mine to a degree. I am the god of desire after all," Eros joked.

"What kind of powers does *that* come with?" Mazz asked.

"Wanna find out?" Eros asked.

"I'm not scared of you," he answered.

"Oh, really?" Eros answered and a sparkle ball appeared in his hand.

"Not glitter!" Mazz said, feigning fright. Eros smiled and threw it at Mazz. Mazz's eyes glazed over and a lazy grin spread across his face. He looked at the table and gasped.

"My gods! What are you doing all the way over there?" he cried.

"Who are you talking to?" I asked him, but he didn't look at me. He was staring at the teapot.

"Come here!" he said and grabbed the pot, gently and lovingly in his hand. He lifted it up and nuzzled it with his cheek. "You gorgeous thing."

"My gods," I uttered. Mazz was in love with the tea pot.

"Okay, very funny you can make him fall in love with an object," Jett said.

"What? Not dangerous enough for you?"

Jett burst out laughing but not for long when he was hit with a sparkle ball too. His eyes widened as he looked with love at the stove. The red hot stove.

"Stop!" I shouted at Eros, who was watching with cool detachment as Jett got up from his seat and crossed the room to the stove and the kettle that was boiling on it.

"I mean it! Stop them, Eros! You've proved your point," I yelled. But, he didn't stop. Jett was getting closer and closer to burning his face on the element.

"Stop!" I hollered and clasped my hands around Eros's head. I pulled.

A sparkly dust started to rise from him, as his eyes shot open. The dust filtered out of Jett and Mazz and the two of them stood, confused, beside the table. That would have been enough for me…if the power within Eros didn't call to me.

But it did…and I listened.

I pulled hard, feeling the power within the god enter me. Seeping into my veins and running wild through me. Again, everything was brighter, more alive. I felt everything. The smallest breeze in the air, the smell of the tea in the bags in the hot water. The sound of every bubble that popped in the boiling kettle. It was amazing.

A hand was placed on my shoulder and I turned slowly toward it. Jett's eyes met mine.

"Let go, Laya," he said.

"But…"

"Let go, please," he asked, nodding and holding out his hands for mine. I looked at Eros, whose mouth was open, the veins in his neck protruding as his eyes bulged. Was this what I had become? A monster that would steal the life from another to satisfy a craving?

I looked back at Jett and pulled my hands from Eros's face. He fell to the ground.

Jett pulled me into his arms and hugged me tightly.

"I'm sorry," I uttered and suddenly I was wracked with tears. They came fast and furiously. I wasn't even sure why. Maybe it was the realization that there was a part of me that I had no control over. Or that I was now addicted to something that would kill another. Maybe, it was the relief that Jett had stopped me before I had done something that I would regret for the rest of my life.

I sat heavily into the chair. Eros laid on the floor. His breathing coming evenly as his unconscious body started to recharge.

"It's okay, Laya. You're okay," Jett said sweetly as he sat beside me.

"It's not okay, Jett," I cried. "What's wrong with me? Why am I doing that?"

"I don't know," he answered and pulled me into his lap, placing a kiss on my forehead as he pulled me to his chest. In his arms I felt comforted, as if his embrace brought calm to my world.

"Whoa!" Eros shouted as he sat up in a blink. "What the heck happened?" he asked looking at me.

"You wouldn't stop toying with Mazz and Jett," I answered, glaring at him.

"Right, sorry about that. Sometimes I forget that you are such fragile creatures. What did you do to me?" he asked, holding his head and stumbling to a chair.

"I...I don't know. It started tonight when I pulled Deimos's powers," I answered.

"Wait...what? You took my power?" he asked.

I nodded sadly. "I'm sorry. I didn't know how else to get you to stop."

"Can you shoot a bow?"

"What does that have to do with any of this?" Jett asked as he hugged me closer.

"Everything!" Eros exclaimed. "Here!" A bow appeared in his hand and he gave it to me. He grabbed my hand and took me outside, to the loud protests of Jett and Mazz. "There! Shoot that bottle over there on the top of the shed."

"That's all the way on the other side of the garden! I have never shot a bow and arrow in my life!" I explained.

"Doesn't matter. We are testing something. Try," he said.

"This is ridiculous," I uttered and strung the bow confidently and naturally, which had me looking at my hands as if they weren't my own.

"Shoot!" Eros exclaimed. I took aim, bringing the bow up to my eye. Looking out over it. A calm came over me as I zeroed in on my target and took a deep breath. I let half of it out slowly and shot.

Ping!

"Wow," Jett uttered. "That was amazing!" he smiled and nodded at me. "I'm impressed."

"I don't know how I did that. It just came to me," I said.

Eros took the bow from my hand and smiled, "*You* know because *I* know how to shoot." With that he nocked an arrow and shot, rapid firing three arrows in a row. For each arrow shot we could hear the *ping* of the bottle as each hit it. "You took that knowledge from me when you placed your hands on me," he explained.

"Oh, I was just hoping that I was a natural," I answered with a sheepish smile. Jett put an arm around me and kissed my forehead. Mazz rolled his eyes.

"What does that mean for her? Is that knowledge going to stay with her or run its course?" he asked.

"I'm not sure. I've only read scant things about a power like hers. It's exceptionally rare...and old, really old," he said.

"Which is why Aphrodite would have wanted to protect it," Jett offered.

"Exactly," Eros confirmed.

"And why Ares wants it so much," Mazz added.

"True. She would be able to absorb the essence of another god, gain their knowledge and their power…who knows what she would be able to do with that," he said and turned to look at me. They all did.

46
KYLAYA

EROS LEFT FOR OLYMPUS, confident that we would be left alone for the night, as Deimos and Phobos would be home licking their wounds for a while.

I went and took a long shower. Eros had cleaned my skin, but I somehow still felt like I needed to get the night off of me. It was the break that I needed. A few moments to clear my head and really think about what the future held. The water over my skin renewed it, seeping into my blood and feeding my soul. It was how the water always felt to the Mer – life-giving.

I wiped a hand across the mirror in the bathroom and looked down into the full sink. A set of black eyes stared back at me.

What?

I blinked and shook my head; but, when I looked back the eyes were still there. A fully formed face appeared as I watched in utter awe. Stunningly beautiful and undeniable deadly, a woman's face appeared. Her black eyes looked at me from behind her seaweed green hair.

"You might have gotten away from me this time, KyLaya Constantilly. But, I assure you, I will have you before long. I have something that you have been looking for."

"What could you have that I could possibly want, Siren Queen?" I asked. I knew who she was. I had heard enough about her to recognize her.

"You will see. Before this over your whole family will fall to me. Mer is at an end. The Prime is dying. The city will fall and you will bring it down for me," she smiled, revealing sharp teeth.

"I will never follow you, sea witch," I hissed at her.

"We shall see," she teased and turned, but then stopped. A smile spread across her face that was cold and sent a shiver up my spine.

"Say. 'hi' to my grandson for me," she said and disappeared.

"Grandson? What? Who?" I asked, looking into the water but seeing nothing but the sink.

I staggered to a fall, landing on the floor. Rubbing my face with my hands, I brought myself back to reality. Had I seriously just talked to the Siren Queen? There was no way that I was going to do anything for her. But her words haunted me. What did she have that I have been looking for? What could it be? Who was her grandson? Was she even telling the truth?

I dressed and left the bathroom. My mind was a mad rush of thoughts and questions, and it was nearly driving me crazy. Her grandson. Did that mean that she had sent someone to infiltrate the Sirenites? Did she really have a grandson that she gave up; and, that was saved and bought there? Was it a lie to drive us apart? What did that mean?

I walked out of the bathroom and thought of the men in that small house. Sam. Jasper. Mazz. Jett. All of them I trusted, completely. How could I tell them what she said? It would devastate them. None of them would want to be related to her. What was I going to do?

Sam seemed to be doing much better, to the relief of Jasper. Rayna was sitting up in the living room and Mazz had brought her in some blankets and food. He was always the gentleman, but I had a feeling that he was itching to talk to her about her mark and their new roles in all this.

I went looking for Jett and found him out on the deck, sitting on the bench and looking out at the field in the moonlight.

"Hey," I said as I sat down. "You okay?"

"Yeah, I mean, as good as you can be after finding out you are being sought out by a god for a reason that you don't know," he half-smiled. "How about you?"

"Same," I said and we chuckled. He reached over, placed his arm around my shoulders and pulled me towards him. He took a deep breath, something that I had learned he did to clear his mind.

A nagging feeling in the back of mind had been plaguing me. I needed to talk to him about it, or it would eat me from the inside.

"Jett?"

"Yeah?"

I opened my mouth to tell him about Midira but then changed my mind. What would that accomplish? It would worry him. We had enough on our plates as it was. I didn't need to be the one to add on another course.

"What is it?" he asked, turning to me.

"Do you-I mean, are you worried that what we feel is more *dream* us than... *real* us?" I asked. It had been playing on my mind, but I had been afraid to ask until that moment. Somehow, with everything else, I needed the answer more.

Since the moment that I met him, I had already loved him on a level that didn't match the time that we spent together. Our dreams had forged a relationship between us and a connection that was there before we had set real eyes on the other. But, did we really care for each other, or was all this just something designed by the gods? A trick of our minds? A fantasy?

"I *was* worried," he answered honestly.

"Are you still?"

He turned to me, dropping his arm. "No."

"How-"

"I knew from the moment that I saw you outside of Triton that we were supposed to meet. But, the feelings that I have for you aren't because of our dreams, sure they help, but that's not all of it. When I look at you I know what I feel is all me, right here, right now."

I didn't know what to say. My heart was racing and my eyes were watering. He placed a finger under my chin and lifted my gaze to his. "This is probably the weirdest way to fall for someone. But, honestly, I'm fine with that, Laya - because it's *you*. Are you okay with that?" he asked, watching me as he drew a delicate line down my cheek with the back of his finger.

"Yes," I said without hesitation. Jett leaned over and rested his forehead against mine and I smiled. Relief ran through me, amplified with a burst of joy.

"Whatever comes next I'm not going anywhere," he said. "You're stuck with me, got it?"

"You sure about that?" I asked, looking him in the eye. He leaned down and kissed me. Sweet, gentle, and yet in a way that claimed me for himself. His kiss was passionate and immediately I was lost in it.

When he broke away from me, my hand rested on his chest and I could feel his heart slamming hard against my fingers. A hunger settled in behind his eyes and I knew it was for me. My pulse spiked and a flurry of butterflies ignited within me.

"I'm yours, Laya, always have been. *Always* will be," he answered against my lips.

I believed him and couldn't have been happier. "And I'm yours. All yours, Jett." I said, smiling against his lips.

"Good, because I've never been a good sharer," he chuckled.

"Me neither," I replied and pressed a kiss to his lips.

I wrapped my arms around his neck and pulled into him. The feel of his arms, strong and steady around me was heaven. I kissed him hard and he responded with a sound from deep in his throat. Then his lips were hot and hard on mine. When I opened to them, I felt a flick of his tongue over mine that sent my heart into spasm. I was convinced in that moment that I would never find another, not like him. And I didn't want to. He was it for me.

I was just too scared to tell him.

I was completely in love with Jett, the Siren's Son.

About the Author

Emory is lives in a world of mermaids and mythology. Escaping into the world of Mer is the best form of self-care she can think of. Who doesn't want to visit with Jett and Darrien? When she's not hanging with her book boys, she teaches Arts Education in Regina, Saskatchewan. Mommy to two adorable boys, she gets lots of hugs and snuggles from her favorite little men. She's lucky to have a hubby that supports her writing to the fullest. Emory dove into writing with the goal of finishing one book…now she cannot stop and doesn't plan on it. Look out for more in her newest series coming in 2019!

KEEP UPDATED...

Keep updated with what is going on in the world of Mer and beyond! I do frequent giveaways and let you know when sales are coming up on my books! Find out more on my site!

http://emorygayle.com

HELP A GIRL OUT...

If you enjoyed *Triton's Daughter*, please review it! Every review is SO appreciated!

FOR THE FUN OF IT...

I am very active on social media and would love to hear from you! Come find me and my crazy ramblings on Facebook, Twitter, and Instagram! Join *Emory Gayle's Siren Squad* on Facebook and get advanced notice on sales, releases and giveaways! We have LOTS of fun in there!

NEW BOOK ON THE WAY...

I am currently working on **Siren's Son**, the second installment inn my new series **The Triton Series**. Stay tuned to my Facebook Page for information on release!

https://www.facebook.com/emorygayle/

HAPPY READING!!!

Also by Emory Gayle

The Water Series:
Water: Book One of the Water Series
Mer: Book Two of the Water Series
Siren: Book Three of the Water Series
Tempest: Book Four of the Water Series

Celia's Journey: A Water Story
Volume One
Volume Two
Volume Three (TBD)

The Triton Series:
Triton's Daughter: Book One (September 2018)
Siren's Son: Book Two (2019)

CPSIA information can be obtained
at www.ICGtesting.com
Printed in the USA
LVHW090017080719
623402LV00001B/133/P